THE GIRLS NEXT DOOR

THE GIRLS NEXT DOOR

Peter Turchi

NAL BOOKS
NEW AMERICAN LIBRARY
A DIVISION OF PENGUIN BOOKS USA INC., NEW YORK
PUBLISHED IN CANADA BY
PENGUIN BOOKS CANADA LIMITED, MARKHAM, ONTARIO

Published simultaneously in Canada by Penguin Books Canada Limited.

The author gratefully acknowledges the following permissions:

HOMER: THE ODYSSEY translated by E. V. Rieu (Penguin Classics, 1946), copyright © the Estate of E. V. Rieu, 1946.

"Cherry Red" Words and Music by Pete Johnson and Joe Turner © Copyright 1941, 1944, 1948 by MCA MUSIC PUBLISHING, A Division of MCA INC., New York, NY 10019. Copyright renewed. Used by permission. All rights reserved.

An excerpt from this novel appeared under the title "Primitive Music" in *New Times*. Copyright © 1986 New Times, Inc. Reproduced with permission of New Times, Inc.

NAL BOOKS TRADEMARK REG. U.S. PAT. OFF. AND FOREIGN COUNTRIES
REGISTERED TRADEMARK—MARCA REGISTRADA
HECHO EN DRESDEN, TN, USA

SIGNET, SIGNET CLASSIC, MENTOR, ONYX, PLUME, MERIDIAN and NAL BOOKS are published *in the United States* by New American Library, a division of Penguin Books USA Inc., 1633 Broadway, New York, New York 10019, *in Canada* by Penguin Books Canada Limited, 2801 John Street, Markham, Ontario L3R 1B4

Library of Congress Cataloging-in-Publication Data

Turchi, Peter, 1960–
The girls next door / by Peter Turchi.
p. cm.
ISBN 0-453-00665-5
I. Title.
PS3570.U6255G57 1989
813'.54—dc19 88-32161
CIP

Designed by Leonard Telesca

First Printing, July, 1989

1 2 3 4 5 6 7 8 9

PRINTED IN THE UNITED STATES OF AMERICA

This book is for my mother,
my father, and my sister,
and it is for Laura.

THE GIRLS NEXT DOOR

JUNE

The most promising words ever written on the maps of human knowledge are *terra incognita*—unknown territory.

—Daniel J. Boorstin
The Discoverers

Yes, the world's a ship on its passage out, and not a voyage complete. . . .

—Herman Melville
Moby Dick; or, The Whale

Chapter One

In the early days of our marriage Donna and I did everything together. When she vacuumed, I held the cord; when I took out the trash, she came along for the walk. But by our eleven-month anniversary, in June of 1963, things had already started to change. While Donna went off with her mother that day, I stayed home and helped prostitutes move into the neighborhood.

Looking back, I see how that should have been a sign of trouble. At the time, everything wasn't so clear.

We were weeding when a new white Bonneville with dealer plates rolled onto the driveway, as quiet as money. Evelyn, Donna's mother, hit the brakes, honked, and waved for her to come over. Evelyn always kept the engine running as long as possible. She liked the sound of a new car.

Donna walked back to me.

"She wants to go shopping," she said.

"Of course she does."

"Mom needs a pocketbook. I could use some buttons."

Donna was tall and slender, she had soft chestnut hair, and the corners of her mouth connected directly to my heart. When she smiled I couldn't say no.

But when they left, I stopped working. It wasn't that Donna spent a lot of money—she would go out for hours and come home with three yards of material and a zipper for a new skirt. What I couldn't figure was why anyone would want to spend a beautiful afternoon shopping. We had decided to have a baby, and it worried me that I didn't understand my wife.

The other thing that bothered me was the weeding. I like to plant—gardening is one of the hobbies Donna and I both enjoy—but it seemed futile for everything to be so healthy. In the fall, when my father died, it had been right that blooms were fading, leaves falling. The chrysanthemums, which normally put on a show into November, succumbed to a freak early frost. In winter everything died off, of course. But spring had been perfect, and by early summer the beds were beautiful. As if out of spite, African violets shot runners across the yard in all directions, the daffodils by the front sidewalk propagated so profusely that I had to thin them out. Even so, when I looked at the flowers all I saw were brown stems, shriveled petals—what they would be in the fall.

It seemed to me the least I could do was to remember my parents by maintaining the garden my mother had started, the house my father had built. But I was having a hard time weeding. I pulled them out by the roots and turned the dirt with a gardening shovel, but when I finished, the row didn't look brown and fresh, the way my mother's had; little bits of weed stuck up everywhere, laughing at me. I couldn't get the beds to look the way they did in my memory.

I was on my knees when a pickup truck pulled into the driveway we shared with the house next door. It was a dirty green Ford, piled high with carpets and furniture—chairs, a table, a dismantled bed, a lamp. A girl in a loose blouse and tight yellow pants stepped out of the driver's side, stretched her arms high, and groaned. Her face was pale, with light brown freckles that matched her hair. She looked to be in her late teens, but when she glanced over, a hardness behind her eyes made her seem older.

The passenger door opened and another girl walked around the front of the truck. She was blonde and thin—too thin, as if she had been sick. She was wearing a man's white T-shirt and cut-off shorts.

"Hey there," she said.

She was talking to Joe, who was watching them from

behind the toolshed. He barked and wagged his tail. The girls walked to the front of the house next door, out of sight.

Over the past ten years I had seen a lot of people move in and out of that house. I wondered if these two were moving in alone, and what they were waiting for. Maybe one was helping—the one with the freckles—and they were waiting for the blonde's husband. Something about the one with freckles made me nervous. She looked angry, as if she were having an argument with someone no one else could hear.

The house belonged to an enterprising man named L. V. Bellshaw, who had a certain notoriety as the owner of Liberty Low-Priced Liquors, the only liquor store in Snyder's Mill. Before he bought it, the house had stood vacant for months. The overgrown yard made it look haunted, and the garage, modeled after a Victorian carriage house, suffered from broken windows and from the dozen or so birds that visited each year. In the first few weeks, Bellshaw had the yard groomed, the garage cleaned, the windows replaced, and the house painted. But the flurry of activity was deceiving; no one came to cut the grass again, and the paint began chipping and flaking immediately. We knew then that Bellshaw wasn't moving in.

Now the gravel in the driveway scattered as a light blue Chevy with a steel-gray hood pulled in behind the green pickup. A third girl got out, short and black-haired and almost chubby. She walked around front as another car pulled all the way to the end of the driveway, near our toolshed. Joe jumped back, then pressed forward, barking, protecting his territory. The second car was a white Cadillac. It was more than a few years old, and it had a rusted dent by the rear fender, but it was the first Cadillac I had ever seen in our neighborhood. The trunk lid was propped open by two big green shrubs like decorated toothpicks sticking out of a tray of hors d'oeuvres. The driver, a man in his late fifties, stared at Joe as he rolled up his sleeves. He didn't take off his hat. He walked around to the front of the house slowly, as if he wished he hadn't come.

The other door of the Cadillac opened and a woman with strawberry-blond hair got out, sizing up Bellshaw's house.

She looked wiry and tough, not like the kind of woman who spent her afternoons shopping. She took loose strides, like a man, and smoked a cigarette that dangled low from her lip. As she walked out of sight she glanced over at me, and I thought I saw her wink. If she did it was in a flash, and by the time I recovered she was gone.

While the new people unloaded, I trimmed back some narcissus, minding my own business. I like to think of myself as friendly, but Bellshaw's past tenants hadn't been the kind of people you'd be in a hurry to meet. Most of the previous family he had rented to had ended up in jail. Even so, when one of the girls shouted and fell, I looked up; the rest were inside, so I ran over.

The blonde was lying in the bed of the pickup, half under an oak dresser. I lifted it back and held out my hand.

"Are you okay?"

"I'm dusty," she said.

"That's all right." I showed her the dirt on my hands. "I'm a mess."

She held on and I pulled her up. Her grip was strong, and when she stood she paid no attention to the scrape on her arm from knocking against the side of the truck.

"My name," she said. "Like dirty. Rhymes with rusty." She smiled and I knew she had used the line before.

"I'm George," I told her. "Looks like you could use some help."

We struggled with the dresser—it was like moving a tree.

"Are you sure this thing is empty?" I stood trapped against the wheel well of the truck.

"It's just shirts and stuff," Dusty said.

"Take out your drawers."

"Do what?" Her voice was high and uneven, like an adolescent boy's. It was the only awkward thing about her, and it gave me confidence.

"Take them out," I told her. "This thing is heavy enough."

I waited, pinned, while she found a place to put them. "I would have come over earlier, but we've been having neighbor trouble."

"Oh yeah?" Dusty balanced a drawer on the arm of a white couch. "Us too."

"It's a shame," I said, sympathizing. "Decent people suffer just because a few others can't be civilized."

The woman and the chubby girl helped us carry the dresser up the front steps and inside. When we were back on the lawn the woman wiped her hand on her plaid Bermuda shorts and held it out.

"I'm Grace," she said. "You married?"

The question caught me off guard; I didn't answer fast enough for her.

"Must be," she said. "Got a big gold ring. And you sure as hell *look* married." Her voice was a loud rasp, the product of too many cigarettes. "You hustled right over to give us a hand. Just being a good neighbor, right?"

"The dresser fell," Dusty told her. "He told me to take off my drawers."

"I didn't—"

"A man of action," Grace said. "I like that. This is Eve"—she pointed—"and that's Kristin." Eve, the big-breasted girl with black hair, gave me an odd look, and I almost checked to see if my fly was unzipped. Kristin, the angry one with freckles, was already walking away.

"I'm George," I said. "George Willus."

"Glad to meet you, George," Grace said. "Everybody around here as neighborly as you?"

"At least. It's a friendly neighborhood. You won't have any trouble with us."

"That's good to know," she said. "We're friendly neighbors ourselves. You never seen people so friendly."

The man in the black hat walked by with a short cigar in his mouth and a lamp in one hand. He looked like a G-man from the forties.

Grace stopped him. "Larry, say hello to our new neighbor."

Larry glared at her, then at me.

"I'm George," I said again. I felt as if I were running for office. "George Willus."

Larry grunted.

"Don't mind him," Grace told me. "The man's got all the personality of burnt rubber."

I gave Kristin a hand with a heavy glass tabletop. As we moved up the driveway, I asked her where they had come from.

She bit her lip, concentrating on keeping a firm grip as we reached the stairs. Her eyes darted, never looking in one direction for long. I wasn't sure she had heard me.

"Have a long drive?" I said, louder.

"Two days."

We turned the glass sideways and edged through the door. "Where's it go?"

"Against the wall," she said; then, "East."

"What?"

"Two days, straight east. Dullsville."

"Worth it, though."

Her look implied otherwise, but she didn't waste words. We walked back outside.

"I mean, you're here," I said. "This is a nice part of the country, don't you think?"

Kristin stood at the bottom of the porch steps, taking in the yard, our house, the neighborhood.

She said, "It sure don't look like much."

When we reached the pickup I handed down a chair so we could get to the couch. A cigar ash fell on my arm; Larry made a vaguely apologetic grunt.

Eve said, "It's hot out here. We should've got a house with a pool."

I told her there was a pond in the backyard, and everyone looked. There was nothing but grass.

"Filled in," I said. "But you could probably fix it up. It was about ten feet from the back steps."

"Deep enough to swim in?" Eve asked.

It had been covered over for as long as I could remember, but I doubted it was deep. She said she wished they had moved near the ocean, and she seemed surprised when I told her it was only two and a half hours away.

Kristin came back from the house. "Hey," Eve told her, "did you hear that? Maryland has an ocean."

"Killer," Kristin said. "Which one?"

As soon as we emptied the pickup truck and the Cadillac, Larry left. While the others worked inside, Dusty and I unloaded the blue Chevy.

"That's a great dog you've got," she said. "What kind is he?"

"Golden retriever. His name is Pokerino."

"What's that, Italian?"

It was a game on the boardwalk in Ocean City. Friends of Donna's family owned one of the arcades, and when their dog had puppies they named them Skeeball, Pinball, and Pokerino. We called him Joe.

"Crazy," Dusty said.

We walked back to the car. She was the easiest one to talk to, and when she asked questions she listened to the answers.

She said, "You lived here long?"

"Always. Twenty-four years." I handed her a box of shoes from the back seat. "What brings you to Maryland?"

"Larry has a friend who owns some bars downtown."

"Are all of you moving in?"

"What's it look like?" It wasn't a rhetorical question; she seemed to want to know the answer.

Grace and Larry looked like an odd pair, and the three girls didn't look like sisters. But I didn't tell her that. Instead I told her about the other people who had lived in that house.

Bellshaw's tenants had never belonged to the neighborhood; they were all destined to move on, like the migrating birds that rested in the garage each spring and fall. When I was in college, a couple in their early thirties lived there. We never saw much of them until, two weeks before Christmas in 1961, the husband crammed everything he could into his bright red Corvette.

"Ooh," Dusty said. "That's my car."

"But he left her," I said.

"What did she do?"

"Another guy moved in."

She didn't respond.

"They weren't married."

"Don't tell me," Dusty said. "Big scandal."

She was the first person I saw react that way to that kind of news. I had been surprised when it became clear that the couple were living together, but then I decided it was their business. Mine was a minority view, to say the least, and I never let on that I wasn't outraged.

The neighborhood had been shocked. When my parents built their house they chose to live near people like themselves: friendly and warm but quiet, politically and morally conservative. There had been a momentary uproar, culminating in a three-and-a-half-hour meeting of the Snyder's Mill Community Association. Our neighbor and her new friend weren't invited. It all blew over when the man, a building contractor, finished his new house and took her with him.

"Sounds like he was loaded," Dusty said. "Good for her."

"Early last year the next people moved in, a family of five." The word on them spread even faster. The three children were boys; a fourth, a girl, was in jail for assaulting a policeman. Their mother worked during the day as a beautician down the street, at nights as a waitress at a diner on Reisterstown Road. Their father was an alcoholic, and I can still remember hearing him drive up in the early morning in their battered black Olds, turning the car in a great drunken arc beginning just past their mailbox and running up onto our lawn, next to the telephone pole. The boys were as bad as their sister. One day in early July, Bill Steinkamp, a neighbor who worked for the phone company, walked out the front door with a cup of coffee in his hand, late for work, and stood staring at the empty driveway. Two days later the police found his truck in Hagerstown. In the fall the three boys weren't at the corner where Mr. Wheatley's school bus stopped, and in October one of them was arrested in the drugstore down the street.

"Sounds tough," Dusty said, handing me a flat box of hangers that had been stuffed under the front seat. I thought I heard sympathy for the family in her voice. Like everyone else, I had been relieved when they left.

I said, "I felt sorry for the mother." I used to see her walking to work the mornings after her husband had come home late. After the youngest was put in a detention center, the neighborhood was quiet for a while, but the day before Christmas the Pattersons came back from dinner at their daughter's to find their presents stolen and the living-room furniture spray-painted. A few days later the other two boys were arrested, and in February Bellshaw evicted their parents.

"Just like that?"

"Sure," I said, wondering what kind of place she had lived in. "This isn't that kind of neighborhood. Until they got here, we never locked our doors."

"Serious?" She shut the side door of the car and walked around to the trunk. I followed her.

"Everybody was angry with Bellshaw. People want him to be more careful about who he rents the house to."

"So now he's being careful?"

"This woman, Virginia Mead—she's the president of the Community Association—she tried to stir up some action against him."

"What happened?" Dusty stacked some dish towels on top of my load of hangers.

"She didn't have much luck. She's not very popular."

The house had been empty for four months. Donna and I were used to seeing Bellshaw drive up on Saturday evenings to make sure that no windows had been broken and that the lock on the rusty gate by the back porch was still intact; he'd wave his cigar to us and leave.

Dusty said, "So we're not even moved in yet, and everybody around here probably wishes the house would just stay empty."

"Not me," I said. "I'm glad you're here."

And I was. It felt right to have people living in the old house again, people who would be part of the neighborhood. Besides, earlier, working in the garden, I had been worrying about weeds, and Donna's mother, and having a baby; since I had walked across the driveway I had forgotten all that.

"Well, good," Dusty said, pulling a box of records out of the trunk. "I hope we pass the test."

Chapter Two

"Good Lord," Donna said.

"What's up?"

"Come look at this."

I was by the fireplace in the living room, tightening the hinges on the leaves of the coffee table my father and Earle and I had made. Donna stood by the window at the foot of the stairs, looking out across the driveway. I walked over and followed her finger to the backyard of the house next door. Two pairs of legs lay on beach towels on the grass.

"They're sunbathing." I turned to go back to the coffee table.

"They're half-naked."

My head bumped the window frame. "How can you tell?"

"One of them just sat up." Donna stared out the window, her lips drawn thin.

I looked at her, then across the driveway. The angle was wrong. "I think I'll get something to drink," I said.

We went to the kitchen and stood at the sink, looking out the window across from their back porch. Eve and Kristin were on their backs, wearing nothing but shorts.

"What do you think?" Donna said.

"What do I think what?"

"What do you *think* what do you think?"

I looked out the window. "I can't really—"

"Hold on." She went into the dining room.

My pulse tap-danced. I had never seen a woman sunbathing topless—Donna wouldn't even wear a bikini. I leaned forward and squinted, trying to see what there was to see. A moment later I heard Donna's footsteps on the linoleum and drew back. She was carrying my binoculars.

"Wait a minute," I said. "I don't think we need to do this."

"You're the one who can't see. Move over." She adjusted the lenses. "Who has the mustache?"

"Eve."

"Look at the size of her."

This wasn't the Donna I knew.

"Honey, what is this for? What are you doing?"

She handed me the binoculars. "Go ahead. Get it out of your system."

I put my eyes to the lenses and looked through the window.

Something was green and grainy. A green towel? Green shorts? I turned the focus dial.

Grass. A bug was walking up the side of one blade.

"These are very strong binoculars," I said.

"You're complaining?"

I looked out the window at the girls, then looked through the binoculars, but I was disoriented. I moved left. Right. Up.

Something was dark blue.

I pulled back my head and looked out the window. There was nothing dark blue in the yard next door.

I looked through the binoculars and moved very slowly to the left.

A giant blister.

"One of them has blue toenails."

"Only you," Donna said. "Only my husband would be looking at their feet."

"Feet nothing," I said. "One toenail. It's huge."

The cliff of the foot dropped to a valley at the instep. Farther up the leg stood a blackened field of stubble, and higher, hairs, blond like Kansas wheat. Amber waves of grain.

"These are amazing," I said. "I feel like an amoeba."

"Where are you?"

"Shorts." A huge patch of faded denim, white and pale blue

fabric with diagonal black valleys. Then flesh, pale brown, a mole, more flesh, and there it was: an enormous nipple, exposed, towering in my sights like Mount Fuji on the distant horizon. I half-expected to see snow on the peak, a wisp of smoke rising slowly—

"That's enough," Donna said sharply.

I looked a moment longer, then handed her the binoculars. "What do you think?"

She said, "If Virginia Mead hears about this, she is going to be in her glory."

Their yard was protected by the house and garage in the front and back, by a thick hedge and two maple trees on the far side. We were the only ones with a clear view.

"What I mean," I said as Donna snapped the covers over the lenses, "is who do you think they are?"

"They don't act like a family." She stared at the binoculars as if there was something to see in them. I had never seen her like this. I had no idea what she was thinking.

She said, "I bet they're hookers."

"Hookers?"

"Prostitutes," she said, only half-joking. "Look at them, lying out there like bait. Luring customers."

"Honey, they're sunbathing. They're in their own backyard."

"You looked, didn't you?"

"Sweetheart, you're the one who saw them. You called me over."

"That's not the point." She stared at them again, then turned away. "They don't look like sisters."

"Maybe they're good friends," I said, following her into the dining room.

"They aren't out looking for jobs."

"Maybe they're teachers," I said. "On summer vacation."

"Maybe they're nuns on retreat." Donna put the binoculars back into the cabinet beneath the china closet. She seemed distant. "It's pretty strange."

"I'm sorry," I said.

"What for?"

I didn't know. It just seemed like a safe thing to say with

two girls sunbathing topless across the driveway. I thought I might have a lot to be sorry about.

"I'm sorry it's strange," I said. Then I went back to work on the coffee table.

Mr. Wheatley stopped his school bus in front of our house late one afternoon.

"That's right nice what they've done over there," he said, motioning next door. "Maybe L.V. will sell it to them. Hell, he ought to give it to them."

In less than a week Grace and the girls had planted flowers, put a set of green metal patio furniture in the backyard, and started scraping the bad paint off the house. I told Mr. Wheatley he was right: Bellshaw ought to give it to them. I didn't mention the sunbathing.

"Yes sir," he said. "It's about time we had some people living here that we don't have to hold our breath when we go to bed. With those boys around I even took the keys out of Fifty-five at night." He rubbed the steering wheel fondly.

Mr. Wheatley was sitting in the driver's seat of his school bus and I was standing in the doorway. He was a big man, all roundness and bulges, like a damp sack of grapefruit. It was hard to look at him without feeling the tension of his seams. During the summer, when he drove for summer school and day camps, his last stop was at the corner of Red Plum Lane and Hobbs Quarry; if I was home I would wave him down and we would drink a beer together.

"It's not like it used to be, George. Back when your mother and father moved in we were all kids, raising families. Now that Linda and Jimmy are moved out, it's just you and Donna and a few dozen old farts."

"You're no old fart," I told him.

Mr. Wheatley tugged on the bill of his Orioles cap. "I wasn't talking about me, George. Mind your manners." Holding his empty beer bottle firmly by the neck, he leaned to the left and dug his right hand into his pants pocket. "I better get going. What do I owe you?"

I waved him away. "Forget about it. I'll put it on your tab."

Mrs. Webb liked the new people too. I walked over to her

house that evening, while Donna was giving a late flute lesson. Mrs. Webb's was a regular meeting place for half the neighborhood, but this was dinnertime. She had eaten, so the two of us sat in wicker rocking chairs on her back porch, sipping mint tea and talking about the new neighbors. I told her what I knew.

"The two bushes they brought in the car are oleander," I told her. "Grace says she's had them for five years." The bushes were in large wooden tubs in the back of their yard, by the garage.

"I don't believe I've seen those here," Mrs. Webb said. "If I remember correctly, it's a southern plant."

"And poisonous. She said just chewing the leaves can blind you. But it's supposed to be real pretty."

Mrs. Webb looked out over her yard, her own small garden. "I believe I'm going to bake them a cake. It makes me so happy to see that woman taking care of that house. I'd say that's a sign of—" She stopped and listened hard at the police radio blaring inside the house.

Mrs. Webb's son, Kyle, was a fireman in the city. He told her about his work, and she didn't let him leave out any of the details. Later she would calmly tell us his grisly stories while she crocheted an afghan. She believed in sending people food, in making Christmas gifts by hand, and in sitting on the back porch talking all afternoon; to sit beside her was to be hypnotized, to be lost in the timelessness of her friendly favors and cushioned rocking chairs.

"What was I saying?" she said. "I lost my place."

"You're going to bake them a cake."

"Yes, I think I will."

"I'll be jealous."

"Listen to you. I just sent Donna home with brownies last week."

I stopped rocking. "You did?"

"Last Tuesday." Mrs. Webb sipped her tea.

"That's funny."

Mrs. Webb looked out across her yard. "Wait a minute . . . now, I know I gave them to her. She came over with some magazines and I—" Then she saw me and broke up. "Go on with you," she said. "I believe you'd lie to the pope."

She baked the new neighbors a German chocolate cake. The entire back-porch crowd was surprised and delighted to hear that Grace returned the favor the very next day; she made Mrs. Webb a loaf of banana bread that we all sampled and agreed was first-rate.

The people of Snyder's Mill kept farmers' hours: they got up before the sun, and by ten o'clock our neighborhood was sound asleep. Donna and I were considered the night owls; we waited until eleven for the news, and sometimes I stayed up for Steve Allen or a movie. The new neighbors seemed to keep late hours too. I saw lights on at their place even after Channel Two had signed off for the night, and when I left for work in the morning the house next door was silent. Donna saw Grace and the girls outside occasionally, but after two weeks she hadn't said more than hello.

Saturday afternoon I trimmed the hedges by the road. As I dragged the clippings to a pile by the toolshed, the gate next door squeaked and Dusty crossed the driveway. She wore a white T-shirt coming untucked from shorts that looked like they would slide right off. She didn't have any hips to speak of.

"Do you think you could give me a hand?" She took off her sunglasses. She had wide eyes and bright teeth that looked whiter because of her tan. I wondered if Donna could see us.

"I can't get the lawn mower started," Dusty said. "I don't think I can pull on it anymore."

I was just being friendly. A good neighbor. We walked over to their garage, which was empty except for the pickup truck, two rusted wheels, and an old gray push mower with a gas can next to it.

I pulled the starter. The cord was so tight I could feel my arm leaving the socket.

"Does Larry have any tools?"

Her face went blank for a moment, as if she didn't recognize the name. Then she said, "I don't think so." She knelt across from me and looked at the engine, hoping to see something. "Do you need tools?"

The mower might have started eventually, but what it really needed was a good cleaning. "Start at the beginning," my father always told us. "Do the job right."

I found an old can sitting on a ledge. Dusty watched as I drained the thick, gritty oil. When I went over to our shed, she followed me.

The metal doors were hot to the touch. The air inside was suffocating, full of that stale summer smell of gasoline and hot metal and dead grass. I stepped inside. The shed was small, and over the years it had gotten so full there was barely room to stand. Dusty stepped in beside me.

She pointed at a brand-new riding mower pushed against the side. Her bare shoulder nearly touched mine; the hairs on my arm felt like iron filings near a magnet.

"Does that work?" she said. "I haven't seen you use it."

"I like to walk." I took an open can of oil off the shelf, but the spark-plug wrench was in a toolbox on the other side.

I said, "Excuse me."

Dusty didn't move; instead, as I reached across her for the wrench, she leaned forward, just barely brushing my arm.

"What do you want?" she said.

I held up the spark-plug wrench.

She mock-smiled. "For doing all this stuff."

The shed had shrunk to the size of a phone booth. I tried to joke my way out of it.

"I usually charge five bucks an hour, but since you're a new customer . . ."

She didn't laugh. I can name all of the people I've ever stood that close to.

"Look," I said, trying not to touch her. "I'm a married man."

"Uh-huh." She sounded impatient.

"I would do this for anyone," I told her. "I help Kyle put up Mrs. Webb's screens every spring, and she's sixty-eight."

Dusty didn't answer. I didn't have to look down to know that her bare legs weren't far from mine.

Quietly I said, "I saw Kristin and Eve sunbathing."

"Oh," she said. Then: "You like them better."

"No."

I answered too quickly; neither of us spoke.

I closed the toolbox, then turned back to face her.

"I'm married," I said again, at least partly to hear myself say it. It didn't mean to Dusty what it meant to me.

We went back to their garage.

"My father was fanatic about cutting the grass," I told her. "He'd cut it two, three times a week."

"You're serious," Dusty said. "You don't want anything."

"He was a real grass cutter."

"Okay," she said, crouching to watch me work. "Crazy."

I could picture my father pushing our old lawn mower, walking quickly and pretending not to be able to hear anything. When Gus Triandos struck out in a clutch situation, or if he really needed to think through something important, he would go out and cut the lawn. As I changed the oil, I told Dusty about one Sunday after church, when a double-header between Baltimore and Cleveland was called because of rain. My father changed his clothes, went outside, and cut the grass. He kept his pipe in his mouth and an old baseball cap on his head, with the brim pulled low to keep the water out. Once the motor started, he was shut off, hidden from the world. My mother would follow him around the yard, trying to tell him that dinner was ready or that someone was on the phone, but he would point to his ear and shrug. We learned not to bother him when he was mowing.

"There were a lot of kids in our family," I told her. "He needed some time alone." I finished adding oil and put the cap back on.

"So why the tractor? Aren't they expensive?"

"My in-laws gave it to us." I took out the spark plug. "Donna is their only daughter. Her mother can always think of something we need. First it was the riding mower, then a dryer, then some kitchen chairs. Now it's wallpaper." I tapped the plug against the concrete to loosen some of the dirt. "Thanks to her, I've bought my way straight across the first floor of Montgomery Ward's."

"Why don't you tell her to bug off?"

I asked Dusty if she had ever been married. She hadn't.

I dipped the tip of the spark plug in gasoline and gave all

the moving parts a drink of lubricating oil. The underside of the mower was caked with dead grass, so I scraped it clean with a garden shovel.

"I didn't know it was going to take all this," Dusty said warily. She still seemed to expect me to hand her a bill.

"Don't thank me yet." I pulled the starter cord. On the second try the engine coughed, hesitated, and turned over. I opened the throttle and it ran smoothly, the noise echoing against the high ceiling of the garage.

"It's still hard to pull," I shouted over the noise, "but it should run for a while. Pick up a new spark plug, and have those blades sharpened." I wasn't sure if it was me talking or my father.

I pushed the mower through the side door and onto the lawn, then turned it over to Dusty. For a moment we both held the handle, then I let go.

"Thanks," she said loudly. "When there's something I can do for you . . ."

I shouted, "I'll let you know."

In an uncharacteristic display of responsibility, Bellshaw sent a professional crew to finish the paint job. This time the paint stayed on, but the color they chose—Grace and Larry or Bellshaw, we never knew which—was a glossy dark green, and the two-story house looked like a giant lime.

With the painting finished they settled into a different routine. Donna didn't see them outside as much during the day, and when Eve and Kristin sunbathed they stayed up against the back of the house, out of sight of everyone except Joe, who barked and wagged when he saw them. We hardly ever saw Larry's Cadillac. Grace and the girls replaced the old white curtains with heavy drapes so dark, pulled together so tightly, that it was impossible to tell whether any lights were on inside.

After dark there were few signs of life around their house. Occasionally we heard the cars of late visitors. And if the air was still, the faint sound of a record player continued long into the night. Sometimes after Donna was asleep I would lie beside her, awake, trying to make out the songs. I recognized some jazz, but most of it was dance music, rock-and-roll. Ray Charles telling everybody to do the Mess Around. Some nights I wondered if I was the only one listening; after a stack of singles played in rapid succession, a half-hour would pass before someone turned them over. Sometimes the same sides played all night.

Chapter Three

My father was a great man. He didn't like to draw attention to himself, and when he was alive I didn't understand that there was anything remarkable in what he did. He was a quiet man. He kept his hair short, wore plain white shirts, and rooted for the Yankees before Baltimore joined the major leagues. He wasn't physically intimidating—three of us grew to be taller than he was—and he never spanked or hit us, rarely raised his voice. He didn't need to. When I first saw the Lincoln Memorial, with its enormous statue of Lincoln sitting, solid and serious, with the weight of the nation on his shoulders and the strength to carry it, I was reminded of our father. Beneath his shirt the muscles in his arms and shoulders were evidence of his strength, and the scars and calluses on his hands told stories of countless small battles fought and won. He wasn't the kind of father who played catch every day, but he came to our games, and he took pride in all our accomplishments.

Since his death, I had begun to realize how much he and my mother accomplished. As I walked through the only house my parents had owned, slept in the room they had slept in, I wished I had known them better. Only six years ago I had been in high school, my parents were alive. Then the future we thought would involve all of us had been pulled out from under me, made instantly a part of the past. Now Donna and I had agreed to have children, and I thought it was what I wanted, but too many other changes were happening. Things I had grown up with were being replaced too quickly.

In the winter of 1953, before Bellshaw bought the house next door, it was owned by commercial developers. All of us in my family were disappointed to hear that the house was going to be torn down; we had always assumed one of us would buy it someday. What surprised us was that the men who had bought it wanted to tear down our house too.

We children heard this at a family meeting on a Wednesday night. We had meetings from time to time, whenever there was an important decision (What should be the new chore squads?) or announcement (Waite has joined the Navy.) to be made. Our house wasn't particularly big, so we spent a lot of time outside; it took something special to get everyone in one place.

There were eight of us. Even though the house was crowded, our father had wanted one more. He worked sixty hours in an average week, and his greatest pleasure when he relaxed, after mowing the lawn, was to sit in the green armchair in the living room with his shoes off, his thin black belt still cinched about the waist of his black pants, listening to baseball on the radio. My mother said she felt blessed to be loved by such a hard-working man; blessed enough that she agreed when he made an unusual, even bizarre, request. He wanted to name their children after the starting players on the 1927 New York Yankees.

The oldest was Mark, after Mark Koenig, the shortstop who had had such a bad year in 1926. Father admired Koenig's recovery—sportswriters thought he would be the one flaw in the Yankee lineup in '27—but he also liked him because he had read that Koenig carried books with him on road trips, and that Homer was his favorite author. Father's copy of the *Odyssey* had seen him through his own road trip, and even at home the worn volume was never far from reach.

Next came Waite, after Waite Hoyt, the pitcher, and then Lou, after Lou Gehrig. Gehrig was the silent star of the Yankees, always under Babe Ruth's shadow. My brother Lou moved to Germany when he got out of college, and we've only seen him once since then.

Bob Meusel was another strong hitter, but my brother Bob was never much good at baseball. My sister is named after Pat Collins, the catcher, and she was a tomboy who would play anything. My youngest brothers, Tony and Earle—second base and center field—don't care much for sports. Tony always wanted to lead a rock band, and Earle prefers to be on his own, taking things apart.

Relatives always told my parents that I looked least like either one of them, the most like some combination of the two. I have our father's angular nose and short, straight hair, but my mother's higher forehead and long neck. Other people—friends from school, their parents, casual acquaintances—weren't always sure the eight of us were related, we looked so different.

Because of the size of our family and our father's penchant for teamwork, he had organized us into squads, each of which was led by one of the oldest boys. That January night in 1953 it was my squad's turn to clear the table. Pat collected the silverware and napkins, I had the greater responsibility of glasses and plates, and Waite, our leader, stacked it all so nothing would break. Normally, the squad whose turn it was to wash the dishes had to begin as soon as that much was done, but on meeting nights cleaning was delayed. The dishes soaked while we pushed together around the long oak dining-room table, arguing and joking, our father sitting patiently at the end, near the window looking onto the backyard, and our mother off to one side, standing in the doorway to the kitchen. Father was the chairman of our meetings, captain of our ship. My mother rarely spoke, but when she did, her opinion influenced us all. If she had found the need to contribute, we knew she must have had something important to say.

The men who bought the house next door had presented their offer to our father in a restaurant downtown earlier that day. After waiting for quiet at the table, this is what he told us:

"They want to buy our house. They want to tear down three houses and buy the lot across the street. They want to put up office buildings."

"Those crudballs," Pat said. "Those dip-wads."

Tony said, "Do we each get our own office?" He was looking for a place to play the three-piece drum kit our aunt and uncle had given him for his tenth birthday. It was an unpopular gift.

"Hey, Einstein," Bob said. "The offices aren't for us."

"Big Duh," Tony said. "I know that."

"Then why'd you—"

Our father held up his hand.

"Do they only have the place next door?" Mark asked. "How do they expect to change the zoning?" He wasn't out of college yet, but he already thought like a lawyer.

After answering our questions, Father spoke again in his calm voice, telling us that, as always, he would do what the family decided would be best.

"They've already offered more than the house is worth," he said, "and they'll offer us more. But what we need to decide today is this: do we want to take the money and move to someplace bigger, where we would all have more room, or do we want to stay here?"

What affected our decision that night was more important than space, more than the thought of losing our friends and leaving our neighbors: our father had helped build our house, and the one next door. He never talked about it, but we knew what he had done. His hands had poured the foundation, laid the floors, and nailed down the roof.

All eight of us agreed to stay.

He looked at us, then toward the kitchen door. "Mother?"

She stood with her hands in her apron, always nervous at the prospect of speaking to a crowd, even when it was her family.

"I want to stay here," she said. Her father had died after the Depression, and the money he had left her, though less than he had hoped, was enough to allow her and our father to build the house when I was born. I was her fourth, the family was already big; she had planned to stay settled. It had only been fourteen years.

Father rested his hands on the table, palms up. The decision was not yet final. "They'll double their offer, in time."

"There isn't enough money in the world," she said. "This is

our home." Then she looked down, embarrassed as we all stared at her.

"We'll stay," Father said.

After Bob's squad finished cleaning, he and I lay on our beds in our basement room. He kept a bag of balloons in the drawer in the night table; we were hitting two of them, playing slow-motion volleyball with an imaginary net. I was winning.

"Do you think we'll move?" Bob said.

"Not if he said no." "He" was never "Dad" or "Pa." We had no informal name for the man. Addressed directly, he was Father.

Bob batted the red balloon so hard it touched the ceiling. My point. He said, "We've got to move, sometime. I'm not gonna stick around here forever." He was thirteen. "Are you?"

"Not forever." Moving away seemed inevitable, but I couldn't imagine leaving for good.

"Five years?" He tapped the yellow balloon higher.

"Sure."

"Ten years?"

"How do I know?" I grabbed the edge of my mattress and made a wild swing, nearly knocking the lamp off our table. Our room was so small it was hard to have much fun without knocking something over.

"In ten years I'll be in Kansas," he said.

Bob spent his free time drawing detailed blueprints, graph-paper designs of small rectangles inside one larger rectangle. He had soft pencils and art erasers and even a template with special shapes for doors, closets, bathtubs, and toilets. He had his best plans thumbtacked to the wall. Some of the houses were long, some square, some were for big families and some were just for him, but they were all ranch houses in Kansas. He had never been there—no one we knew had been there—but he was always talking about it.

"Not in a town," he would say, "but on a ranch. Near a town." Relatives and teachers said Bob was mature, a good planner. Kids at school thought he was weird.

I started one of my favorite games. "If you could take a trip anywhere in the world, where would you go?"

"Besides Kansas?"

I told him it had to be outside the United States. He held the balloons in his hands and looked up.

Our ceiling was covered by an enormous map of Western Europe. The north of France didn't quite make it, and southern Spain started down the wall, just over the door. Seville was in the crack. East to west the ceiling ran from Portugal almost to Warsaw. We had a lot of choices.

"Maybe Switzerland," Bob said. "They have a lot of snow."

"What about an island?" I had been reading Robert Louis Stevenson. "Corsica." I pointed to a spot above the door.

"No good. What if it sinks?"

"Islands don't sink."

He threw one of the balloons at me, but as soon as it left his hand it stalled out, then floated to the floor. "You're nuts. Islands sink all the time."

"I'd stay in a house on stilts. With a diving board on the porch."

"I'd go to the Amazon," Bob said. South America was on his side of the room. "In Social Studies we read you can die from an insect bite down there."

"And piranhas," I said. "They have piranhas in the water." The Amazon sounded perfect.

We kept on like that, looking at the maps and batting the balloons back and forth. We considered huts in Africa, igloos in Alaska, and wigwams in Australia (we knew there was a desert; it sounded logical). Bob settled on Kansas.

"It's the best," he said. "You can come visit."

We heard footsteps coming down the stairs.

"Halt," Bob said. "Who goes there?"

"William Faulkner." Mark stopped in the doorway. "Where's my dictionary?"

"How should I know?" Bob batted a balloon at him.

Mark caught it. "I told you yesterday that you could borrow it if you brought it right back."

"Hit the balloon."

Mark dropped it instead. Then he walked over to Bob's

bed, took an ankle in each hand, and lifted until Bob's feet were nearly touching the ceiling. An eraser fell out of his shirt pocket and bounced on the mattress.

"Hey," Bob said. "Cut it out." He gurgled.

"Where is it?"

His face was turning dark red, like the bulb at the bottom of a thermometer. "Under the bed."

Mark tipped Bob back so that his feet were leaning against the wall, then knelt down and pulled out the thick black dictionary. "Good boy, Bobby."

Bob was still balancing on his head and hands. "If you were like this, you'd have to step up to get through the door."

"I'll make a note of that," Mark said.

I turned around and let my head hang over the end of my bed. Mark was upside down.

"Where do you think we'll be in ten years?" I asked him.

"You two clowns are going to be in the loony bin."

"I'll be in Kansas," Bob said.

"I bet you will." Mark sounded as if he meant it. It was hard to tell with him.

"Not me," I said.

"In ten years? You'll be right here, holding down the fort."

We listened to Mark's footsteps as he climbed the stairs. I tried to swallow and couldn't.

"I'm getting dizzy," Bob said.

"Me too."

"Are you going to stop?"

"Not yet."

The wind howled against the basement window. It was supposed to snow again. I looked at the maps on the walls, upside down, patches of color with names I couldn't read.

"What's he know?" I said. "I could be anywhere."

Chapter Four

Donna was wearing her bathing suit, lying on a lounge chair on the patio, humming along with a piano concerto on the radio. She started when my shadow fell over her.

"What's this?"

"I got finished early," she said. "Kim Daniels has a fever."

"That's too bad." I leaned down and kissed her, then dropped into a lawn chair.

Donna said, "She's a sweet little girl, but she couldn't play a scale if I put a gun to her head. I should tell her mother to save her money."

I leaned back and closed my eyes. "Forget about it. We're too poor to be ethical."

She turned down the radio. "I blew it. I wanted to meet you at the door like this."

She was a sweetheart. *Happily married*, I should have told Dusty. *I'm a happily married man.*

Donna went back to humming the concerto. The sun felt good. I thought of a mildly indecent calendar in my employer's office, hot days on a beach. I wondered what Dusty looked like in a swimsuit.

"Hey," Donna said.

"Hey what?"

"Hey hey hey."

I opened my eyes. She had slipped her arms out of the suit and pushed it down to her waist.

"What are you doing?"

She grinned up at me, her breasts pale as teacups in the sun. "I thought I'd work on my all-over tan."

She had never done anything like this before. I didn't know whether to pull her suit off the rest of the way or wrap her in a blanket.

"I think the sun's a little low," I said, wide-awake.

She kept grinning.

"I'm serious," I told her. "Roll that back up."

"Why?"

"Because. We're in public." I was starting to feel nervous.

"What are you talking about? We're in our own backyard."

"We're *outside*," I said. "People can see us."

Her grin was gone. "Are you serious?"

"Somebody could see you."

She propped herself up on her elbows. "Who?"

The patio was tucked up against the house; the porch hid us from the street, the house separated us from Bellshaw's, the hedge in back screened us from the Pattersons'. Our yard stretched off to the north, but on the border was a long line of ten-foot-high lilacs; beyond them, almost entirely blocked from view, was Mrs. Webb's house.

"I don't know *who*," I said. "That's not the point."

"I was only trying—" But then she stopped. She rolled up her suit and slipped her arms through the straps. She picked up the radio and went inside.

This was a whole new level of anger for Donna—like a fire that turns bluish white, she was so angry she looked calm. I was afraid that if I followed her inside I'd be scorched.

I knew it was a bad move to tell a woman—any woman, but especially my wife—not to take her clothes off. But she had pulled down her suit to compete.

I slumped back in the chair.

Of course, the irony is, she was prettier than any of them. Kristin's freckles were so pale and dense they made her look like she had some kind of skin disease, and meanness was etched into her face. Eve had a dark complexion, she was heavy, her eyebrows were thick, and she had a mustache. She looked vaguely Spanish.

Then there was Dusty.

Dusty was bony, her hair dirty blonde, her lips too thin. But her teeth were straight and white, and she had an electric smile, a smile with more power than she could have controlled. Still, she wouldn't have stood out in a crowd. She always looked a little undone, as if she had gotten dressed in a hurry, and her voice squeaked at the beginnings of sentences. There was something about her, but it wasn't what you would call beauty. It was more important than that.

The three of them reminded me of the girls Waite had told Bob and me about when he was on leave. Once he showed us a black-and-white photo of a girl he knew—not naked, which is what we had hoped, but sitting on his lap in a bar. Her hair was stringy, stuck to her forehead, and her nose had been broken. Waite told us about the bar, and then, seeing that we weren't quite impressed, said that the girl never wore underwear. ("Ugh," Bob said. "Gross," I said. It sounded kind of *clammy*. Waite shook his head. "You guys are perverts.")

Bob and I talked about that picture later. We had seen other photographs, the kind one kid would keep in his locker until lunch and then charge everyone a nickel to look at. For a while it was exciting to see naked women, but then we told Terry Gleason, who said he got the pictures from a shoe box in his father's closet, to get some of women *doing* something. He made promises before finally admitting that he couldn't; soon only the little kids crowded around his locker.

In college there were more photographs, and magazines. The photographs were in color and the women were prettier, though none of us ever described them as pretty, and they were doing things, or at least pretending to. There were even black-and-white films, silent and grainy and poorly made. In the films the women were ugly again, but they did everything, with everyone (everyone, that is, but us—where were those women hiding?). We would go to whatever fraternity house had gotten the movies and start with some beers, talking without saying much. Then we'd pay someone standing at the stairs to the basement and go down and watch two or three of the films, which were short and predictable, and afterward we'd come back up and drink more beer. Everyone made bad jokes, everyone laughed. Outside, when we saw the girls we knew from our classes, even being drunk couldn't keep us from seeing that they were undeniably different from the women in the movies; more than that, there was something about us down in those basements that we never carried out onto the campus.

I had two girlfriends before Donna. The first was Linda Koestler, the girl behind the candy counter at the Ambassador movie theater, where I worked as an usher during my senior year of high school. While the film was running I would help her box popcorn and clean up spilled soft drinks. After the last show of the night we would clean up the theater, then walk down to the front row and sit for a few minutes, thinking about starring in romantic movies of our own.

In college I met Beverly Clark, an eternally tanned junior from Connecticut. Some friends of mine had invited me to an early Thanksgiving dinner at one of the dorms. Beverly was easily the most beautiful girl in the room, and while my friends never believed it, it was true nervousness that made me spill the gravy—a thick, primordial ooze straight out of a Japanese horror film—down her blouse. Like another alien creature, I offered to have it cleaned. We dated through that summer, then she transferred to a college in Colorado. We wrote for a while.

I met Donna on a hot Sunday in August the last fall Father lived in Baltimore. Pat and I were taking care of him since everyone else had left home. The next spring, when Pat graduated from high school, she left too, and our father went to spend his final months with Mark and his wife in Tennessee.

Chuck Estrada was pitching for the Orioles at Memorial Stadium. Our father had decided at the last minute that he wanted to see the game; after he started treatments for the cancer, he didn't often feel like going out, so when he did we tried to please him.

It was a beautiful day. We were in lower-deck seats on the third-base side and we had already had conversations with most of the people around us. That wasn't unusual when we went to a baseball game, even when our father wasn't feeling well. At first he would try to restrain himself, then he would mutter about the doctors, and by the top of the second inning he'd be balancing a beer between his knees, squeezing three packets of mustard on his hot dog. For the rest of the game he'd eat peanuts, crushing the shells and scooping the nuts into his mouth in one smooth motion, and he'd shout out to the players in a way he never did when he watched games at home. Later I'd try to explain it to Donna by telling her Pat and I were like page turners for a master pianist: we would flag down concessionaires and keep score in an official lucky-number program, attending to our father, who took a rare opportunity to indulge himself.

It was in the fifth inning. Jim Gentile watched two balls, low and outside. On the third pitch he hitched his left arm, started to swing, then tried to stop; in an instant the ball glanced off his bat, over the Orioles' dugout, the crowd stood, our father's arm rose high above the rest, and the ball smacked into his palm.

The crowd roared—a line drive caught one-handed—but our father would have none of it. He flipped the ball to Pat and yelled, "Straighten it out, Jimmy. Wait for your pitch." And then, with a magic I believed our father possessed, Jim Gentile nodded vaguely, got set, and drove a high fastball into the right-field stands.

We were on our feet, with Gentile about to touch third as he rounded the bases. From the row ahead of us, the girl I had been watching all afternoon turned and said, "That was some catch." I didn't quite hear her; I assumed she was talking about Gentile's hit, and I said it sure was.

"Has he ever done that before?" she asked as we all sat down.

"Gentile?" He tipped his cap in our direction as he reached the dugout.

"Your father."

She was older, and so attractive that I wouldn't have had the nerve to approach her anywhere else. But she wasn't at home—she wore a light skirt and ruffled blouse, too formal for a baseball game—and I was.

"I don't know how he does it," I said. "He catches fouls all the time." An exaggeration, but it felt like the truth.

"Doesn't it hurt?"

"Ground ball, six-to-three." My father frowned over at me as he dictated the last out of the inning. I made the notation on the scorecard as the Orioles took the field. "You have to know how to catch it," he told her. "Let your hand give just as the ball gets there. It still smarts, though. Sure it does." Before he finished he caught a peanut vendor out of the corner of his eye and whistled, reaching deep in his pocket for change.

Donna and I talked for the rest of the game. The shadow of the upper deck, which had crept over us in the third inning, along with gusts of wind caught in the curve of the stadium, made the heat bearable. At first we talked between innings, then between batters, and soon we only stopped long enough to watch solid hits and long fly balls to the outfield. In the top of the sixth she told me her name, and that she was a graduate music student at the University of Maryland. In the bottom of the eighth I scrawled her phone number across the extra-innings section of the visitors' side of the scorecard, between beer stains and the thin red skins from roasted peanuts.

It had only been two years.

"Honey?"

No answer.

I pictured her upstairs, lying across the bed, crying. I wondered if she had gotten that dramatic.

"Honey?"

I found her sitting at the kitchen table, staring at the salt and pepper shakers, wearing my trench coat.

"I'm sorry," I said.

Her face was blank in concentration, as if she were trying to remember something important. My coat covered her completely.

"I mean it," I said. "I don't know what I was thinking about."

There was a long silence. The refrigerator motor clicked off, rumbling to a halt.

"You don't think I'm pretty." She wasn't asking.

"Of course I do." I couldn't believe my luck when she agreed to go to a movie the first time I called her. I proposed six months later, before she had a chance to come to her senses.

"But you didn't have to do that," I said. "Forget about them." I was saying it to her and I was saying it to myself.

"I'm going to be pregnant," Donna said, strangely calm as the floor dropped out from under me.

"You are?"

She half-smiled at my panic. "*Going* to be."

She turned, the same calm, intent expression on her face. "Do you know what's going to happen? Do you know what I'm going to look like after five months? Seven? You're going to look at me in the morning and you're going to throw up."

I tried to imagine her ugly. I thought about the way the hair on my arms had stood on end when Dusty moved beside me in the toolshed.

"No I won't," I said, pushing the thought away.

"*I'm* going to throw up. I won't be able to eat, and then I'll eat like I'm starving. When I get fat I'll be wearing bags made to look like dresses. My skin will break out. I'm going to look like a pig."

She locked her gaze to mine, not letting me get away.

"You're going to roll over and see me," she said, "and you're going to think to yourself, 'Why did I marry her?' You're not going to want to *touch* me."

I had never been one to fall asleep easily, but more and more I found myself lying awake long hours, thinking. That night the air was muggy, thick with humidity. The top sheet, damp, clung to my skin. I pushed it down to the foot of the bed.

Donna was asleep. She could drop off in a minute, no matter what the weather, no matter what was on her mind.

We had been aware of our differences from the start. She was three years older, an only child, and I was from the middle of eight. She was in music education, I was in engineering. But she sewed, and I did woodwork—skills we admired in each other—and we both liked gardening. She wasn't very athletic, but she cheered for me at softball games. I didn't know anything about music, but I applauded loudly at her concerts. I explained how to place-hit, how to slide, how to judge the backspin on a towering foul. She talked about the structures of concertos and symphonies, about melody and tone, about intonation and character. Our differences had been something to explore.

Those nights I lay awake, I saw it all more coolly, without the warm filter of romance. Donna had tried to give me lessons on her flute, but I never even learned to do a scale. I convinced her to play softball at the picnic before the wedding, but she was embarrassed because she couldn't hit.

My brothers and I had spent endless afternoons in the yard, playing catch and hot box and pepper and other games that didn't have names. The rose of Sharon in the corner of the yard marked our home plate, the lilacs along the side were our first-base foul line. We had each gone from frustratingly bad to competent to a kind of nonchalant amateur ease.

I remember Brian Lindbaum's father, who was driving Brian and my brother Bob and me to an Orioles game, telling us that one day we would get tired of baseball, that instead we would like girls. We looked at him in disgust. But there had come a time for each of us when we stopped waiting for the first day in March just warm enough so that we could go outside in a loose jacket and start throwing, a time when we put our gloves away in the fall without first wrapping a ball in the pocket. The smell of saddle soap disappeared, and our gloves grew dry and brittle.

I had never heard classical music before meeting Donna, never been to a concert; no one in our house mentioned Bach or Chopin or Mahler. I couldn't follow the intricacies of the solos she described before playing them. I understood that classical music was more sophisticated and articulate than the blues I liked, but there was a difference between knowing that and wanting to listen to it.

So when I went to her concerts, at the university or at places around the city, I listened for something else: for mood, for something that would carry me off the way Big Joe

Turner's voice and Count Basie's piano could. Afterward I would remember the way one conductor had stood in front of the orchestra in his rumpled suit, arms poised, like a bear balancing on his hind legs, ready at any moment to drop onto all fours and lumber off the stage. I would remember the attitudes of the musicians—the lesser ones looking either nervous or self-consciously bored, the better ones anticipating, smiling—and the way they applauded the conductor and the soloist, violinists and violists holding their instruments in one hand as the other fluttered like a fish against one knee.

Now Donna and I quietly accepted the routine of day-to-day living, and the bond that held us together had become a silent one. When I got home I did odd jobs around the house; Donna gave flute lessons, cooked and cleaned.

It was faint at first, but as I lay in bed I heard a drumbeat, then bits and pieces of a melody. Music from the house next door.

Seeping through the walls of Bellshaw's house and the new heavy drapes, the music crossed the driveway and passed through our screen window soft as a warm breath. You had to listen for it.

I shifted my weight, the bedsprings creaked. I watched to see if Donna stirred. Moving slowly, I got out of bed and put on a pair of pants.

The music wasn't much louder outside. I looked at their windows, but there was no light. I looked higher. The night was quiet, breezeless, the stars dim and out of focus in the haze. My bare feet were warmed by the rough concrete of the sidewalk.

I had hoped coming outside would help, but there was nothing out there. The same thoughts that had kept me awake returned. When my mother died, I actually hurt, I was sore; I couldn't think. But cancer killed our father slowly, and by last fall I thought I was prepared for the end. Yet in the months since then I had realized how much I didn't know—who our parents were before they were married, what the family was like before I was born. I wished I had asked him to tell me how to be a good husband, a good provider. Anyone who had raised eight children so well must have known the secret. My mother had told me that when she was young she had been named queen at a parade; one of her prizes was a puppy, and it died within a week. Now I wanted to ask her: What kind of dog was it? How did it die?

I heard footsteps. Someone on the road.

The man stopped when he saw me. Feeling friendly, I called hello.

He hurried on without answering, proceeding not down the road, but straight toward our driveway. It was after midnight; for all I knew, he was a burglar. Before I could decide to challenge him, he opened the gate to the backyard of Bellshaw's house.

When I turned to watch him, I saw something that hadn't been there before. Up in one of the front upstairs windows, muted by the heavy drapes, shone a dull blue light.

The man, who looked to be in his forties, stood on the back porch and knocked on the door. After a moment it opened. He spoke, then listened, then went inside. When I looked back at the upstairs window, the blue light had been turned off.

That was the first time I gave the possibility serious consideration. A whorehouse. It couldn't be, I thought—that was Bellshaw's house, the one my father built, right next door. A whorehouse would look like something special. Besides, Dusty and the other two didn't act like whores. Though I wasn't sure exactly how whores were supposed to act.

Exactly what would they do? I assumed it had to be something exotic, if men were willing to pay for it. All three of them at once? Whips and chains? I started to imagine Dusty in a fraternity-house movie—then I stopped and went inside.

Climbing upstairs in the dark, I thought of myself in front of the television, watching baseball, while Donna listened to Mario Lanza in *The Student Prince*. When I told her I had found one classical composer I liked, she said Gershwin wasn't classical, he had little understanding of the major problems of form and continuity. I didn't know exactly what she was talking about, but I knew what she meant: Gershwin didn't count.

I undressed and lay beside her. She slept curled in a ball,

her back to me. She liked me to slip one arm around her breasts and the other around her waist, but lately that had bothered me; it was hot, and her hair kept getting in my mouth. So we slept back to back. She liked to press against me, wrapped in the sweet gift of sleep. I lay there wide-awake, wondering what had happened since that afternoon in Memorial Stadium, slowly being pushed toward the edge of the bed.

Chapter Five

We heard honking and went outside.

"So here it is," Donna said to her father. "Your second childhood."

Her parents were in the front seat of a shiny dark blue convertible with a sparkling white interior. There were letters on the grille: GTO.

"New for sixty-four," Ed said. "Climb in."

Before we had the door closed he was backing up, turning onto the road in a squeal of rubber.

"Slow *down*," Evelyn said, flinching.

"Cut it loose," Ed told her. "Live a little." Evelyn held her hair as if it might be blown from her head.

As he sped down Hobbs Quarry and turned hard onto Red Plum Lane, Ed shouted to us over his shoulder, "It's an option package for the Le Mans. Wide wheels, the 389-cubic-inch V-8. Kids are gonna eat it up."

"You know what they say," Evelyn yelled as we rocketed down the lane, leaving barking dogs and clouds of dust in our wake. "The only difference between men and boys is the size of their toys."

"Price," Donna corrected, but her mother couldn't hear.

"Hold on!" Ed shouted, swinging into the sharp turn that would take us to Liberty Road. With a wide grin on his face he called out to the world at large, "You're looking at a big nine-point-five on the fun meter." He slowed down on Liberty, but he accelerated into the turn for Hobbs Quarry.

We skidded onto the driveway and he stamped the brakes, throwing us forward. "Better than the roller coaster at Gwynn Oak."

"And almost as safe," Evelyn said, checking to make sure her eyes and nose were where she had left them.

Ed got out and held the seat up for us, puffing in excitement. He had a paunch from too many slow days in the showroom.

"What do you think? Ready for a trade-in?"

"It smells good," Donna said. "That new-upholstery smell."

Ed waved it off. "I can get you a can of that stuff. You can make your sofa smell like that."

"This kind of car could get you into trouble," I said.

He wiped his face with a handkerchief. "You're only as old as you feel. I guess that makes you about a hundred and ten." He grinned. "That's a joke, son-in-law. I'm here to tell you, I'll eat my hat if these things don't sell literally like hotcakes."

"Literally?" Donna said. "With syrup, and a pat of butter?"

"Literally," Ed said. "It's a figure of speech."

After we got settled in the living room—Ed and Evelyn each liked to have a Bloody Mary before dinner—they asked what was new, and I said I was thinking about asking for a week off sometime soon. I was an inside man for Harry Reynolds, an industrial manufacturer's representative. I had decided in the spring that I had to get more money or leave, but Harry never came through with the raise he had mentioned, and I didn't quit. He had promised the vacation a year ago.

"So," Ed said, "where are you going?"

Donna came in carrying a tray of cheese and crackers. "We haven't really talked about it."

Evelyn leaned toward the coffee table to spread some cheese. "Just because he's got a vacation doesn't mean they have to run off somewhere." She turned to Donna. "Maybe you'll have time to refinish those floors upstairs. The longer you wait, the harder it is to sand them down." She took a sip of her drink. "Now, maybe a weekend at the ocean—"

"Forget the floors," Ed said. "Get away from home, see what the rest of the world is up to."

"I thought we might visit some of my family," I said.

He nodded. "I can see those wheels spinning now."

"What you need is a pool," Evelyn said. "One of those aboveground pools. We had one when Donna was young. We'd lie in the sun, then play in the water. A small one is all you need."

Ed stirred his celery until tomato juice splashed up over the side of his glass. "What *you* need," he told Evelyn, "is some imagination. Let them go now, while they're young." He turned to Donna and me. "Best thing I know is when you get to be our age, if you make it, just to sit and roll back the miles. Take a look at every place you've been, what you've done. I read somewhere that traveling slows time, and it's true. You remember the trips you take together. They're like frozen moments, like little . . ." He tried to find the words, then shook his head. "Go now. You get old, you never know what's going to happen. One day you'll be driving along and suddenly—pow."

Evelyn winked at me to change the mood. "If I had known he was going to grow old, I never would have married him."

Ed wasn't listening. "Remember that time we went to Rehoboth with your brother? That was on my vacation that year. And remember when you went up to New York with Dottie Kaye and that girl she knew from Owings Mills?"

"I certainly do," Evelyn said. "I still have the picture of the three of us standing in those fake-fur coats in that booth near the Empire State Building."

"If you remember, the reason you could go was that you and Dottie had both quit your jobs down at Lexington Market. Just like that."

"We saved all summer for that trip," Evelyn told Donna.

Ed leaned back in his chair. "If it's right for us, why isn't it right for them? They can refinish floors when they're a hundred and two."

Evelyn finished a cracker quietly. "I guess I'm no fun anymore." She smiled, but it didn't stay.

Ed asked Donna, "You remember your Uncle Connie?"

"Barely."

He looked over at me. "My oldest brother. I hardly ever hear from him. Anyway, he's a wild man. When we were young he bought a motorcycle, and he'd ride that thing up the front porch, through the living room, and into the kitchen. Used to scare the living bejesus out of Mother. She'd say, 'What the hell are you doing, riding that motorcycle in the kitchen?' "

"She never said any such thing," Evelyn said.

"Well, words to that effect. And Connie would say, 'Just wanted to see what's for dinner,' and ride out the back door and down the steps.

"But that's not the story. He had all kinds of schemes, and one year he actually made pretty good money. He bought himself a thirty-nine Terraplane, a trailer, and a brand-new camera. Packed up everything he owned, and took off for California. Halfway across the country, somewhere in Missouri —maybe Kansas, somewhere out there—he lost control of the car, and it tumbled down the side of a hill, trailer and all.

"He was in the middle of nowhere, so there was no use waiting for someone to find him. He worked his way out of the car, which was totaled, pried open the trunk with a rock, found the camera, and took a picture of the wreck. Then he climbed back up to the road, still carrying that damned camera, and thumbed his way out to Los Angeles.

"And did he sit around and cry over it? No sir. He traded the camera for two months' rent and went back to business. I think about him some days. He had his faults, but when he got an idea in his head, he wouldn't let anybody tell him no."

After dinner we played bridge. The three of them were teaching me. I wasn't much good at remembering tricks, but I was learning. Once in a while Donna and I would win a game. Around ten, after Ed and Evelyn had won a rubber, Evelyn was in the kitchen getting a drink. We heard a knock on the side door.

"Don't get up," she called in to us. "I'll get it."

She took the steps down and opened the door. We could hear a man's voice.

I walked in and stood by the refrigerator, out of sight of whoever was there. Then I leaned forward to see him.

"I don't understand," Evelyn said.

The man moved closer to the screen door. The porch light cast a long shadow over his face.

"Larry told me to come around," he said.

Evelyn paused, curious. "Who's Larry?"

The man peered in through the screen. "What is this, some kinda joke? I ain't got all night."

Evelyn reached for the doorknob. "You had better turn around and leave before I call the police."

"What?" He pressed harder against the screen, glaring at Evelyn. "That son of a bitch," he muttered. He turned, then stopped. "You tell that son of a bitch Larry—"

I leaned out over the steps. "Next door," I said.

The man stood back and looked at the side of the house. He mumbled something before backing away.

Evelyn told the story to Donna and Ed as soon as we got back to the table.

"Uh-oh," Donna said.

Ed picked up his cards and fanned them. "You've gotta be kidding. What've they got going over there, a cathouse?"

Neither of us said anything.

Ed was reading his hand, looking for an opening bid. When he found it, he rapped the cards against the table once, then looked up. He read our faces even faster.

"You're kidding me," he said. "No fooling?" He looked from Donna to me and back to her; an enormous smile lit his face. "I'll be damned. Hurt me Bertha."

"What was that?" Evelyn looked up from her hand. "What did I miss?"

"A goddamned cathouse," he said. "Right across the driveway."

"We don't know for a *fact*," I said.

Donna told them what we did know: three girls who didn't look like sisters lived with a woman who didn't look like their mother, they didn't go out during the day, and at night there were visitors. She didn't tell them about the sunbathing.

I said, "There's one other thing." Donna glanced at me,

trying to remember what she had left out. I kept my eyes on her parents as I told them about the blue light.

"That's wrong," Ed said. "They'd have a red light."

"This one's blue."

"No," he said. "They used to call them red-light districts. Like the Block. Still do, some places. They have red lights in the windows."

"What for?" Evelyn asked.

Ed frowned. "Sometimes I think you grew up in a convent. A red light—stop and go. Controls the traffic."

I said, "I know all about that, but—"

Evelyn raised her eyebrows.

"I've heard that," I said, "but the light next door was blue."

Ed thumbed his cards. "I think you probably didn't—"

"It doesn't matter." Donna's voice was flat and hard.

"You're right," her mother said. "What matters is when are they going to stop. When did you call the police?"

Donna and I looked at her.

"You did call," Evelyn said.

"No," Donna said. "Not yet."

"We're not even sure that's what they're doing," I said. "Maybe they're just friendly."

The three of them looked at me.

"Absolutely," Ed said. "What you and I need is to go on a little fact-finding mission. Collect some hard evidence."

"Edward."

"What do you want them to tell the cops, there's a red light in the window? Maybe they're getting ready for Christmas."

"Blue," I told him.

"They need to tell the police what they just told us," Evelyn said. "I don't see how you can joke about something like this. Right next door, as we speak, people are getting—"

"Laid," Ed offered.

"—corrupted!"

"Who?" he said. "The broads? Not if they're doing what we think they're doing. The johns?"

"All of them!"

"Mother," Donna said, "calm down."

"I will *not* calm down! I don't believe what I'm hearing. Of course *they* don't understand, but you . . ." Suddenly Ed and I were the enemy. "Don't you know what they're doing in that house?"

Ed sat back and sighed. "You told me you handled all that when she was in seventh grade. One diamond."

Evelyn ignored him, leaning close to Donna. "Women are selling themselves next door," she said in a low voice. "*Next door.*"

"Get your mind on important things," Ed told her. "One diamond."

She played, but before she regained her composure, Donna and I won two hands. After that she concentrated long enough to win the rubber, but she wasn't finished telling us what to do.

"This won't be the end," she said as we walked them to the door. "Think how it will look if you don't stop this. You could even go to jail for—"

"—for living next door to a cathouse." Ed stood by the car as Donna walked her mother around to the passenger side. While they were talking, he turned to me and said, "Do me a favor, will you? If they start giving away free samples, give me a call." He tapped me on the stomach. "That's a joke, George."

Chapter Six

I wanted to tell someone about the girls: someone who wasn't going to hand me a pair of binoculars, or laugh it off, or be outraged that I hadn't called the police. My brother Lou seemed perfect.

I only heard from Lou at Christmas, when his wife sent a copy of a letter typed on red stationery with their news from the past year. From the red letters I knew where he worked, for an engineering research laboratory, and I knew he had gotten a promotion last October. His wife said they had modernized all the plumbing in their eighteenth-century house, and they were becoming so fluent in French and German that they almost forgot to write their "friends in the States" in English (but I was his *brother*, back home). Each year, in a handwriting different from the one that signed the names on the mimeographed letter, was "Thanks for writing. Happy Xmas," followed by a vertical line and a horizontal squiggle that I guessed meant "Lou." The note only made me feel worse; I could hear his wife making him write it. "Look at these letters," she would say, holding up a thick pile of airmail envelopes. "Write *some*thing."

I learned letter writing from my mother. She liked to listen to what other people had to say, and she liked to get mail from places she could only imagine. I didn't write as much as she had, but as my brothers moved away I started a correspondence that never stopped. After college it included twenty relatives and over a dozen friends. I kept all their letters, and I began to feel like a cartographer, charting the course of other people's trips to Europe, job searches, love affairs, and marriages.

I wrote Lou everything we had told Ed and Evelyn. Then I told him about Eve and Kristin sunbathing topless, and about standing next to Dusty in the toolshed. Maybe she *was* just trying to be friendly, I told him—but then I nearly crossed it out. She had needed her lawn mower fixed.

Donna hung up the phone in the kitchen and walked past me, into the living room, carrying a skirt she was hemming.

"How's your mother?"

She spread the skirt across her lap and held a needle up to the light. "I think the only reason she called was to see if the paddy wagon was in the driveway."

"And?"

"And nothing. I changed the subject." She knotted the thread.

After a minute I started writing again.

"Have you thought about next week?" Donna said.

"What?"

"The Fourth of July. I thought we might invite Press and Cindy over."

I stared down at what I had been telling Lou, wondering what the women were like in Germany.

From the living room Donna said, "Should I call them?"

"Call who?"

"Press and Cindy." She sounded annoyed. "We can talk about it later."

"No," I said, "that's fine. I'll ask him at work."

"Do you mind if we listen to some music?"

She was always good about asking; sometimes I couldn't concentrate with music on.

"Go ahead." I thought about what else I needed to tell Lou, trying to explain why I didn't think everyone should be so excited.

"What do you want to hear?" Donna said.

"Anything, sweetheart."

I told Lou what Ed and Evelyn had said, and that I wasn't

sure how Donna felt. I didn't know how to bring it up. When we sat across the kitchen table from each other, or lay in bed, I felt I should *know* what she thought, it should have been obvious. Or maybe what I should have known was something else: there are some questions you can't ask your wife.

As I wrote I was dimly aware of orchestral music in the background. Suddenly a violin soloist went wild. I tried to ignore it, but it was like ignoring an albino on a bus.

"Honey?"

She didn't hear me.

"Honey? What *is* that?"

She was engrossed in her sewing. "What's what?"

"That music."

"Paganini. Concerto Number One. Why?"

"Isn't there something a little less dramatic?"

Donna let the material sink to her lap and looked over at me. "I guess so." She walked over to the record player and lifted the tone arm. "Do you not want to hear classical? It doesn't have to be. I'm just in the mood for music."

"Great," I said. "Fine. Play anything you want."

"You're sure? We could listen to Big Joe—I don't care."

"Anything," I said. "Let her rip."

She put the record in its jacket and looked through our albums.

I wrote, *If this had happened last summer, we would have talked about it. She wouldn't have handed me binoculars eleven months ago; she wouldn't have*—but I couldn't tell him about her pulling down her bathing suit. Some things you don't tell even your brother.

"I'm sorry," Donna said, "I know you're busy. Mozart?"

"Sure. Mozart. Great." I lost my train of thought. I considered asking Lou if he had heard from Pat about her boyfriend. She had written me a long, carefully worded, almost apologetic letter explaining that they were living together. She seemed to expect me to be shocked, but I had gotten over that with Bellshaw's old tenants. I felt sorry for her, so I reassured her that I didn't hate her for it, that I understood why she didn't want to rush into marriage. But she seemed obsessed with explaining their living situation, and reexplaining it, and she never got around to telling me much about the guy.

My pen was making a pond of ink on the paper—I couldn't start the next sentence.

"Hey," I said. "How do you expect me to concentrate with this?"

Donna looked up. "It's Mozart."

"It sounds like something from a circus."

"The twenty-fifth symphony is *not* circus music."

"It sounds like—" I stopped. "All right, it's not. But could you turn it down?"

She walked quickly across the room. "We don't have to hear anything—that's why I asked you in the first place." She switched the record player off.

"You didn't have to do that."

She sat down. For a minute the house was quiet.

"Who are you writing to?"

I finished my sentence. "Lou. Then Ken Bukowitz."

"I didn't know you had heard from him."

"I haven't. That's why I'm writing."

"I see." She poked the needle into the skirt and let it rest. She smoothed out the material as she talked. "Who have you heard from lately?"

"I got that letter from Bob last week. And Barbara sent the postcard from San Francisco." Barbara Heathrow was a friend of ours from school.

Donna came into the dining room. Sheet music from the day's lessons was stacked neatly on the corner of the table. Usually when I came home I'd find two chairs pulled off to the side, a music stand in front of one of them forming the third point of a triangle. The closeness of the chairs and the loose music made the rest of the house seem empty. Some days I felt the house had been rented out from under me, strangers had moved in.

She leaned against the table. "Did you ever think of keeping track of the letters you send?"

"Why?"

"I bet you send five times as many as you get."

"What's the point?"

"It's just that . . . I thought it might bother you that people don't answer. Sometimes they do—I don't mean that—but not very often. You sit here and you write letters and you tell everyone what's happening, you're some kind of alumni magazine and family newsletter combined, and they don't write back."

"Sure they do." I put the cap on my pen. "Maybe not every time, but most people don't write a lot of letters."

Donna picked up the pen. "I don't know. Maybe it isn't important. But some nights, when you sit here while I'm in the next room waiting to talk to you, I wonder what it is that you're saying to all those people. I wonder if you've got another life you're not telling me about."

Looking back, I see that as our first discussion about the girls next door.

JULY

Where we walked that day
The ice cracked, a long summer
Of frozen lightning.

—Nick Nappo

Chapter Seven

Kristin and Eve were stringing Chinese lanterns along the edge of the fence. Piled on the back steps were other supplies: paper tablecloths, red-white-and-blue bunting.

I said, "They're having a party. They're putting up decorations."

Donna took her robe from the closet door and came over to the window. We watched Eve and Kristin hang the lanterns.

She said, "This whole thing is very strange."

"What I want to know," I said, "is why aren't we invited? We're neighbors."

As it turned out, we were. After breakfast, when I went to feed Joe, Grace called over. She was taping a paper tablecloth to a picnic table pushed up against the house.

"We're having us a cookout," she said. "You and your wife want some hamburgers, come on over."

I told her we were having company.

"Bring everybody," she said. "We got beer for an army, and plenty of food. The way the girls have been inviting people, you'd think weinies grew on trees." Grace finished with the tablecloth. "Come over for a beer, anyway."

I told her I'd mention it to Donna.

Press and Cindy pulled up early in the afternoon with their daughters, Beth and Kimberly, and their golden retriever,

Belle. There were already a dozen people in the backyard of Bellshaw's house. Belle sat on the grass and scratched, then trotted back to visit Joe.

"You should get this to the refrigerator," Press said, handing me a six-pack. "We had to buy it warm."

"This should stay cool too." Cindy was carrying a bowl covered with tinfoil. "Let's go inside, girls." Beth and Kimberly, two and three, each had a redheaded doll.

"Looks like a party next door," Press said.

I took four bottles of cold beer to the living room and Donna brought milk for the girls. "Those are our new neighbors," she said, setting out the coasters. "Hasn't George told you about them?"

Press turned to Cindy. "Did you hear this?"

As Donna and I finished telling the story, Press wiped the sweat off his beer bottle. "The house of blue lights."

"It sounds like a mystery," Cindy said. "Do you sit by the windows all night, looking over there? I would."

Donna said, "They aren't even close to pretty. There's a fat one with boobs like balloons and a very bitter-looking girl, and then there's the skeleton—all skin and bones."

I had never heard any of this.

"That's not true," I said.

Donna and Cindy looked at me.

"I'm just saying, she isn't skin and *bones*. In the name of accuracy."

Cindy said, "My dad used to say, 'No boy is going to buy the cow when the milk is free.' Which was his idea of a father-daughter conversation. But he never said anything about cows for rent. Can you imagine, sleeping with just anyone who took out his wallet? I can't even see how men can do that. Pay them for it. And they get all those diseases?" She shuddered. Then turned to Press. "Could you do that?"

He said, "I am fundamentally incapable of such an act."

"Seriously," she said. "If you weren't married."

Press ignored the question as completely as if he had been struck deaf.

Cindy turned to me.

"I think I hear Joe," I said. "I should let him run for a while."

Press stood immediately. "I'll check on Belle."

We went out to Joe's house. It was six feet long by four feet wide, divided into two rooms, with a slanted roof. Joe loved it. As a puppy he kept getting sick in the basement, so the vet told us to let him stay outside. I built him a house he could live in.

I slipped the choker over his head and he and Belle ran off to explore the yard.

"You have papers for him, don't you?" Press asked.

We did.

"You ever put him out to stud?"

"We don't give him the car or anything, but I don't know what he does on his own time." Every few months Joe managed to slip his leash, but he always came back to his house at night.

"Belle's going to be in heat in a week or two. We're thinking of breeding her."

"Just say when."

Press looked over my shoulder, across the driveway. "Which ones are they?"

I didn't recognize the people in the yard. "They must be inside."

We walked back to the patio and sat in lawn chairs. The dogs wandered and we drank our beer.

"Okay," I said. "We're both happily married men."

"Very happily married," Press said, with the slightest hint of a question in his voice.

"Very."

"And next door," he said, "in fact, within one hundred feet of us, as we speak, are three young women whose lives revolve around sex."

"Three, maybe thirty. Who knows about their friends?"

"Let's not confuse the issue." Press held the beer bottle to his lips, thoughtful. "More specifically, unlike some, perhaps even most young women, and in clear defiance of all traditional social and moral codes, these young women seek to have sex with any number of men."

"Some of whom, we must assume, are married."

"It's always dangerous to assume, but we feel safe in doing so here."

"Some of whom have children."

"Certainly."

"Some of whom have dear sweet mothers waiting up late at night, praying for them to return home from their bowling league safely."

"Perhaps."

"So here's the question," I said. "What's the difference between them and us?"

"Could it be that they are *un*happily married?"

"I suppose." Neither of us was satisfied.

Press thought it over. "Could it be that they are low and despicable creatures?"

"Certainly."

"And if that's true—if we are, in fact, not only more content, even more than content, with our chosen mates, not to mention intellectually and morally superior to those creatures—then why is it that we wish we were in their euphemistic shoes?"

"Euphemistic shoes," I said. "I'd love to have a pair."

Press leaned back in his chair and propped his feet against the house. He was dark-skinned—he had West Indian blood on one side—and strong. He had cleared the lot his house stood on, and he lifted weights in his basement.

He said, "We don't really wish we were them."

"No."

"But we envy them this . . . particular freedom."

"We do."

Press took a sip of beer. "Back in Virginia, when I was fourteen, I went with my brother and some of his friends to a house they knew about. There were five girls sitting around in bathrobes, watching TV."

"And to change channels?"

"Ten bucks."

"Ten?"

Press nodded. "It's a wonderful country."

"And?"

"There were several important factors. For one, I was by three years the youngest in the group. There was some fear among the others that I might squeal."

"So?"

"They paid."

"And?"

"It was my first time, and I was clumsy, excited, all of that. But about halfway through, I was staring at the headboard of this old, stinking bed that felt like it was going to collapse any minute, trying to find the rhythm, and I thought to myself, 'This is bestiality.' "

"Because it was so crude, so impersonal."

"Because she was a moose. We had gotten drunk first—the rest of them knew the girls were ugly—and I tried to keep from looking at her, but I felt like a lonely farmboy. Three seconds after I finished I was waiting out by the car, trying to get the hell out of there, scared to death I was going to die of the clap."

"But you went back?"

"Oh no. Never." He started to drink but laughed before the bottle reached his mouth. "I never paid for it, ever."

"So what's the moral of the story?"

"Are these three as unattractive as Donna makes them out?"

"Only two."

He was silent for a long time.

"I never went back there," he said. "The ugly part kept me away. And believe me, all her parts were ugly."

"But—"

"I had begged my brother to let me go, I had nagged him for months. It was all I wanted. But I had better times locked in the bathroom with some one-handed literature."

"That's a piss-poor moral to the story," I said.

"I used to wonder what it would have been like if she had been one of those fifty-dollar women from Alexandria. Just to see what it's like in the pros."

"Big-league ball."

"But now," he said, "we're happily married men."

Neither of us said anything.

"You play the field much in college?" Press asked.

"A little." I looked down at the patio.

"And you've got three whores next door, one of them half-pretty, and she tries to jump you in your toolshed?"

"Well, not exactly."

Press shook his head. "These are the times that try men's souls."

I scraped at the label of my bottle. "There's one more thing, just to confuse the issue. We're working on making babies."

"Looking for pointers?"

"It's not the making I'm worried about." I finished my beer and set the bottle on the patio. "It seems impossible. All the money, all the clothes, the doctors . . ."

"I thought having a kid was going to be hard," Press said. "We both did. We were excited about having Kimberly, and we did all sorts of stupid things. Having two, that's when you find out what it's all about. Having one was almost like being single."

"Being single," I said.

"You'd think two would be just twice as much work, but it's not. You've got all the baby gear, all the outfits and toys and things, and you know what to worry about and what not to. Most of the time. But some things are worse. It's like juggling. It's a geometric progression."

"What if something's wrong with the kid?"

"Three eyes or something? Antennae coming out of its head?" He tipped the bottle for a long last sip. "You'll have enough to worry about if it's healthy. What do you want—girl or boy?"

"I don't know. I haven't thought about it."

"Sure you have."

"Girl."

"It'll be a boy. Assume that from the start."

I went inside to get more beer, and when I came out, the crowd across the driveway had grown. It took me a minute to pick out Dusty. She was wearing a red-and-white-striped shirt with blue shorts. I stared for a moment, and suddenly she looked straight at me and waved.

"Hey, George," she called out. "You want to play softball?"

I tried to speak softly, so Donna wouldn't hear. "Now?"

"We're going to get up a game."

I told her I didn't think so. "Anyway, there isn't enough room."

"You let me down," Dusty said, pouting. Two girls near her booed. "Boo, George." They said it loudly. I was sure Donna could hear them.

Press was scratching Joe's neck when I got back. "What was all that about?"

"They're trying to get up a softball game."

"You kidding me? Are they whores or Girl Scouts?"

"Something in between, I guess. When you're done, they sell you cookies."

The spring on the door stretched loudly as Donna and Cindy came out behind the girls. The dogs walked over and sniffed them.

"He's a nice doggy," Cindy told the girls, "it's okay."

"What's his name?" Kimberly asked. Donna told her. "Hi, Joe dog," Kimberly said. "Hi, Joe." She held her doll tight to her chest.

Beth stepped down onto the patio, concentrating on each step. Joe licked her forehead. "Yeech!" Kimberly said.

Cindy and Donna pulled up two chairs.

"It's a beautiful day," Cindy said. "Warm but not too muggy."

"Baseball weather," I said. "This is the kind of weather . . . you'll be listening to a game on the radio between two teams you don't really care about, it'll go on forever, and it seems as if nobody scores—no home runs, no close plays. You barely hear anything from the stands—it's too hot to be noisy. The announcers sound a little tired. There are long silences between pitches."

Press said, " 'Barber takes the sign, sets—but now he steps off the rubber, and the runner moves back to the bag.' "

"Exactly."

"What are you two talking about?" Cindy turned to Donna. "Do you know what they're talking about?"

"I was going to say it's a great day to be at the beach," Donna said.

Cindy nudged Press's foot with hers. "Hint hint."

"Hint hint," Donna said.

"The beach," I said.

Press winced. "Ocean City on the Fourth of July. Terrible idea."

"Why'd we marry them?" Donna asked Cindy. "Do you two have anything in common?"

"Not us. You?"

"Opposites attract," I said.

Just then Dusty, another girl, and two guys came around the corner of the house.

"Hey," Dusty said, "you sure you won't play?"

"We need four more," one of the guys said. He had blond hair and a wide brass belt buckle that said "Kurt."

I looked at Donna. I couldn't read her expression.

"Where's the game?"

"Across the street," the other guy said. "We're going to block it off."

"You have to play," Dusty said. "Your front lawn is left field."

"I don't think so."

Donna said, "Why don't you? Cindy and I'll watch."

Life is full of complicated decisions. Either you play a game or you prove to your wife that you'll choose not to, just to make her happy. But what kind of world is it where you choose between marriage and softball? I decided to call her bluff.

"Are you sure?"

"Certainly. Go ahead."

I turned to Press. "What do you think?"

"I say you're slipping one foot into a euphemistic shoe."

"What?" Donna said.

"He's like this all the time," Cindy said.

"But I'm willing," Press added. "You call it."

"Play," Cindy said. She told Donna, "It's either that or listen to baseball stories all afternoon."

"We're in," I told Dusty.

"Great. We'll meet you over there."

Press and Cindy carried the lawn chairs around front while I went to dig out two gloves. Donna followed me inside.

"You're sure it's all right?" I asked again.

"Sure." She opened the refrigerator. "Why shouldn't it be?"

I waited for her to look at me.

"Am I going to hear about this for the rest of the week? I'm serious."

"So am I," she said. "Is there some reason I shouldn't let you near them?"

"It's only softball. Just a friendly game."

She poured the milk into the girls' plastic cups. "Exactly. You love softball."

"We're going to be outside," I said, still testing. "Right in front of the house. In plain view."

"Indoors would be a little tricky."

"It's just a Fourth of July picnic."

"And Cindy and I will be right across the street, watching." She snapped the lids on the cups. "Hit a home run for me, Babe."

Two cars blocked off the street. The road forked just before Bellshaw's house, so anybody who had to could get around. Dusty and a short girl named Sheila picked teams. Press and I stood off to the side.

"Dusty," he said, "is not your ten-dollar woman."

"I want him," Sheila called out, pointing at Press. "I want him bad."

Some of the others laughed. I looked across the street at Donna and Cindy, but they were out of earshot. Donna waved.

Dusty picked two others before she picked me. "I almost let you get away," she said. When they finished there were eight on each side, five guys and three girls. We were in the field first; I played third base.

"Billy Mendini," our shortstop said. He held out his hand. dark with grease. "Sorry. Just changed a fuel pump."

"Car trouble?"

"I'm a mechanic. Working at the Sinclair station in Mondawmin." He grunted and missed a practice grounder our first baseman had thrown.

"Listen up," Kurt shouted. He held a bat in the air. "First

base is that piece of cardboard, second and third are the trashcan lids, home plate is this baseball cap."

"Home is where the hat is," I said. Somebody booed.

"No balls and strikes. The foul poles are that tree"—Kurt pointed to one near the porch of the girls' house—"and the telephone pole."

"Too many rules," someone said. "Play ball!"

The girls on our team were Dusty, a redhead named Alice, and Brenda, a tall girl with dark hair that came to her waist.

"Hum fire," Billy yelled. "Burn it by 'em."

Brenda stopped and looked over. "We're pitching underhand, right? I can't throw overhand."

"It's just an expression," I said. "Baseball talk."

The first pitch was hit straight at my head; I caught it just in time. From across the street, Donna and Cindy applauded. "Around the horn," Billy said. I flipped it to him and he made a bad throw over to first.

"Cut the fancy crap," Kurt said, coming up to bat. "We'll be here all day."

The game went on for three hours. People kept arriving next door. Some played, some stood in the driveway and drank beer. Someone eventually dragged a keg over to the field. People quit, others took their places. The crowd was about even: there were slightly more men than women. I couldn't figure it out.

When our team was at bat I asked Billy how he met the girls.

"That guy in right field, Kevin—he knows Eve. He works down at the station."

"How's he know her?"

"He dates her."

"Dates?"

"Yeah," he said. "You know. Goes out with."

"They go on dates?"

"Yeah," he said. "You know—movies, hamburgers. That kind of thing."

"Are you kidding?"

"What do I know? I don't hide in the trunk or nothing.

This is what he tells me. Go!" he yelled. "Run hard!" Alice got thrown out at first.

I tried again with Brenda. She played with the ends of her hair the whole time we talked. "I met Kristin at a party," she said. "She hangs out at my place some nights when she gets stuck downtown. Which one is your wife?" She was looking over at our front yard. Cindy and Donna were braiding the girls' hair.

"On the left."

"She's cute."

Dusty came over and put her arms around both of us. I felt an electrical charge run from her arm down to my toes.

"This man," she told Brenda, pointing at me, "this man saved my life."

Dusty was drunk. I ducked from her arm and stepped away before Donna could see us.

"Saved me from a falling tree," she said.

"After it had been made into a dresser," I added.

"*And*," she said more softly, as if she were sharing a secret, "*and* he fixes my lawn mower." She still had her arm around Brenda. "Cleans my plug. Lubricates my parts."

"Her real lawn mower," I told Brenda. "Really."

Dusty said, "You two getting to know each other? Working on that team spirit?"

"He's married," Brenda told her.

"Our sacrificial husband," Dusty said. "We'll roast him over the grill."

"Press is married too."

She ignored me. "Don't we make a great team?"

"We're losing," I told her.

"Jesus." Dusty leaned closer to Brenda, still in fine spirits. "What a spoilsport."

Billy hit a fly ball that Press caught for the third out.

"Last inning," someone announced.

We walked out to the field. "Let's hold 'em." Dusty patted me on the rear.

"No fraternizing," Billy said, pointing his glove at me. "Whatever the hell that means."

The other team scored three runs—it was our best inning defensively.

"Twenty-seven to twenty-six," Kurt said. "Last at-bats for you suckers. Then it's chow time."

Grace took her place behind the dark spot we were calling the pitcher's rubber. "Sounds good to me. I'm too old for this horseshit."

Our first baseman stepped up to the plate, his belly hanging over his belt. "I'm gonna smash one right here. Gimme something to hit."

Grace lobbed the ball in and he popped up to third base.

Mike, our left fielder, came to bat.

"No stick," Eve said from behind the plate.

"I'll show you a stick." As he said it he hit a grounder to second base. Sheila bobbled the ball, then lobbed it underhand to their first baseman. Two gone.

Dusty came up. "Give her the high hard one," someone said.

"Do it," she said. "Higher. Harder."

I didn't know where to look. Hundreds of pickup games I had played with my brothers, and I had never heard batters talk like this.

Grace lobbed the pitch. Dusty swung hard, popping the ball into the air between third and home. The third baseman stopped short, waiting for the bounce, but the ball hit the ground and rolled backward. Eve picked it up and threw it past the first baseman. "Stay there," Billy yelled. "Stay on the bag."

Someone watching from across the street threw the ball in. "All right, Georgy boy," Grace said as I came to bat, "time to eat."

"Do it, Babe," Donna yelled from our front lawn. I was surprised she was still paying attention, rooting for me.

"Right here," Press called from our driveway, deep center field.

"Hit it," Dusty said from first base. "Bring me home."

Grace lobbed the ball up. As it reached the peak of its arc I felt something I hadn't felt in a long time: my left foot moved back, my right leg tensed, my left shoulder tilted down, my arms moved forward. I caught the ball on the fat of the bat; it cleared the street and hit our house on the fly.

"All the way," my teammates yelled, "go all the way!" As I turned first I saw the ball bounce off the corner of the house and richochet past Press. Dusty was stopping at second. "Go!" I said. "Run!" She started toward third, but I had almost caught up with her.

"Go hard," Billy yelled from foul territory. He made huge circles with his arm. "Play at the plate!" Turning third, skidding on the grass, I nearly ran into Dusty—I reached out and pushed her forward. Off to the left I could see the ball sailing toward home.

"Slide!" I yelled. Dusty jumped headfirst, reaching for the base, and I dove in on top of her, hitting Eve in the shin with my shoulder. She collapsed across us.

"Out!" Kurt said from the field.

"No!" Billy shouted. "She doesn't have the ball!"

I turned and saw Sheila chasing after it. Dusty sat on the baseball cap that was home plate and pulled me toward her, but Eve was pinning me down. "Oh, no you don't," she said, pulling me back by the pants. Dusty's fingers dug into my side. I strained forward, Eve lost her grip on my leg, and as I flopped into Dusty's arms I felt a softball jammed against my neck. "Gotcha!" Sheila said, her chest heaving.

"Safe!" Billy called.

Across the street Donna yelled, "Out! Out at home!"

Chapter Eight

At seven the next morning Grace's hair was undone. She wore a loose yellow top and baggy plaid pants, her eyes were red, and she was halfway through a cigarette. She stopped cleaning up the yard long enough to sniff a white oleander blossom, inhaling deeply.

"Lord, Lord, Lord," she said in appreciation. "If stale beer smelled like that, I'd have led a perfect life." She sniffed again. "You smelled these?"

I told her I hadn't.

"Come on. You've got to. Worth being late to work for."

I left my briefcase by the car, opened the gate into their backyard, crossed the grass, and leaned my face into one of the bushes. The scent was amazing. Vivid but not overpowering. Better than roses.

"I read smoking can ruin your sense of smell," Grace said. "These right here are what I'd quit for."

I asked her if they were hard to grow.

"They're real hearty," she said, "but of course you've got to bring them in, in the winter. Can't survive up here."

I inhaled again, breathing in the fragrance, trying to hold on to it.

"You're up early, aren't you?" I asked.

"I couldn't sleep five minutes. My head's still ringing from last night."

"Too much beer?" I started back toward the car.

"George, I could drink from yesterday to tomorrow and still pull a grain of pepper out of a pile of antshit. It's that damn music." She walked over to the gate with me and picked up a soggy paper plate. "You ever listen to Benny Goodman?"

"Sure I do."

"That man is an artist," Grace said. "He doesn't stand there and shout and wriggle his crotch at you. That son of a gun can *play*." She poured the contents of two paper cups onto the lawn, then dropped them into the trashcan. "I don't get to listen to much real music anymore—the girls are always playing their crap. But I saw him once."

"You saw Benny Goodman?"

"Carnegie Hall. I turned around to Jackson, my first husband, and I said, 'If you could do anything that good, I'd follow you the long way to hell.' He couldn't, so I'm taking the short way." Her laugh was like sandpaper on gravel.

"Did you know Dave Brubeck is coming to town?"

"I'll tell you who else I like," she said. "Les and Larry Elgart. I bet they're too old-fashioned for you."

" 'Music to Watch Girls By,' " I said. " 'Stella by Starlight.' "

" 'My Heart Belongs to Daddy.' "

" 'When I Take My Sugar to Tea.' "

Grace laughed again and took a long drag on her cigarette. "You're all right, George." She pulled the trashcan beside her as she moved down the yard. "I'd like to find me a man who can dance to Les and Larry," she said. "The only ones I see anymore just want to drink and screw."

Donna wasn't in the house when I got home from work. I went up to the bedroom and took off my coat and tie, then went out across the lawn and looked through the lilacs. Mrs. Webb sat on her back porch, sewing, with Mr. and Mrs. Wheatley rocking by her side. Donna sat across from them, on the porch swing, and Mr. Duncan, a barrel-chested man in his sixties who worked for the gas company, stood near the steps.

I can picture my parents with those same people—the Duncans, the Wheatleys, the Webbs—sitting and standing on that porch, talking, laughing, drinking iced tea. They were people who gave serious consideration to the instincts of dogs and migrating birds, who trusted completely their belief that the events of the world were controlled by forces greater than themselves.

I had worried that Donna would be like my brothers, that she would think Mr. Wheatley and Mrs. Webb and the rest were old and dull. I was afraid she wouldn't enjoy their stories, wouldn't want to spend slow hours on Mrs. Webb's porch. But she got along with them just fine. She traded recipes and solved sewing problems with Mrs. Webb, talked teaching with Mrs. Wheatley, and played music with Mrs. Patterson. In some ways she knew them better than I did.

Mr. Duncan nodded and smiled when I reached the porch. "Hey there, George. How's things?"

"Pretty good." I kissed Donna on the cheek. "A magazine is going to publish some of the research I've been doing."

"That's wonderful!" Donna smiled beautifully.

"What exactly is it?" Mr. Wheatley asked.

"Pretty dry, really. A sort of history of the way energy has been used in the state. Steam, hot water, electricity. This is just the first section."

Mrs. Wheatley rocked with her hands in her lap. "And where will this first section be published?" She enunciated too carefully, the result of years spent addressing second-graders.

"The Delmarva Energy Journal."

"Never miss an issue," Mr. Wheatley said, poker-faced. "Keep it in the can, right next to *The Saturday Evening Post.*" His wife frowned at him.

"We get it at the office," Mr. Duncan said. "You know what month your piece'll be out?"

I told him I didn't, yet.

"I'm happy for you," Mrs. Webb said. "You'll have to bring me a copy." I knew she meant it.

But then Mrs. Wheatley said she knew someone who edited a magazine, and the others shifted their attention to her. My moment was gone.

Mrs. Webb offered me a piece of the lemon cake on the

table beside her. "I haven't told you-all about the new man at the firehouse," she said at a break in the conversation.

"This isn't nasty, is it?" Mrs. Wheatley asked. "I don't think we want to hear a nasty story on a nice day like today."

"Pass a slice of that cake, George-o," Mr. Duncan said softly, trying not to interrupt.

"They were in the station last night when they got a call for an accident." Mrs. Webb was working on a pillow cover, a country scene with a lot of green. She sewed effortlessly while she talked. "It was a car accident back on Marriotsville Road. A truck had stopped there at the corner of Marriotsville and Liberty, and this little sports car slid right under it." She directed the next sentence at me: "They think the boy who was driving might have been drunk."

"That's a terrible story," Mrs. Wheatley said quickly.

My mother was killed by a drunk driver, and our neighbors tried to avoid talking about accidents like hers in front of me. What I couldn't tell them was that there was no accident like my mother's.

Mrs. Webb continued. "It took the top of the car clean off. The passenger, the driver's girlfriend—her family is the Walkers, from Owings Mills, they owned that seafood place that burned last year—she was hardly hurt. When Kyle and Craig—Craig's the new man—when they got there, the Walker girl was out of the car, and she was trying to put her boyfriend's head back onto his body." Mrs. Webb snapped a piece of thread.

Mrs. Wheatley had gone white. Mr. Duncan tapped me on the arm. "Just one more," he said. "A little piece."

"What did they do?" Donna said.

"Kyle talked to her until the ambulance came, and Craig stood behind the truck and got sick. It was his first fatality."

She went on with her sewing. There was a long silence, long enough that I saw the rhythm in the movement of the shadows of the leaves over the porch steps. Mrs. Wheatley finally said something about how so many young people today were careless, just plain careless. Mr. Duncan said, "Those sports cars aren't safe. Couldn't give me one. I'd rather walk."

Before I could mention my article again, Mr. Duncan said, "Anybody read any poetry lately?"

That had become a standard conversation filler in the neighborhood, along the lines of chatting about the weather or asking about somebody's dog or grandchildren. The joke had started after Mr. Mead's performance at Talent Night in May.

Mr. Wheatley laughed. "I read Emily the clues to a crossword puzzle backwards."

"That counts," Mrs. Webb said, smiling. "That counts."

Talent Night had started when Mr. and Mrs. Patterson's daughter came home after playing a year with a touring orchestra. They wanted to celebrate, so they invited the neighbors. The night was like other pot-lucks we had, except that Christie played the violin and her mother played a song on the piano. Everyone was polite, but there weren't many classical-music fans in the neighborhood. No one else played an instrument, unless you counted the women who could beat out Christmas carols and "Sweet Little Buttercup" from old piano lessons. Still, the night was a success for two reasons: because the Pattersons, who normally seemed uneasy at neighborhood parties, clearly enjoyed themselves, and because a lot of people seemed to think it proper for everyone to do a sort of cultural penance. That second thing bothered me. Why smile and applaud for music you didn't enjoy? It was one thing to be polite, but they didn't have to pretend to want more. The honest thing was to admit to being uncomfortable and to try to understand why.

This year had been different. At the April Community Association meeting someone mentioned that Christie Patterson wouldn't be in town. One of the women asked if anyone would be interested in doing some kind of skit. No one was. One of the men said he could sing three songs composed by his college football team, but his wife told him to hush up. Just when it appeared as if only Mrs. Patterson and Donna would perform, Mr. Mead glanced up from his notepad and offered to read a poem he had written.

It was an unexpected suggestion from a usually quiet corner. Virginia Mead was a tenured philosophy professor, but no one was sure exactly what her husband did. They only occasionally made appearances at our pot-lucks or on Mrs. Webb's back porch, and their visits always reminded me of something I had read about anthropologists doing research on backward natives. We were surprised when Mr. Mead made his offer to join in; we looked around and someone said: Well, yes, certainly.

On the Saturday of the dinner Donna played a short, cheery piece she had been teaching one of her students, and something else I liked, a Scott Joplin rag she had transposed for the flute. Mrs. Patterson went on too long with some slow Schubert, so Mrs. Coleman and Mrs. Duncan sneaked into the kitchen to set out the dishes for dessert. They knew everybody would be ready to stretch out and eat. After Mrs. Patterson finished and everyone applauded dutifully, she turned and introduced Mr. Mead, who walked to the end of the living room, in front of the fireplace, laid a few pages on the piano, and began to read.

Donna guessed later that most people in the room had never heard a poem read aloud, with the exceptions of "Trees" and "Casey at the Bat" and limericks about girls from Nantucket. What they got was more like Ezra Pound. If the poem had a title, I didn't hear it. Mr. Mead began reading in an unnaturally low, strained voice, something about dust, bones, and ashen faces. He seemed to be describing a landscape, but it was hard to tell if he was talking about a place or a group of people. He started rambling in Greek and Latin, including a few bits I recognized from church, then came back to English to praise "fallen warriors/ and the dauntless, homeless hungry" before skipping along into French. When he got back to English he was still talking about some sort of war, and after an allusion to Homer—a soldier struggled to find "familiar fields,/ fragments of the mind's earlier day/ And a woman weaving?"—he described the seduction of a prepubescent girl by one of George Washington's officers from the point of view of a cannon. Everyone would have been shocked if they had had the first idea what he was talking about. He kept going back to wars and to the sea, and to dust, scattered bones, and ashen faces. He sang one verse with a deep Southern accent, then spoke the final solemn lines in what I recognized from an introductory literature class as Old English. Then, keeping the same basic rhythm, he tapped evenly on the top of the piano. Tap. Tap. Tap.

Mrs. Coleman and Mrs. Duncan had come out of the kitchen when they heard the singing; now they were standing behind the crowd, mouths open, Mrs. Coleman holding the leftovers of a three-bean salad.

After a noticeable silence, I saw Mrs. Webb, deep in the middle of the group, begin to clap. I banged my hands together steadily, loudly. Virginia and Donna were next, and in a moment everyone was doing it, clapping and sighing with relief. Mr. Mead looked up from his manuscript, coughed into his hand, and said, "I see. I suppose it's time for dessert." Everybody smiled; that was the best thing he could have said.

There were a lot of poetry jokes after that. Back on Mrs. Webb's porch, Mr. Wheatley said, "I don't understand those people."

His wife agreed. "I know we had to be polite, but sometimes I wonder if it wasn't a mistake to encourage him. Next year he'll probably read two or three of those things—I can't call them poems. I don't know what they are."

After Mr. Mead read, everyone realized how relatively comfortable they felt with flute and piano music. Donna tried to keep her pieces lively, and Mrs. Patterson would know better than to go on so long next time. Mr. Mead hadn't understood the rules of the game.

Mr. Duncan wiped his face with a handkerchief. "What scares me is that there are more where he came from. I bet Virginia was just eating it up." He turned to me. "What about it, George? Are all those college people like that?"

I stood on the bottom of the porch steps with one arm on the railing. "Like what?"

"Are they as crazy as Mead? They all go around singing about death and naked women?"

Mrs. Wheatley rocked slowly. "It wasn't that way when I went to school."

Mr. Wheatley rolled his eyes. "When you went to school the alphabet only had nineteen letters."

I pushed a chip of old paint off the railing. Maybe I had

gotten tired of the joke, or maybe I was still thinking about my article; for some reason, I didn't feel like playing along this time.

I said, "He isn't all that bad."

Mr. Wheatley rubbed a spot on the porch with the toe of his hard black shoes. "Come on now, George. You don't go for that gibberish, do you?"

"I think I could see what he was trying to do. I took a class once where we studied poets who did that sort of thing."

Mrs. Wheatley held out her hand as if she were checking for rain. "The Lord knows I try to be open-minded," she said, "but I just don't see the point. What's the purpose in that man standing there and talking to us in languages we don't even know?"

There was a pause as they all silently agreed.

"It's no different than opera," I said, as interested as anyone in hearing what I was going to say next. "Opera's in French or Italian, but people still go to hear it."

"You know what I say about opera," Mr. Duncan said. "Only place where when a woman gets stabbed, instead of dying, she sings."

Mrs. Wheatley said, "I confess, I'm not a fan of the operatic art."

"Neither is George," Donna said.

I felt betrayed. "Just last week I listened to *Porgy and Bess*."

"That's in English," she said.

"What if it is? You still can't understand what they're saying."

They were all staring at me. I didn't know why I had taken up for Mead. It was true, I had taken a course in twentieth-century poetry, but I had hated it. I didn't like Mead's poem either. But they weren't even willing to give him a chance. I couldn't help wondering what they had said about Mrs. Patterson's piano playing. I wondered what they said about Donna's flute music when we weren't around.

When I looked up I saw dull, stony faces. I blinked and they were old friends again.

I changed the subject. "What did I miss? Any big news today?"

Mr. Duncan took a sip of tea and answered with the glass

still up to his lips. "Donna's been telling us about the people over in Bellshaw's house."

I glanced over at her. She wouldn't meet my eye.

"Yep," Mr. Duncan said.

Mr. Wheatley rocked in his chair. "It doesn't sound too good. I've been pulling for them ever since they fixed that place up, so I'm sorry to hear about it."

"I don't understand why this always happens," his wife said. "That man seems incapable of finding decent people to live in that house. We never had any trouble before he bought it."

I leaned away from the railing, angry. "Maybe they aren't like you think," I said. "Everybody's got these stereotypes in mind, they judge people before they even meet them. No one has proven that they've broken the law."

Mrs. Wheatley looked as if she had been slapped.

"No one said anything about breaking laws," Donna said quietly.

Mrs. Wheatley recovered. "There's no reason to take this personally. It's not your fault that you live next door to them."

"But it's true," I told her. "Just because they've got a blue light in the window, that doesn't mean—"

"What was that?" Mr. Duncan tugged at the back of his collar.

I turned to Donna.

"I told them all about the fireworks," she said. "Mrs. Webb heard them go off." After the softball game, after dinner, someone in the crowd next door had set off about a dozen rockets and a roman candle. Joe and all the rest of the neighborhood dogs had barked for hours.

"It's terrible," Mrs. Wheatley said. "Donna says they left trash all over the yard."

"What was that about a light?" Mr. Duncan asked.

"Nothing," I said. "Just a . . . Nothing."

Mrs. Wheatley said, "Helen Campbell says they were drinking beer in the street, cars blocking the road. What if there had been a fire? They've been moved in under a month and you'd think they owned the neighborhood."

"They cleaned up the trash," I said. "The next morning."

"Is that so." Mrs. Wheatley sniffed. "If I were you, if I saw any more of that behavior, I'd tell Kyle."

"Kyle's a fireman," her husband said. "What's he going to do, drown them?"

"We'll do that," Donna answered Mrs. Wheatley.

Mr. Duncan checked his pocket watch and let it drop back into his pants. "I better get going," he said. "Dinner's on the plate at six. Good thing I've ruined my appetite."

"Good-bye, David." Mrs. Webb took his glass. "Say hello to Carol for me."

He said he would, then waved good-bye. He turned at the end of the flagstone path and headed down the lane.

"We should go too," Donna said.

We were halfway home when she kissed me.

She said, "You've got a big mouth." She kissed me again. "And that's for getting your article published. We should celebrate."

"I thought you had told them everything."

"Why would I do that?"

"They would call the police. They're just like your mother. Or *my* mother. And father. That's what you're waiting for, isn't it? For someone else to make the call."

"We even have a bottle of wine in the refrigerator," she said, walking ahead of me. "Let's celebrate."

Chapter Nine

That's how it was: one minute Donna was telling me to play softball with them, the next she was angry at me; after that she seemed to forget about them entirely. Sometimes we'd be discussing a completely different subject, and she would get upset for no reason at all.

For instance, there was the Japanese-beetle problem.

Donna wanted to dig up the African violets that had grown over the edges of the flowerbed and into the lawn, but I convinced her to cut back only the new growth. My mother had liked the way they took over everything—she didn't mind letting her beds run a little wild.

When we were finished, I took care of the bleeding heart by the patio while Donna weeded around the rosebushes. That's when she saw that Japanese beetles had been eating through the leaves.

"How bad is it?" I said.

She slipped off one glove so she could scratch a spot near her shoulder blade. "Not very, yet, but it doesn't take long."

"We've had them before."

"Don't tell me they've got to stay too."

I sat back to look up at her. "Nobody said anything about keeping Japanese beetles. My mother tried all sorts of things."

"There's something you can put on the leaves," Donna said. "Some sort of powder."

"Poison."

"Isn't that allowed?"

"What's the matter with you?"

She didn't answer.

"It's a nice day, we're outside, the yard looks great—what's wrong?"

Donna gripped a short shovel with a green handle. "I want to plant something."

I told her that's what we were doing.

"We're weeding," she said. She brushed flecks of dirt off the shovel with her glove, then stopped. "I want to wallpaper the bedroom, you say no. I want to get new rugs for the bathroom, you say we have to keep the same color. You won't even let me put anything in the ground. What I want to know is, what do you think you're saving? I understand why you'd be angry if I was trying to ruin things, or tear them down, but I'm trying to make them nicer."

"I never said you couldn't wallpaper the bedroom."

"You said it was a stupid idea."

"I never said you couldn't do it."

"What's stupid about wallpaper?"

"The walls are painted," I said.

"Can we paint them a different color?"

"Sure we can. But what's wrong with white?"

"See?" she said. "See?"

That's what I mean: suddenly she was angry.

Donna said, "You argue against anything I want to do."

"I do not."

For a violent second we could both imagine her garden shovel as a weapon.

"You make me shirts," I said. "I wear them. I let you make all kinds of clothes."

"Let me? You let me?"

"You know what I mean." I tried to steer her back to the flowerbeds. "What is it that you want to grow?"

"It's not the plant, it's the point."

"But if there isn't anything you want to grow, what's wrong with keeping what we've got?"

She shook her gloves at me. "Sometimes I just want to—" She put her hands on her hips and looked at the flowerbed behind the house. There was a rosebush at each corner and one near the clothesline, snapdragons and peonies in between. My mother was keen on symmetry.

"Beans," she said.

I couldn't tell if it was a curse or a choice.

She said, "I want to plant beans."

"What kind?"

"Who cares what kind? Food beans. I want—"

"You can't just plant beans. You have to plant a particular kind."

She pressed her gloves between her hands. "String beans." She stepped closer, looking straight down at me. She was taking this bean thing very seriously.

"Okay," I said.

"I can plant beans?"

"Dig away."

"You won't mind?"

"Not at all." I pulled a weed from the pile I had been making on the edge of the grass. "The only bad thing is, whenever you eat string beans, there's always one piece of fiber, I guess that's what it is, stuck between your teeth, and you work at it and work at it with your tongue—"

"Don't do this to me," Donna said.

Joe barked and pulled at his chain.

We heard a voice from the driveway. "Elvis," Kristin called. "Here, Elvis."

Joe whined and pawed the ground. Trotting around the shed, heading toward us, was a tiny black poodle with that bizarre poodle haircut. From a distance something seemed to be very wrong with its fur.

As it got closer we could see the problem: it was wearing some sort of shirt. Brown with white trim. It sniffed a pile of weeds, stepped into the flowerbed, and did its business. Elvis was a girl.

Kristin came around the house. When the dog saw her it ran between us, and Kristin walked over to pick it up. I think she would have gone back to her place without speaking to us if Donna hadn't said, "Elvis is your dog's name?"

Kristin nodded, as if she couldn't afford the words.

"It's a girl," I said.

Kristin's eyes caught on mine for a moment, held, then dismissed me.

Donna asked, "Isn't that shirt a little hot?"

Kristin spoke, but her expression didn't change. I wondered if she had been angry so long that the look had stuck. "Cotton," she said. "Feel."

Donna did.

"I made a cap," Kristin said. "She don't like it."

We didn't have anything else to say, but Kristin didn't turn to leave. We all looked at the dog. The dog stared at Joe.

"Where did you get her?" Donna asked.

"Friend." Kristin scratched Elvis's neck and burst out with a speech: "I took one look at them hips and said, 'If Ed Sullivan saw you he'd have a heart attack.' "

"Like Elvis Presley," I said.

"I'm not talking to you," Donna said.

Kristin glanced at Donna, then at me, and for a moment I thought she almost smiled. Then she was snarling again. I half-expected her to show her teeth and spit.

"Eve draws patterns," she told Donna. "We're making a vest. Dogs like clothes."

"They've got fur," I said.

Kristin turned and fired, "*You've* got fur."

Donna glared at me.

"Right," I said.

Kristin started across the yard, ending the conversation. Elvis looked back over her shoulder, as if she expected us to save her.

When Donna and I met, she was impressed by the drop-leaf coffee table my father and Earle and I had made. It was sturdy and functional, thanks to my father, but no work of art, thanks to me. Our father made beautiful furniture on his own, but he strongly believed in letting us learn by trial and error—his trial, our error.

I did better on a jewelry box with a carved lid I gave Donna as a wedding present. After that I built a cabinet for her sewing machine, and Joe's doghouse, but I hadn't made anything since my father died. Every time I went to the basement to start something, I ended up thinking about him. If that wasn't enough, I got the impression Evelyn thought making furniture was backward, a way for me to waste time and avoid spending money on the things her daughter deserved. So I had stopped.

I was going to build a bookcase in the basement and leave it there, against the long wall near the furnace room, out of the way. We had a lot of books stored in boxes around the house, so it would be a practical gift. A peace offering. It was going to be a surprise.

The first book I owned was a 1952 Hammond *World Wide Atlas*. Even before I started reading, earlier than I can remember, my mother and I shared a passion for travel. Since we didn't go anywhere, we had to be satisfied with talking about the places we wanted to see. I would sit at the kitchen table after the dishes had been put away, while Mom cleaned up after whichever squad had cleaned up, and we would quiz each other about places we dreamed of visiting. I had never been outside of Maryland. Except for one trip to Atlantic City in 1921, neither had she. My ideas about other places came from pictures I saw in magazines, but my mother had a better imagination: she pieced together a geography of the country from the letters she received.

"New England," she would say, folding a tea towel.

"Leaves," I said. "Big piles of red and yellow leaves, and trees with poles sticking out of them." I had read an article on maple syrup in *National Geographic*.

"The air is so crisp that you can snap it," my mother said, looking out the window, "and in the air there's always the smell of something burning somewhere."

The only book I ever saw her look through at any length was that Hammond *Atlas*, which she gave me as a Christmas present. She was fascinated by the meticulous work of cartographers, the careful, abstract detail of maps.

Bob and I moved into the basement when I was twelve, and almost immediately I began covering my half of the room. Beside my bed the enormous Michelin map of the United States was dotted with pins marking the places where we had relatives or friends. The maps on the other walls—Asia and Africa, South America and the Pacific islands—were from *National Geographic*. Europe, on the ceiling, was another Michelin.

The few black pins on the United States map and the black line that wandered around the edges of the others showed me where Father had traveled. He had jumped onto a merchant ship in 1916, when he was only fourteen, and during the next fifteen years he went, he told us, everywhere he had to go. In his natural voice, he would speak another language: "What happiness for the few swimmers that have fought their way through the white surf to the shore, when, caked with brine but safe and sound, they tread on solid earth."

Father often quoted the *Odyssey*, and he read us to sleep with it when we were young. The meeting with the Cyclops and the battle in the hall were early favorites, but later we leaned toward the horrific: Scylla and Charybdis, and the Book of the Dead, which he warned would give us nightmares. Left to choose for us, he would read either Odysseus' reunion with Laertes or his parting with Calypso, when he decides to attempt the journey home rather than to live forever on an island.

When Father came to Baltimore in 1931 he won my mother with stories of exotic places he had seen. His savings, which had traveled with him, made him one of the few spared by the Depression. They lived in an apartment near Druid Hill Park while he did maintenance work and waited to find a man to help him build his house.

I found out about the houses—ours and the one Bellshaw bought years later—from my mother. Building them wasn't something he talked about, and I still don't know why. His early silence about his travels was more understandable. When he settled down, he meant to raise a family, and I think he was afraid that talk of his independent days would intoxicate him; either that or he worried about what it would do to us. If one of us children talked about running off somewhere, he would remind us of the Lotus-eaters, who tricked Odysseus' men and would have kept them from returning home. He never acknowledged my mother's desire for us to travel as a family, ignoring it the way a reformed alcoholic will politely but flatly refuse a cocktail. "They say the beaches won't be so crowded this year," she'd say, looking out the living-room window. She'd turn to whichever one of us was in the room. "How long is that drive out to Crumpton?" We would tell her, but she already knew the answer. She was waiting for Father to speak up, for him suddenly to decide to go. He never did.

He grew more relaxed about his memories as his feet became more firmly planted. When I was twelve, when the youngest of us were old enough to listen, he began to tell us about his trips. From those stories, told at no predictable times and in no certain order, I was able to piece together the nearly continuous line that crossed the maps in the bedroom. My charting had to be done secretly, because when we showed too much interest in his stories he would say, "Surely a tramp's life is the worst thing that anyone would come to."

One of the first stories he told us about his own travels, the first story of our father's that I knew by heart, was about the *Odyssey*. He told us that he found an English translation in Palermo while his ship was being repaired, but he didn't have time to look at it until he got shore leave in Piraiévs. There he read the entire story of Odysseus' journey in a single afternoon, sitting within sight of the ruins of the Parthenon. Our father described that as a magical day, a milestone of his earlier life, the first time a book had won his attention from the world. He didn't tell us the rest, but as we got older it became clear: he saw the *Odyssey* as his story. When his ship returned to the U.S., our father ended his travels, staying home to establish the close family that, as a boy, he had been denied.

After releasing that memory, he allowed himself to talk about his other trips, telling us the stories that had enchanted our mother. For a while I copied them, waiting until he left the room to scribble down what sentences and phrases I could remember. But when I'd return to those notes, they seemed shallow, passionless, fragments that held none of the power of our father's tales. So I began memorizing them, repeating the stories to Bob in our room. ("You left out the cat they taught to swim," he'd say. "You forgot the cook with arms like coiled rope.") I told them to Donna in the months after we met.

When we were too old to be told stories at night, our father read to himself, sitting in his green armchair in the living room, oblivious of us as we did our homework or listened to the radio. He didn't read Homer straight through, and sometimes he didn't seem to be reading at all: he'd prop it open on his lap and stare out across the room.

Eventually our father saw the contradiction between what he had done and what he wanted us to do: he was full of encouragement for us to explore by the time Waite joined the Navy. He told each of us, as we finished high school, to do what we thought best. But even then, when we went out at night, he would call to us as we headed for the door, "Be warned yourself, my friend. Don't stray too long from home."

It couldn't have been much of a surprise when nearly all of us, raised on the world's greatest travel stories, headed off. By the time I graduated from high school my three older brothers were gone. I decided to stay home and commute to college, but first there was a trip I wanted to make: after graduation a group of my friends were going to drive to Ocean City, where their families spent the summer, then to Texas, by way of Florida, and back through Missouri, Tennessee, Kentucky, and Virginia—six weeks on the road.

My mother was the one who said no.

She still wanted me to wait so we could all go on a trip, so we could travel as a family. But we knew that wasn't likely to happen, and I didn't want to wait. I got angry, and I gave my mother the cold shoulder. I'd be talking to Bob at breakfast about one of his teachers and Mom would try to join in, saying something like, "Remember how you worked to get through algebra?" And I wouldn't answer. I pretended I hadn't heard a word. After dinner I'd pass her in the kitchen. "Hawaii," she'd whisper. I kept going.

But there was a limit to how mean I could be to my mother, and one evening just before the end of the school year I sat down to tell her how I felt. I had gotten my graduation announcements that day; they were still on the kitchen table. Mom was wearing an apron and wiping the top of the stove with a washcloth.

"Something could happen," she said, not looking at me. "What if you got into an accident?"

"I could get into an accident on the way to school." I was impatient. "I thought you'd be happy for me."

"Does it have to be this summer?"

"What am I supposed to wait for?" I rapped the box of announcements against the edge of the table. "I don't understand why it's such a big deal."

But I did. I was the son she had been closest to, and I was leaving. It was only for six weeks now, but it might be for good sooner than we wanted to admit. At the time I told myself that's the way it was: we all leave home.

She helped me pack, and she was even happy for me. I promised to send postcards. On the morning we left, she said "Just be *careful*" about seventeen times. Father kidded her about being so worried, and as we pulled out of the driveway I saw him turn to her and begin another one of his quotations: "I do assure you that the gods, who live such easy lives themselves, do not mean you to be so distressed, for it is settled that your son shall come home safe." She laughed. Before we turned the corner he walked her to the door. I never saw my mother alive again.

Chapter Ten

"Apple pie," Mr. Duncan said, handing Mrs. Webb a bouquet of snapdragons. "Smelled it all the way over at our place this morning. Must have had it cooling out on the windowsill."

"I guess I would have if I wanted bugs stuck to the crust," she said, standing. "Help yourself. I want to get some water for these beautiful flowers."

I had been working in the yard when I heard a dinner bell ringing. Mrs. Webb was standing on her porch, and when Joe and I walked over, she invited us to lunch. I had mint tea and a sandwich; Joe had cold cuts. Mrs. Wheatley saw us and came up to talk, and Mr. Duncan managed to show up just in time for dessert.

When Mrs. Webb went inside, he winked and cut himself a slice of pie.

"Where's Donna?" he said, digging in.

I told him she was shopping with her mother.

"They're looking for wallpaper," Mrs. Wheatley added.

"Sounds like trouble," he said.

"I told them to look all they want."

He nodded, chewing. "It's a mess, all right."

"When did you ever put up wallpaper?" Mrs. Wheatley asked him, knowing the answer.

"Never, but I hear it's a headache. I say, paint a wall once and leave it alone. Wipe it down when it's dirty."

"Not everything will wipe off," she said.

"Hang a picture over it." Mr. Duncan grinned at me. "I don't need to be doing no painting every year."

"Any painting," Mrs. Wheatley said, "and even that doesn't make it grammatical. You know better—you don't repaint walls every year." She turned to me. "Don't let his bad habits rub off on you."

Mrs. Webb came back out to the porch with the snapdragons in a white vase and set it on the table.

"I wish—" Mr. Duncan began.

"Chew," Mrs. Wheatley told him. "We'll wait."

He swallowed, then said, "I wish you could teach Carol to bake. Last time she made prune turnovers I just about cried. Dry, burnt crust, soggy innards—I wouldn't have fed 'em to a dog." Joe looked up without lifting his head from the grass, panting softly.

Mrs. Wheatley looked shocked. "Why would you say such a thing? Carol's a fine cook."

"Maybe meatloaf," he said, "and corned beef—she's okay with the food you put on the big plates. But not desserts."

"Have you ever told her?" I said.

Mr. Duncan stopped mid-chew. "No, I have not—and neither will you, if you don't want to see me horsewhipped. When she put that turnover on my plate, I cut a piece about as wide as a waffle—she makes 'em big—ate it, and said, 'If this isn't the best prune pie I ever had.' I thought I was going to need a stomach pump."

"David," Mrs. Wheatley said. "That's not even funny."

"You're telling me. It's all I got for dessert three nights in a row."

Mrs. Webb fanned herself. "I'd be glad to give her a recipe, but there's nothing special to it."

Mr. Duncan set his cleaned plate on the table. "Her pies aren't all that bad, but they don't taste like yours. I never had apple pie like that anywhere else."

"Tell her, before she pours the filling, to grind about a cup of those cinnamon red-hots, the little candies, and mix them in."

"That's what it is." Mrs. Wheatley congratulated herself. "I knew it was something about the cinnamon."

"Clarence was a big pie eater," Mrs. Webb told her, "and so is Kyle. But they about bore me to tears. You've got to do something to give them a little punch."

Joe rolled over and sighed, but I was suddenly impatient.

"Well," I said, "I hate to eat and run, but I have to do some work on the car."

"Take it to the shop," Mr. Duncan said. "Cars are a big headache."

"Hush now," Mrs. Wheatley told him.

When we got back to the yard I dug a box of spark plugs and the wrench out of the toolshed, then raised the hood on the station wagon. The car was hot just from sitting in the sun; the wrench slipped in the sweat on my hands. Joe yawned, then lay in the grass in the shade of the car, picking up where he left off. I popped off the first cable and loosened the plug.

The wagon was running fine, but my father was a firm believer in regular maintenance, and not just for cars. I changed the oil every three thousand miles, replaced the plugs and rotated the tires every six, replaced the screens in the house with storm windows the first of October, drained the lawn mower and took off the blade the weekend before Thanksgiving, put the snow tires on the week after. Maintain the things around you, our father used to say, and you'll avoid unpleasant surprises.

But it wasn't the fact that it had been sixty-one hundred miles since I had changed the plugs that made me antsy at Mrs. Webb's. As I sat and listened to them talking about pies, it had all started to go bad on me, like a favorite record you hear once too often. Mr. Duncan had always seemed friendly and funny, but today I saw him as a fat man who worked for the gas company, the neighborhood mooch. At pot-luck dinners he balanced two plates on his lap, and he was always helping himself to second and third helpings at Mrs. Webb's.

It wasn't just him. When I was young, Mrs. Wheatley had seemed polite and correct, the resident schoolmarm, but now she just seemed condescending. What was the point of correcting Mr. Duncan's grammar? Being in classrooms most of her life had stunted her growth. She saw us all as second-graders, long on potential but short on discipline. I had always enjoyed talking to Mr. Wheatley more than to his wife, but now I even wondered about him. What lack of pride and ambition would allow a man to be happy as a school-bus driver?

I gapped a new plug. Those people had been my parents' closest friends. They had worked together, raised families together. But I was starting to feel I wasn't one of them. It had begun when we talked about Mr. Mead's poetry, and it was even clearer when they talked about the girls next door. Not even Grace's banana bread and oleander earned her the benefit of the doubt. I wondered if there would ever be new people the neighborhood would accept.

Had my parents felt the same way? If those neighbors were such close friends, why couldn't I picture them in our house? They had all come over a few times, when my parents had hosted cookouts, and at Christmas everyone went from house to house, the women inspecting decorations and nodding over gifts while the men drank eggnog spiked with whiskey. But I never heard our parents talk to them about the issues we discussed in our family meetings. The conversations they had with our neighbors were about simpler things: How to cure sleepwalking. Where the poison ivy was bad this year. When the tomatoes would start to ripen. Recipes. The weather.

I pulled off another cable.

The people closest to our parents were us. The eight of us. But where did that leave me now? I wasn't truly close to my neighbors, I couldn't share with them the things I really cared about, and my brothers and sister were gone. I didn't hear from Lou anywhere near as often as I heard from, say, Mrs. Patterson. And I shared a bedroom with Bob for seven years, I gave him the notes from every class I ever took, and I still didn't understand his fascination with blueprints. Since he left he hadn't called or written more than a dozen times. Mark was my oldest brother, the closest to our father, and he seemed to know me. At least, he had been right when he said that I would never leave home. But maybe that had been a lucky guess.

I slipped the last cable back on and set the wrench and the old plugs on the grass next to Joe. He wagged once, brushing the lawn with his scythe of a tail, hoping for a ride. I lay back on the gravel and wormed my way under the car. The hood was still open, and the sun shone around the engine in patches. I rested my head in the shade of the carburetor.

Donna encouraged me in everything I did. She listened to and remembered everything I told her about work, every story about my family. No one had ever cared so much about me, and I wanted to be everything she wanted me to be: strong, brave, loving, wise. But we listened to completely different music.

"Hey there, neighbor."

Something blocked the sun near my left shoulder. I turned and saw bare feet by the front tire.

"Whatcha doing down there?"

Dusty.

"Looking for a leak." I turned back to the engine. Donna thought she had seen something dripping.

"A real handyman," she said. "Mr. Fixit. The lawn mower runs real good."

"Great." The engine in the Catalina wasn't very complicated; I ran out of places to pretend to look. I was considering sliding out from under the car when I caught Joe's eye. He had one golden eyebrow cocked, and I could tell he was thinking of Homer: *There is no homecoming for the man who draws near them unawares and hears the Sirens' voices; no welcome from his wife, no little children brightening at their father's return*. No dog, either, Joe added.

Ever since the softball game I had tried to keep my feet out of those euphemistic shoes. I thought avoiding her would be easy, but here she was, elbows on the car, holding her hair back with one hand. I looked around for a mast to lash myself to.

"Hey," she said, leaning down until her face was near the battery. "Where's your ring?"

"What?"

"Your wedding ring."

I looked at my left hand. My ring was gone.

I turned and looked in the gravel, but even as I pushed the stones aside I realized that I didn't remember having the ring on earlier, my hand had felt strange that morning. I looked at my finger again; there was an indented circle of flesh where the wedding band should have been.

"That's funny." My voice cracked.

"You didn't know?"

I shook my head as if it were no big deal, I lost things all the time. The truth, of course, was that I was instantly worried. Donna would kill me.

"Let's see." Dusty wrinkled her forehead, concentrating. Off to my left I saw one bare foot scratch the back of the other ankle. Her feet had thick calluses.

She said, "Do you take it off when you go to bed?"

"Nope."

"When you take a shower?"

"No."

"No?"

"I never take it off."

She looked down. "I know a lot of married people. They all take their rings off sometime."

The stones in the driveway bit into my back. I wanted to move, but I didn't dare get out from under the car. I wanted to grab her by the ankles and pull her down beside me.

"So," I said loudly. "Did you want something?"

"Wedding rings," she said. "They remind me of those African women, the ones who stick those big pieces of wood into their lips. The whole marriage scene is incredibly weird."

"Yeah," I said. "Weird." I shifted under the car. "How come you get stuck mowing the lawn?"

Dusty didn't answer right away.

She said, "So do you and your wife, like, tell each other *everything*?"

I bent my neck and looked up at her. The battery blocked the right side of her face. With her hair pulled back, she looked like a girl I might have known in school. She might have grown up down the street.

"You know," I said, surprising myself, "we're not even related."

"Who?"

"Donna and I."

Dusty stared down, confused. "You're *married*," she said.

"Well, sure. But we're not actually *related*. See what I mean?"

Dusty shook her head.

"I'm related to my parents, and to their parents, and to all their brothers and sisters." Lying under the car, staring up at the engine, talking to her was like talking to myself. "I'm related to *my* brothers. I'm more related to my sister than I am to my wife."

Dusty's eyes widened.

"I mean, we all share blood. We were born from the same people, we're biologically connected. But Donna and I, we just met, and then one day a priest said some things in Latin, we traded jewelry, and then somebody downtown signed a piece of paper. We're not even related."

"You're married," Dusty said. "That's as related as you get."

"I don't know," I told her. "It doesn't make any sense. I should be closer to her than to anyone else. But I grew up with my brothers and sister. And our mother and father *made* me. And then there are all these neighbors I've known all my life." I picked up a stone in each hand and weighed them. I didn't know *who* I was related to. (*To whom you are related*, I could hear Mrs. Wheatley say.)

A telephone rang. Not ours.

Dusty peered down at me. She was squinting now, as if she had been missing something before.

"That was a wild softball game," she said.

I had replayed the scene in my mind a hundred times: watching the pitch come in, swinging, feeling the ball hit the bat, seeing it hit our house on the fly. I remembered running the bases, Press chasing the ball, everyone yelling, Billy Mendini waving his arm in imitation of some third-base coach he had seen on television. I remembered sliding in on top of Dusty, how strong her body had been under mine, the small blue marks from her fingers Donna had found on my ribs that night.

A screen door squealed and I heard Grace's rasp.

"Phone," she told Dusty. Then, louder, "That you under there, George? How's tricks?"

"That hit was a real surprise," Dusty said. "You didn't strike me as the kind of guy who could get the job done."

"What's that supposed to mean?" I asked.

But she was already walking away.

Chapter Eleven

We were on our way downtown that night, listening to the Orioles on the radio.

I said, "Did you ever think about how things happen, and then you try to make them say something?"

"What's that?" Donna said. "Sorry, I wasn't listening."

I turned the volume down low.

"You know how sometimes something will happen early in the day, like you'll spill something at breakfast, and then a little while later something else happens, like you realize you need gas and you're already late, and you say: So that's what kind of day it's going to be."

"I've had bad days," she said.

"What I mean is, the only reason it's a bad day is because you decide it is. If you weren't worried about having jelly on your shirt, or being a few minutes late, there wouldn't be anything wrong. And even then, just because it's a bad day for you doesn't mean the day itself is bad—it's just *your* day, by your definition."

"Should I be following this?"

I tried again. "A lot of what happens in this world is random, unplanned. But in an attempt to make sense of it all, we try to give things meaning."

Donna said, "Are you talking about your ring?"

Am I the only one who does this? She guessed what I was trying to hide, so I denied it.

"It's just things," I said. "We give importance to things, when instead we should concentrate on—"

"This isn't about your ring?"

I held up my hand. I could still feel it—the weight below the first knuckle, the slight indentation of pale red flesh. I had never worn much jewelry, but I had gotten used to the wedding ring. When we played bridge I liked to spread my fingers along the edge of the table—the thick gold band made me feel like a Mississippi riverboat gambler.

"I lost it."

She looked at me, confused, and for a few seconds I had no idea what either one of us was talking about. Then Donna sort of jumped in her seat, laughed, and kissed me.

"You lost it?" she said happily. "You lost it!"

I nodded.

She put her hand to her chest. "Be still, my beating heart." She kissed me again. "What happened?"

"Wait a minute," I said. "What's going on?"

"I thought you had taken it off. When I saw you weren't wearing it last night, I didn't know what to think, and you didn't say anything. . . . You lost it. That's the best news I've had all day."

"Last night?"

"In bed."

I tried to follow the new evidence, but I still couldn't remember when the ring had come off. I tried to think if I had had it on at the office, but wearing a ring isn't the sort of thing you keep track of. Then something else struck me.

"You thought I had just taken it off?"

Donna half-shrugged, lifting her hands. "I didn't know what you were trying to tell me. All day I felt sick, wondering when you would—"

"You thought I would do that? Just take off my wedding ring?"

"I didn't know," she started.

"That's terrible." I felt indignation rising. "That's awful."

"Let's not worry about it. The good news is, you lost your ring. It doesn't mean anything if you lost it."

It sounded as if she was accusing me of being the sort of person who would hide his wedding ring.

"It *could* mean something," I told her, just to make a point. "Maybe it was subconscious. Maybe I *wanted* to lose it."

"Don't even say that."

"That's not what happened. But it's a possibility."

Donna sat quietly, thinking. When she spoke again her voice had grown angry.

"You didn't say anything about it last night. If it hadn't meant something, you would have told me right away."

"Hold on," I said. "I didn't know last night. I only realized this afternoon that I had lost it."

"You mean to tell me you didn't even know you had lost your wedding ring? Don't tell me *that* doesn't mean anything."

"Honey, how could it mean something if I didn't know it?"

"You *did* know." She hissed the word: *"Subconsciously."*

"You're accusing me of being subconscious?"

"Talk about *accusing*," she said, picking up momentum. "Over at Mrs. Webb's the other day you thought I had told them about those people next door. *You're* the one who thought I was telling them our personal problems behind your back, and now *you* accuse *me* of accusing *you* by saying—"

"Personal problems?"

"Don't play innocent," Donna said. "You know exactly what I'm talking about."

I did and I didn't.

At the time I thought the best I could do was to ride it out, to let things cool down. After a few minutes had passed, I turned up the baseball game.

The parents of one of Donna's students had invited us out to dinner. For some reason, parents never invited us to their homes, as if that wouldn't be enough for a music teacher. The truth was, we rarely ate in restaurants.

The conversation always got worked around to the student's progress, and the parents would do what they could to get Donna to say nice things about their child, who was usually a thin, frail girl with wispy hair and pale skin. Flute students were the only people I ever saw who could make a flute look heavy. The mothers and fathers of less talented students were desperate to hear that their money was being converted directly into high art, but the parents of the best students understood that musical skill took a lot of time and patience.

Roxanne Chapman was one of the best. I hadn't met her—her lessons were in the early afternoon—but Donna said Roxanne was a pleasure to teach, she worked hard and listened to criticism. The pride of her high-school music department, she'd recently been accepted to start at Peabody in the fall. Her parents suggested we meet them at Haussner's, a German restaurant on Eastern Avenue.

I never felt comfortable at those dinners. Someone would usually ask me if I played an instrument. Then they would ask what it was like to live with a talented musician, and make jokes about all the scales and the squeaking and shrieking they imagined I had to put up with from the students, and they would ask what I thought of such-and-such a concerto or such-and-such a piece for flute and piano. Usually if I just smiled and turned the conversation back to Donna they would let me off the hook.

We reached Haussner's just before seven. The waiting area near the doors was crammed, so we ducked into a bar called the Rathskeller. There was a crowd there too. It took a minute before we noticed that the walls were filled, ceiling to floor, corner to corner, with paintings of nude women: nudes sitting, nudes standing, nudes lying across plush red cushions. They were old-fashioned nudes, sickly white, with no hair anywhere on their skin. They had doughy stomachs and broad thighs. Their nipples were violent red with rouge.

"Get a load of this," I said. "I think I see a motif."

"Let's get out of here," Donna said.

"Don't you want a drink?"

"I'm leaving." She excused herself as she made her way through the crowd to the doorway.

We found a place to stand near the cash register and I apologized. "I thought you might want a drink."

"Look," she said. "I don't believe this."

Virtually every inch of every wall of the restaurant was

either covered by a painting or hidden by statuary: landscapes and seascapes and portraits and still lifes, all tending toward the romantic and pastoral, hung frame-to-frame on the walls; decorative plates and saucers lined shelves; busts on pedestals stood among the tables, and life-size statues guarded the doors to the rest rooms. It looked like a clearance sale at the Walters Art Gallery.

Donna saw Roxanne with her parents. Mr. Chapman, a big man in a light blue suit, said, "Sorry if we kept you waiting." He shook my hand and I thought I felt a bone snap—he was one of those. The hostess took five menus from a stack beside a foot-high statue of the Three Graces. Roxanne and her mother went first, followed by Donna.

"After you," I told Mr. Chapman.

"No," he said. "You." I went, and all the way to the table I saw people staring behind me. He was about six and a half feet tall, and people seemed to think he was someone important.

Above our table was a painting of a young man courting a coy young woman in a blue dress. She was seated, her feet propped delicately on an elegant footstool.

"Look, Milt," Mrs. Chapman said. "Isn't that French?"

The painting was behind me. I unfolded my napkin while they stared over my head.

"The clothes are your first clue," her husband said. "And the light. It's popular, done before the Impressionists. I'd say late eighteenth or very early nineteenth century."

"Do you study art?" Donna asked.

"Not me," Mr. Chapman said. "Betty is taking a course down at Johns Hopkins, and she gets me to ask her the study questions. Flash cards, that sort of thing. Can you believe that? A woman her age sitting at home worrying about a test?"

Mrs. Chapman beamed. "Don't let him fool you—he enjoys it. By the time he finishes drilling me, he knows the answers better than I do."

Donna smiled and said something polite about how she admired people who never ended their formal education.

Three pages of single-spaced typed entrées filled the menu. There was a lot of German food I couldn't pronounce, and seafood, and a few odds and ends—black-eyed peas, fresh pig knuckles.

The waitress, a motherly type in plain white, smiled and asked if we'd like something to drink. Before anyone else could speak, Mr. Chapman asked if we would mind if he ordered some wine. He choked something off in German.

The waitress looked at the wine list over his shoulder. "One bottle of number seven," she said, taking it from him.

Mrs. Chapman turned toward her daughter. "Honey, you haven't said a word."

Roxanne Chapman was built along her father's lines: tall, with strong, square shoulders. She was well-developed and tanned, and in a white blouse she looked healthy and young and enthusiastic. Just looking at her made me tired.

She was saved when the waitress arrived with our wine.

Mr. Chapman studied the label on the bottle, then nodded. The waitress uncorked it and poured a few drops into his glass, probably used to most people smiling and waving for her to keep pouring. It was that kind of restaurant.

"Just a moment." Mr. Chapman picked up the cork, passing it under his nose. Setting it down, he held his glass up to the light. Satisfied, he brought the glass to his nose and sniffed.

Under her breath, Roxanne said, "Let's just *drink* it." I looked around; no one else had heard.

The waitress looked at Mr. Chapman as if he were conducting a primitive religious ceremony right there at her table.

"Is everything all right?"

Mr. Chapman moved the glass to his lips, took a very small sip, held it in his mouth for a moment, then swallowed. He looked up. "Fine."

The waitress poured the rest and left.

Donna raised her glass. "Should we toast the Peabody student?"

"You're out of turn," Mr. Chapman said. His glass was almost completely hidden in his hand. He could have palmed a pumpkin. "First, a toast to the tutor."

"To the tutor," his wife echoed.

We drank.

"To Roxanne," Donna said. We drank again.

When we set down our glasses I could feel it coming.

"Tell me," Mrs. Chapman said. "Have you had many other students accepted by Peabody?"

"Roxanne's the first," Donna said. "She played a wonderful audition, too. There wasn't any doubt."

"Have you had many other students apply?"

"Don't start," Mr. Chapman told his wife. "Look at her. She's blushing already." Roxanne was starting to turn red under her tan. She looked like the center of a medium-well prime rib.

"Don't mind me," Mrs. Chapman said. "I guess I'm just proud." She laughed nervously and played with her earring.

"You have every right to be," Donna said. "She's good now, and she's far from her potential."

Mr. Chapman turned to me. "What about you, George? You have an instrument? Tickle the ivories?"

I told him I played the radio. It was my stock response, but Roxanne laughed. She was sitting directly across from me, between Donna and her mother.

Our waitress returned, pulled a pad out of her apron, and took our orders. She kept an eye on Mr. Chapman. After she left, he polished off his first glass of wine. "I always have *hasenpfeffer* here," he said. "I used to shoot rabbit when I was a kid. Don't get much of a chance anymore."

"He was quite a hunter," his wife added.

Roxanne spoke up for the first time. "Let's hear all the gory details while we wait. Maybe we could ask them to skin it at the table." She emptied her glass, keeping pace with her father.

We chatted until our food came, then the Chapmans dominated the conversation. Mr. Chapman told a long story about his cousin, a violist, and he and his wife talked about a cruise they would be taking in the fall.

I looked at the walls. Some of the paintings, like the one of a castle perched in the mountains on the edge of a pine forest, and another of a small girl measuring herself against a patient St. Bernard, were simple. Pop music. Others were more difficult. Across from me, above two elderly couples, was a painting of two young girls. A visitor had just entered the room, and one of the girls was offering him a goat's head on a platter. Was she trying to scare him? Was it a joke? Or was the painting set in a country where it was considered an honor for a hostess to give her guest a goat's head?

I thought of Donna's concerts. I could listen for a melody in Beethoven or Bach, but after a few minutes I'd be sliding away, slipping on the surface. Donna would say, "Listen," and I would, but I didn't hear what she heard. Donna and Roxanne, even Roxanne's parents—they all understood something that was a mystery to me.

Off to my left was a winter landscape, a frozen river cutting through the snowbanks. Beside it was an enormous painting, at least five feet high, called *Aurora of 1876*. A tall, yawning nude looked down on us. I imagined having dinner with Dusty at Haussner's.

We drank three bottles of the German wine. Donna began refusing refills, and Mrs. Chapman nursed hers. Her husband drank because he liked the wine; Roxanne and I drank because we didn't have anything else to do.

At one point the table fell silent. I had been avoiding the conversation, drifting away. A picture above Mrs. Chapman showed a golden-haired girl wearing an apron, surrounded by dogs, cuddling a puppy on her shoulder.

"Tell me," she said to Donna. "I've wondered all along what made you decide to teach instead of continuing your own career. You're so young, and obviously talented . . ."

"You've heard the old saying—those who can't play, teach."

"Come now," Mr. Chapman said. "Don't expect us to accept that. Bernard Shaw was full of those gross generalizations."

I sat back, looking at the picture of the bored nude, and wondered if Mrs. Chapman had taken a class in literary aphorisms. The conversation seemed to be piped through a public-address system.

Donna looked at Mr. Chapman, then at me, as if she were trying to tell me something.

"I took lessons beginning in grade school, through junior high and high school, and all the way through college. My junior year, my teacher told me that I was one of the best students he had ever had, and he got me an audition with the Baltimore Symphony."

The Chapmans were listening intently. Even through the fog of the wine, I knew the story: Donna had told me just before we were engaged.

"It was on a Saturday morning," she said. "I got there early and waited over an hour. I was so nervous . . . first my hands would sweat, then that would stop and my mouth would go dry, then I'd get cold and start shivering."

Roxanne smiled and nodded.

"But when I got inside and started—I was playing the Mozart Concerto in D—I realized that being scared probably helped. I played from deep inside. It's cliché, but I really felt as if I were playing it for the first time.

"The odd thing was that I don't think I heard a note of it. I could feel every part of me working, I could feel my lungs and my lips and tongue and even my legs vibrate with the notes, but I didn't actually hear anything. The music wasn't out there to hear—it was inside of me. It was the best I had ever played."

We were parked in front of her parents' house, late at night. We had been dating for three months. She said, *Tell me something you've never told anyone else*. I confessed about watching those cheap fraternity-house movies, and told her how I had finally stopped going to see them—something I considered a personal victory, a sign of character. *Your turn,* I said.

Mrs. Chapman spoke softly. "What did they say?"

" 'Thank you.' " Donna smiled. "And when I left I knew I couldn't do better than that. But I loved playing, I couldn't quit. So I played with other groups, and I kept taking lessons. But it wasn't the same."

"You had given up," Mr. Chapman said.

"Maybe. But I got better. And I know that if I auditioned for the BSO today I could get a job. But I don't want to be a mediocre player in a mediocre orchestra. I played with my heart once, and it wasn't enough."

Donna was staring at something in the distance, something the rest of us couldn't see. This was what she had told me that night—the story of her greatest failure. I had been bragging, but she trusted me with her pain.

Roxanne leaned toward her.

"So you decided to teach?"

Donna looked up. "It helps me stay in shape. And one day, I tell myself, I'll listen and I'll hear someone else play the way I wanted to."

My heart fell. I had thought it was our story, about the two of us falling in love. Somehow, it had turned back into a story about playing the flute.

Mr. and Mrs. Chapman continued the interrogation. I smiled and nodded, feeling sick. I took another drink and wondered if Donna was still simmering, angry over what I had said about losing my ring.

I blanked out, and a few minutes later I realized I was staring at my spoon. I looked up to see if anyone had noticed. Roxanne was watching me. Glancing away, she licked her lips deliberately, the tip of her tongue turned up. I imagined Dusty doing that: sitting across from me in a crowded restaurant, licking her lips. I imagined her foot moving to meet mine under the table. The wine pulled my face into a mile-long smile, an idiot's grin. Roxanne grinned back.

"George," Mr. Chapman said.

I jumped. "Sir?"

Roxanne laughed, then looked away.

"What type of work is it that you're in?"

We were eating dessert; he paused between spoonfuls of ice cream. I wondered what he would do to the first boy he caught necking with his daughter. Gouge the kid's eyes out with his thumbs.

I took a sip of wine, barely able to taste it. "Industrial sales. With Harry Reynolds, over in Pikesville."

"Is that so?" Chapman refilled his glass. He looked sober. "I used to see Harry down at Bethlehem Steel. That's been about twenty years now. He was a real character, tough as nails—he'd do anything for a buck. Come in at seven in the morning, come in at night, stand on his head and twirl a pipe wrench in his teeth." He took a drink. "He must be an old bastard by now. Hell, he was old then. How is he?"

"The same," I said. "Older."

Chapman gave me a hard look, but he didn't ask me anything else.

Mrs. Chapman said, "You certainly are lucky, getting to hear Donna. Roxanne won't play for us. If she knows I'm listening when she practices, she stops."

Roxanne ignored her. "What's your favorite piece?"

I reached for my coffee cup and nearly knocked it over. "It's hard to say. I have trouble renumbering the manes." Mrs. Chapman looked over curiously. I tried again. "Remembering the names. There's one . . . something by the French guy—"

"Debussy," Donna said. "Syriax."

"That's pretty," Roxanne said.

"I listen to a lot of jazz and blues. Traditional."

"I like to listen to other things too." Roxanne stared intently at me, as if tonight were the start of something.

"Lately I've been listening to one blues singer in particular. Joe Turner."

"He's *great*." Roxanne nearly reached across the table. " 'Shake, Rattle, and Roll.' 'Honey Hush.' A friend of mine has some of his albums. Do you know 'Cherry Red'?"

"Sure."

"I love that one. 'I want you to boogie my woogie, 'til my face turns cherry red.' " She laughed.

Mrs. Chapman glanced around nervously. "That old music certainly was colorful."

Her husband said, "Does he call himself Big Joe Turner? Boss of the Blues?"

"Sometimes," I said. "That's the one."

Mr. Chapman sat back. "Is he, what, about fifty now?"

"That's right."

"I saw him perform back in the early forties. He used to sing in a bar in the old Negro district in Kansas City. Fellow named Pete Johnson played the piano."

"You heard Joe?"

"Back then they billed him as one of the Kansas City Shouters. Something like that."

"He's got a wonderful memory for details," his wife said.

I tried to match his nonchalance. "So how was he? What was it like?"

Chapman smiled patronizingly. "I suppose it was all right, if you like that sort of thing. There were a few people back then who got all excited about it. It's very primitive music, actually."

I looked at Donna to let her know that I felt no obligation to continue the conversation.

When we were ready to leave, Mrs. Chapman said something to her husband. He stood. The elderly couples across from us stopped their conversation as his shadow fell over their table.

"I just told Milt that you might want to see the little museum they have here," Mrs. Chapman said. "We're going to get some pies to take home with us. While they're boxing them up, we can look around."

I was glad for the chance to walk. My head was floating.

We climbed a flight of stairs to the gallery. The first thing we saw was a small sculpture on a pedestal. A naked woman, connected to the ground only by a blanket that stretched to reach the top of her legs, stood proudly, suspended in the air, breasts thrust forward, her hands pushing back her hair. "Oh," Roxanne said, "that's *beautiful*."

The museum was a collection of odds and ends: sculptures, a four-foot-in-diameter ball of string, paintings, busts, clocks—pieces of the Haussner collection that had overflowed from the dining rooms. After we looked at some of the artwork, Mrs. Chapman excused herself and went to the ladies' room.

I stopped at a corner of a piece of something called *Panthéon de le Guerre*. A sign said that, in its entirety, it was the largest mural ever created—four hundred feet long and forty-five feet high. I stood in front of one of the sections, studying the cracks in the paint on a horse's back. Mr. Chapman was discussing one of the clocks with Donna.

Some of the art in Haussner's *was* beautiful. Some of it, like the painting of the little girl and the St. Bernard, was junk. What about the woman with the goat's head? I had wanted to laugh—it looked absurd. But to laugh would have been just like Mr. Duncan and the rest making fun of Mr. Mead.

But maybe the painting *was* ridiculous. Maybe Mr. Mead's poem really was awful. It certainly sounded awful. And even if the poem was good, it was a mistake for him to read it when he knew that no one in the room would have the slightest notion of what he was trying to do. He could have tried to explain—and Haussner's could tell us something about their paintings, and Mr. Chapman could have told us what he was looking for in that wine. Standing in a grab bag of a museum, half-drunk, I thought: Knowing about wine or poetry or music isn't any great virtue in itself. The important thing is to try to understand more, and to share what you know.

"Do you like horses?"

"Not particularly. I was just thinking that if I stand here and stare at this long enough I might not throw up."

Roxanne laughed too loudly.

"Did you ever hear about Catherine the Great? She died trying to hump a horse. It crushed her." She pressed her breast against my arm.

"That's a very interesting anecdote." I didn't move. "Do you read a lot of history?"

Roxanne's mouth nearly touched my ear. I could feel the warmth of her breath. She sang softly, "I want you to boogie my woogie."

Mr. Chapman walked up to us; Roxanne stepped back just in time. "Well, George," he said, "what do you think?" He was studying the mural.

"Very big," I said. "Big horse."

Roxanne hadn't gone far. "Wouldn't you like to have it for yourself?"

Mr. Chapman answered. "Of course he wouldn't. That would defeat the purpose of placing art on public display—this way, everyone can enjoy it."

Roxanne said, "Don't you want just one piece?"

Her mother and Donna were walking over to us.

"There's no room," I said loudly. "The house is already crowded."

Donna drove me home.

Chapter Twelve

"That was the one. I think we're talking triplets." I had worked up a sweat; it was a muggy night.

Donna kissed me, smiled blissfully, and rolled over. "Good night, babe."

" 'Night."

I pushed the pillow away from my shoulders and lay flat on my back, staring at the ceiling. I raised up and flipped the pillow over, then settled in. I needed a good night's sleep, because the next morning I had to be in at seven to get a bid together for Harry.

Too warm. I pushed the spread down to the foot of the bed, then concentrated on being quiet, listening for the music from next door. One night I had heard Billie Holiday. I wondered if it was Grace's choice or the girls'.

"You asleep?" Donna said it softly, under her breath.

"I'm hot."

"Roxanne was flirting with you tonight."

"She's only a kid."

"She's beautiful."

I knew Donna wanted me to contradict her. "She just got out of high school. She's what, seventeen?"

"Nineteen in August."

"Really?"

Donna didn't answer. If I had met a girl like that in high

school . . . Why was I even thinking about it? I stared at the ceiling. I thought I could make out a drumbeat.

Donna said, "Are you sure you want to have a baby?"

My heart fell for the second time in five hours.

"Yes," I said with more confidence than I felt.

"It's a big step," she said. "Sometimes I wonder if we're ready."

I turned onto my side, looking at her back in the dark. "Press said one is a breeze. Two is when the fun starts."

"You two talk about babies?"

"That day they were here—I told him we're trying."

Donna jumped up. I thought something had bitten her.

"You told Press that we're going to have a baby?"

I considered crawling under the bed.

"I haven't told anybody," she said. "We didn't say anything about telling people."

"I thought that's what you and Cindy were talking about."

"I asked her some questions, but I never told her we were going to have a baby."

"What do you mean, *were*?" I sat up.

Donna rolled back onto her side, looking away from me. She wasn't talking now.

I lay back. "You haven't told anybody?"

She didn't answer for a long time. I picked up the drumbeat from across the driveway before she said softly, "My mother."

"There you go—you told your mother, I told Press."

"It's not the same," she said.

"I can't tell my father. Press is my best friend."

"It's not the same."

"You told the audition story at dinner."

Donna froze. With one sentence, I had turned her anger.

Then I heard a sound, a sound so soft that I moved closer to try to make it out. I had my nose in her hair, my ear by her shoulder, when I heard her say, softly, her voice trembling, "I'm sorry."

"I take it back," I said. She was on the verge of tears. "I didn't mean it."

"I'm sorry," she said, louder. "I did it on purpose."

A lead weight sank in my stomach. I was beating up on my wife, she was twisting knives into me. Was this how other people lived, walking a treadmill of arguments? It had never been that way for us.

"It's all right," I said. "It's your story. You can tell it however you want."

"I'm sorry," she said again.

"It's okay." We're even, I thought. Let's stop this.

There was another long pause. I felt a crick in my neck. I moved back onto my pillow.

"This is special, between you and me," she said. "If we have a baby, everybody will be asking questions and giving us advice, but it will be ours, something we share. I don't want the whole world in on it."

I thought about that.

"If we have a baby," I said, "we'll be related."

"Exactly."

"I've only told one person."

"He'll tell Cindy."

"That leaves a few million."

She didn't laugh, but this was better. I steered for a safe subject.

"They're going to breed Belle."

"Really?" She sounded interested, even relieved to get off the argument.

"Press asked if Joe would be willing to do the honors."

"When?"

"About a week."

She rolled over and slipped her arm around mine. "Are they bringing her here?"

"I think so."

"Our dog had puppies. I was in junior high. They're supposed to do it twice, with a day in between."

"What if they don't like each other?"

"When a dog's in heat, they all like each other. Did you tell him we want our pick?"

"What?"

"Our pick of the litter."

I thought she was joking.

"That's what you do," she said. "Ginny, our dog, had four puppies, and the man who owned the stud picked my favorite. I wanted to hide it in the closet, but Mom wouldn't let me."

"What do we want with another dog?"

"Either that or a fee," she said. "That's the way you do it."

"It's not costing us anything. They get puppies, Joe has a good time."

Donna said, "We'll have another dog to take care of for a few days, and when they sell the puppies they'll be making money—the fee is our percentage."

"They're going to keep one and give one to Cindy's sister." I wondered how they knew there would be two. "How many do they have, anyway?"

"Didn't you ever have a dog?"

We hadn't. There were too many people in our house for us to need a dog.

"Five or six," she said.

"That many?"

"Your parents had eight children."

"I appreciate that little analogy." I moved down in the bed and slipped one arm under my pillow. "So now we're pimps."

"We are not."

"We're selling the sexual services of our dog."

"Compromising his virtue." She was in a good mood now.

"He'll be a canine of the evening."

"We're teaching an old dog to turn tricks." She shifted toward me and we kissed.

A shotgun went off.

I jumped awake. Silence. Then a brilliant flash of lightning, a loud rumble. My heart drummed against my chest.

"It must have hit something," Donna said.

I got up and looked outside. Nothing but darkness. Slowly, rain began to fall against the screen. I lowered the windows.

"The one in the bathroom is open," she said, trying to make herself small under the covers.

I turned on the light on the dresser. Before I reached the

doorway there was another bright flash outside—the light flickered and went out.

"Hurry," Donna said. "Come back."

I walked down the dark hallway to the bathroom. The floor near the window was already damp, a shallow puddle forming on the sill. As I closed the window the clouds let loose: rain beat on the roof. I walked back to the bedroom, the floorboards my father had nailed down creaking under my feet.

"Listen," Donna said.

The rain came hard, in waves, washing over the house. It was the sort of rain that made you glad to be inside; it made you want to snuggle with someone. I climbed back into bed, too tired to think. "Rain," I said.

"I'm serious," she said. "Listen."

I listened. High above the pounding of the rain and the rumble of the thunder, a dog was howling.

"Is that Joe?" she asked.

"It's some other dog. He just hides in his house."

We listened longer. It was Joe.

Donna looked over at me in the dark. "What are you going to do?"

"I'm going to sleep."

"He's caught in the storm!"

"He's just scared." I put my arm over my eyes. "He'll stop in a minute."

Rain came down harder, lightning flashed, thunder shook the house. Above it all, Joe howled.

"Do something," Donna said. "Please."

"It's only rain," I told her. "Water from the sky. He'll be all right." Another flash of lightning, more thunder. Donna looked scared. "Dogs belong outdoors. They love this sort of stuff."

Joe howled until I could make out the words: *I hate you,* he was saying.

"Okay okay okay." I rubbed my eyes, got up, and went over to the closet. "Where's my robe?"

"You're going to wear your robe?"

She was right. I went downstairs, taking the steps cautiously in the dark. The lightning was close: the whole house flashed bright white, and when it stopped I couldn't see a thing. I felt my way into the kitchen, certain I was about to jam my toe against something nasty. When I got to the door I considered running outside buck naked—after all, it was the middle of the night, it was only water—but I pulled my trench coat out of the closet. No shoes. I opened the door and stepped outside.

I was drenched before I had taken two steps. As I ran to Joe's house, my feet slipping in the wet grass, the wind blew through my coat, making me feel at least as naked as I would have without it. Man in his original state, I thought. Man runs to save trusty steed.

Joe was standing four feet behind his house, howling as if he had been stabbed. When he saw me he leapt into the air, only to be yanked to the ground by his chain.

"Hey," I said. Joe jumped up, leaving long muddy streaks on my good coat, and howled in my face. "I'm here!" I said. Then, feeling bad, I rubbed his head. "Hang on, buddy."

The bare dirt around Joe's house had already turned to mud, reddish-brown ooze squeezing up between my toes. I squatted down to find the problem, trying to see between the lightning and the darkness, but Joe was going out of his mind—he ran in circles, twisting the chain around my ankles, and I fell to all fours. "Hey," I said, "hold still." Thunder cracked the sky like a cannon blast, and Joe jumped onto my back.

That's how Dusty and two of her friends found me.

I tried to duck so Joe would slide over my head, but after his front legs slid over my shoulders and hit the ground, he wouldn't move. I was trying to get the chain untangled from my ankles and the jagged edges of a tree root Joe had dug up when I heard someone call my name. I thought: That's odd. I looked up and saw Dusty and two older men, fully dressed, huddled under an umbrella.

"Damn," one of the men said. "What are you doing to that dog?"

I pushed Joe off to the side and tried to stand. I was covered in mud. "His chain is caught."

The five of us looked at each other: the three of them under the umbrella, still fairly dry; me in my raincoat, soaked, the chain cutting into my ankles; Joe, his fur plastered to his skin, waiting for one of us to do something intelligent.

"This is my uncle," Dusty said, introducing the man on her left. "Uncle Pete."

"Yeah," the man on her right said. "I'm his brother, Repeat."

It's surprising how long some people laugh at their own jokes.

I wasn't sure who was being fooled, but I played along. "I'm George."

Joe turned and shook, spattering all of us with muddy water.

"Well," I said, pushing my hair off my forehead, feeling water dripping down inside my trench coat, "I'd love to chat—" Thunder drowned me out.

"Help him," Dusty told Uncle Pete. The shorter of the two men, he seemed to be in charge.

"No dice," he said. "This place is a goddamn pigpen."

The sky flashed white and I saw Dusty's face. I couldn't be sure, but I thought she was embarrassed for me. And there she was with two strange men in the middle of the night.

"Hold this," she said, handing the umbrella to Uncle Pete.

"Hey, doll, don't do that," Pete said.

"Don't do that," Repeat said. "You'll have to change. We gotta make time."

She came over and squatted down beside me. "What can I do?"

"Just hold him." I knelt and pulled at the chain. It was slippery, covered with mud. Joe stood next to Dusty, whimpering, trusting us to save him.

"Hey," Dusty said, "what've you got on under there?"

My raincoat was hanging open. I pulled it tight.

"Some of us," I said, "were asleep." Under cover of thunder I added, "Who are those clowns?"

"Clowns," Dusty said. She pulled the dress up over her knees and knelt in the mud.

Joe shook again, and I brushed dirty water from my eyes. "You don't have to do this," I told her. "I'll be all right."

"I owe you," she said.

Uncle Pete called out from under the umbrella, "You should put that dog in your basement."

"In your basement," Repeat said, amusing himself tremendously.

"He won't go in," I said. "He gets sick in the house." I couldn't get the chain loose, I was drowning, and I was kneeling in the mud in front of strangers.

"You sure?" Repeat said. "I never heard of no dog that wouldn't go indoors."

"This is the one," I said.

Lightning flashed and Joe jumped away from Dusty, ripping the chain through my hands. My palms began to bleed.

"Hey," Dusty said, "can't you just take off his collar?"

Idiot, I thought. I slipped the choker off. Joe shook once, surprised to be free, then ran straight to the kitchen door.

Uncle Pete shouted over the noise of the rain pattering on the shed, "Looks like you might get him inside tonight."

I unwound the chain from around my ankles and Dusty helped me up. She was soaked, her dress pasted crookedly against her body.

"Mr. Fixit," she said. "I'm disappointed in you."

Chapter Thirteen

July 18, 1957, was the day I got the call from my father. My friends and I had only been in Ocean City three days. We were about to go out for dinner when the phone rang. I was the last one home. Waite had been on a ship docked at Newport News, but he took emergency leave and got a fast ride home with a truck driver. That's how we knew there was real trouble: our father had told Waite to take the leave, to come home. Mark and Lou, on vacation from college, were with Father at the hospital.

Mom had gone out after lunch to pick up some dry cleaning. She had asked Lou to go, but he was waiting for a phone call from his girlfriend. Pat had said she would go with her, then changed her mind. "I should have been there," Pat kept saying. She sat in one of the yellow kitchen chairs, her head down on the table, eyes shut. "I should have been with her."

We didn't meet the car in the driveway. Without saying anything, we all took our places at the dining-room table. Mark and Lou sat near the end.

Father came in quietly. He rolled up his sleeves, making neat parallel folds, stopping with the cuffs just below his elbows. He may have been stalling for composure, but he seemed calm, thoughtful, in control. We waited. He looked out at us, his children. Then he took the floor for the entire length of our last family meeting.

"As long as heaven leaves us in prosperity and health, we

never think hard times are on their way. Yet when the blessed gods have brought misfortune on our heads, we simply have to steel ourselves and bear it."

Our father took us with him as he told a story about pain, injustice, and the reasons to continue. He talked about his father, his past: baring himself. He told us about running away from home, finding a ship. He told us about France and Morocco and Portugal, and about anger, blame, and regret—as if they, too, were countries on a map we needed to know. He told us we needed to stand strong in the face of overwhelming challenges, to do what we knew was right. He paused for a moment, then returned to Homer, searching for the words to tell us.

"Incontinent grief serves no useful end. It is our common lot to die, and the gods themselves cannot rescue even one they love, when Death that stretches all men out lays its dread hand upon her."

The next few minutes aren't very clear. It still hurts. Pat and Earle started crying loudly, and Tony hid his face against my arm. Lou didn't cry, but later that night he announced that he was responsible for our mother's death. His own judge and jury, he had found himself guilty beyond a doubt. He never let us forgive him.

I didn't cry either. Crying starts slowly. When Father stopped talking, something worse happened, something snapped; strong muscles failed. Tears poured out, uncontrollable, steady as rain. A hole had been punched through me, and I fell—falling, falling—to a place I had never wanted to see.

I wasn't sad. I was angry. I had wanted Father to go on. As long as he was telling his story, the end was far away. I wanted him to talk and talk and talk, telling us about his father and his trips and his family and his losses. I wanted him to go back and tell all the stories he had ever told us; I wanted to fall asleep with him talking. I would wake up with his lips moving against my ear, whispering a story about pain and sorrow and the courage it took to be strong. His voice would drown out the world around me, and his story would never end. Nothing he said could be as painful as what I heard when he stopped.

Father stood at the head of the table, watching us: Mark, his head bent low; Bob, his face in his hands; Lou, behind Bob, holding him, strong in his complete acceptance of failed responsibility; Waite, hugging Pat, looking guilty for being in uniform, looking like one of us; Earle, trying to wipe his eyes dry as the tears kept coming; and Tony, beside me, his arms wrapped around his stomach as if he could hold the pain inside.

For a brief moment I saw Father's eyes register something other than sorrow as he looked at us, his children. Then the look left, and I saw the sadness that held the edges of his face for the rest of his life.

"Anything wrong?"

Janie, my secretary, stood in front of my desk, holding her jacket and pocketbook.

I wiped my eyes fast, before I looked up. "Are you leaving early?"

"It's after five." Janie searched my face. "Are you okay? I put this order on your desk ten minutes ago."

"I'm all right." I reached for the papers.

"You need anything before I go? I'm taking the mail."

I said I didn't and she left.

I hunted through some ragged slips of paper in my top desk drawer before I finally found Mark's office number. A girl with a Southern accent answered, all soft vowels and honeyed drawl.

"I'm sorry," she said, "Mr. Willus is on another line. Would you like to wait or should I have him call you back?"

I told her I'd wait. I hadn't talked to him in months, and he rarely wrote. His wife, Lisa, told us the news about them and their two daughters in friendly notes on green stationery.

"Mark Willus speaking." The voice at the other end sounded tired but professional.

"Do you handle whiplash?"

"Not for you, you cheapskate." His voice relaxed. "How are you, slugger?"

We traded family news. It always took a few minutes to

settle back into the old patterns. I tried to picture him in a three-piece suit, sitting behind a walnut desk.

"When are you going to get off your can and come down here and see us?"

I picked up a pen and started doodling. "Some of us can't just hit the road. Some of us work for a living." I drew a childish outline of Tennessee on the blotter.

"Tell me about it," he said. "I'm so backed up I can hardly see straight."

We talked about work. He had to break away occasionally to talk to someone in the office. Finally the conversation slowed, the tiredness crept back into his voice.

I put the cap on my pen. "You remember what today is."

"It can't be one of the birthdays—I've got them all on my calendar."

There was a moment of silence when I didn't answer. I looked up at Miss July on the Sure-Seal calendar. She was sitting on the beach, a few feet from the water, holding a length of two-inch pipe in a way meant to appear obscene. I looked down at the date again: July 18.

"I don't know, slugger. What did I miss?"

"It's the day Mom died."

I could hear faint static through the silence.

"I always remember the twenty-second," he said. "The funeral." He waited, listening, playing the older brother now. "Is that why you called?"

I nodded.

Neither of us said anything. I uncapped the pen and colored in the outline of the state.

"She was a wonderful woman."

"I've been thinking," I said, trying to control my voice. "I might go to the grave. Take some flowers."

"You still go out there?" He didn't say anything else. The static was interfering.

"Sometimes," I said, louder. "I think about her and take flowers."

"George, it's important to let go. Once a year is one thing. I wouldn't make a steady habit out of it."

"You would too. You would if you were here. They don't

cut the grass often enough. They keep it nicer when they know people come to visit."

"Maybe so." He didn't sound convinced.

We were silent again, and I could think only of things that separated us. Mark's law degree. Our ages. His daughters. The distance from Baltimore to Nashville.

"How are the girls?"

"Fine," he said. "Healthy, happy. If you want to be their favorite uncle, you better get down here soon."

"Good Lord." I kept forgetting that I was somebody's uncle. Uncle George. It didn't sound good.

I said, "What's an uncle *do*?"

"If I were you, I'd send money."

"I'm serious." I kept hearing the word in my mind: uncle. Uncle. It sounded like an Eskimo word for slush.

"It's not a job," Mark said. "It's just a thing. You're it."

"A thing?" I said.

"But *favorite* uncle . . . you've got your work cut out for you. When Tony and Earle were here last month, the girls couldn't get enough of Tony. And they're crazy about Lisa's brother."

Another relationship. I wanted to ask him what I should do, what it was like being a father. I wanted to keep gathering information, case studies. I wanted somebody to say: piece of cake.

"You should come down and visit, we could talk."

"I would," I said. "I really would. But I can't get a vacation."

"Two years and you can't get a week? That's a real slave driver."

I traced a paper clip on a sheet of scrap paper. "He promised me ten days last year, then he never said anything else about it."

"So ask."

"It's not that easy." Harry was hot-tempered, unpredictable, and at least a little senile. He only kept promises when the mood struck him.

I wanted to ask Mark for advice about a lot of things, but instead I said, "I guess you've got work to do."

He dropped back into his professional voice. "No end to it. You know how that goes."

"I sure do," I said, adopting the tone I used with customers. A moment later we hung up.

Chapter Fourteen

Joe jumped down, his tail high, front paws spread, daring me to take it away—then dropped the tennis ball at my feet.

"Good dog," I told him. "Good work."

Press and Cindy were bringing Belle over, so we had started our walk earlier than usual. I took him all the way to Snyder's Mill High School's field and stood at home plate, throwing imaginary hits.

"Pop-up to short," I narrated, heaving the ball. "Circle under it, circle—" The ball hit a pebble and bounced crazily, Joe in hot pursuit. He snared it and raced back to me.

"Last one." Joe wasn't even breathing heavily, but I wanted him to save his energy. "Left-handed batter, a line-drive hitter. Man on first, two outs. Cut off the run at the plate." I spun once, keeping him from getting an early start, and hurled the tennis ball into right field. Joe raced away, low to the ground.

"He's off with the crack of the bat," I shouted to thousands of listeners pressed close to their radios. "But no—he loses the ball in the corner—the runner's turning second and heading for third!" Joe panicked, overran the ball, fishtailed, and found it. "They're sending him!" I shouted. "He's trying to score!" Joe raced toward me, tennis ball trapped tight in his mouth, sprinting through the infield. "Here comes the relay, the play at the plate, he is . . . Out! *Out at home!*" Joe celebrated, dancing, jumping up for the ball. "Oh my goodness, ladies and gentlemen, what a finish! An amazing play by Joe the Dog. . . ." I faked a throw and he ran ahead of me, fooled. "What a day! What a player! What a game!"

Press and Cindy stood by the side door, talking to Donna.

"Where's the lucky lady?" I said.

"By the shed." Press patted Joe. "You ready for some action?"

"We just had some," I said. "You're looking at the original one-man defense. Golden retriever, golden glove."

"Do you want to lead Joe around back," Donna asked me, "so we know they see each other?" She turned to Cindy. "We've got some cheese and crackers inside."

"Oh," Cindy said. She looked at Press.

Press squatted next to Joe. "We're supposed to watch."

"Watch?" I said.

"It's in the book. It puts them at ease." No one answered. He said, "I know it adds something for *me*, anyway."

Donna said, "When I was in eighth grade we bred our dog, and we never watched. We just locked them in the basement."

Press shrugged. "It's what the book says."

"We've been reading up," Cindy said.

"Exactly what kind of book is this?"

Donna asked Cindy, "Are you going to watch?"

Cindy nodded guiltily.

Donna turned to me. "I *know* you'll watch."

I could hear her telling me that we should have charged a stud fee. The look on her face said we should have charged five hundred dollars.

"Well," she said. "I guess I'll get the cheese and crackers."

Press and I took some lawn chairs to the backyard. A minute later Cindy and the girls followed Donna, all of them parading out with beer and milk and food.

"This is the way to do it." Press opened a bottle. "Better than the ballpark."

"Are you sure the girls should see this?" Cindy asked nervously.

"It's never too early to show them a little about the birds and bees."

"These are *dogs*," Cindy said.

Donna said, "If they don't get interested in each other before the sun goes down, I'm going in. I'm not sitting out here with flashlights."

Belle had been on the other side of the house, and Joe was sniffing back by the shed, where Belle had been earlier. When she came around the corner of the house he gave up the scent and ran over to her, his nose low to the ground.

"Good boy," I said. "Make friends."

Joe sniffed Belle's hind legs, lifted his head, and mounted her.

Press said, "That's one horny dog."

We all stopped drinking and watched. Cindy held a cracker over the tray table, forgetting about it. Beth and Kimberly stopped playing.

Joe thrust forward, trying to get a good grip with his front legs. Belle ducked her head as if she were crawling under something, or wincing at a loud noise. She stepped forward and Joe slid off.

"Fumble," Press said.

"Illegal motion downfield." I took a sip of beer.

Joe wasn't certain what he should do next. Belle walked over to a corner of the toolshed, ignoring him.

"Is that it?" Cindy asked. "The end of the romance?"

Joe approached Belle from the side. He sniffed her belly, then put his legs over her back and began humping wildly.

"What the hell is that?" Press said. "What's he doing?"

"Offsides," I called. "Offensive interference."

Belle stood still, not moving away but not showing much interest either.

Donna cut a piece of cheese. "Doesn't he know what to do?"

"How do I know?"

"I thought you two had a talk."

I called over to him. "No," I said. "Bad dog."

Without getting down, Joe swung around and began thrusting at Belle's face.

"I'm not sure the girls should be seeing this," Cindy said.

Donna called out to Joe, "Bad dog. Get down."

"Down!" I said.

Joe looked over at us, speechless.

He dropped to the ground. Belle trotted over to Press and rubbed her head against his leg.

"It's all right," Cindy said. "You're a good dog."

Joe stayed by his house, confused.

"Hang in there," I told him. "Wait for your pitch."

Kimberly looked up from her barrel of plastic monkeys and pointed to the driveway. "Look, Mommy," she said. "A black dog."

Elvis trotted over to us. She was wearing a pink vest with lime-green stripes.

"Hi, precious," Cindy said. "What a pretty sweater."

"That's Elvis," I said. "From next door."

Press took a swig from his beer. "It's a bitch."

"Let's not go into it," Donna said.

Cindy scratched Elvis's ears. "They make clothes for her?"

Elvis and Belle sniffed each other, then Belle sat next to Press. Elvis lost interest. She walked away from us, her nose low in the grass.

"Poodles," Press said, "are silly-looking dogs."

"I think they're kind of cute," Cindy said. Beth couldn't keep her eyes off Elvis. Cindy asked her, "Do you like that doggy?"

"Uh-oh," Donna said. "Look at this."

Elvis moved toward the back of the yard. Joe approached her cautiously.

"But she would have to be in heat," I said.

Press nodded. "Ineligible receiver."

"He's four times her size," Cindy said. "He wouldn't. Would he?"

"I don't know," Press said. "I think this poodle is a loose dog."

Joe and Elvis sniffed each other, nose to tail.

I called him. "Joe! Come here!"

Joe looked over at me.

I said it louder. "Come here!"

Usually he listened. Usually he was a good dog.

"She's presenting herself." Cindy turned to Donna. "That was in the book." She paused, watching them. "Shouldn't we do something?"

"Too late," Press said.

Joe had accepted the invitation. He put his front paws up around Elvis's shoulders, bent low, and thrust his hips forward. Belle's ears went up. She stood and walked over to them.

Press finished his beer. "I want to be the first to say that I am completely disgusted with everything that's going on here. This dog of yours—"

Just then we heard a screen door open and bang shut. A voice called, "Elvis?"

"I think I'll go in now," Donna said. She didn't move.

"Ell-viiis." Kristin was barefoot, wearing shorts and a T-shirt. She came down their porch steps and looked around their backyard. Then she saw the three of them.

"Elvis!" she said. "Come here!" She ran across the driveway.

"Stop!" she yelled at Joe. "Blow off." Belle ran to Press, but Joe and Elvis ignored her. Kristin grabbed Elvis by the front paws and Elvis bit her.

The screen door opened and banged shut again. Grace stood on their porch, a cigarette between her lips.

"Holy God, George. What have you all got going on over there?"

Kristin stood to inspect the teeth marks on her hand, and when she did, Elvis ran into Joe's house. Joe followed her in, Kristin running after them. "Get your dog!" she shouted to me. "Don't you know what they're doing?"

Grace called out from across the driveway, "I think we've all got a pretty good idea, Kris. Let her go. She'll come home when she's done."

Kristin got down on her hands and knees and reached inside the doghouse. "Elvis!" she said. "Come!"

"Have a beer?" I asked Grace.

"Thanks," she said. "Next time." She flicked the butt of her cigarette over the fence and onto the driveway. "Try to keep it decent over there, will you?" She laughed that hoarse laugh of hers and went inside.

I heard a yelp and turned to see Kristin standing with Elvis in her arms, holding a piece of cloth, so angry that her voice was shaking. "This vest," she said, "is *ruined*."

Chapter Fifteen

Ed carried the reinforced grocery bag sagging with steamed crabs to the picnic table and waited while I spread the newspapers. "They're running heavy this year," he said. "Meat's real firm, too. You had any yet?"

We hadn't. Donna liked the meat, but she didn't like breaking the crab open and scraping through the shell, working for the meal.

"Must be from her mother's side," Ed said. "I could eat blue crabs eight days a week." He dumped the dull orange crabs spotted with clumps of seasoning onto the table. "I showed her how to clean them when she was real little—slip the knife under the flap, pull it back, pop out the body, scrape it, and snap the halves. I'd do one or two for her, then the next time she'd say she forgot how. It took me most of one summer to figure out she just didn't like busting them open."

"Women," I said, feeding him his line.

"That's not what I'm saying. It's surprising sometimes what you don't know about the people you know best. My own daughter, and I couldn't figure it out."

"So," Evelyn said after we sat down at the picnic table, "what's new next door?"

"We haven't been over lately," I said.

Evelyn looked at Donna. "Is he always like this? Or is it only when he's with me?"

"It's his sense of humor," Donna said.

Ed pushed a shell to the side. The heat and thick spice of Old Bay seasoning rose from the table.

"Maybe," he said, pulling the meat out of a claw with his teeth, "it's none of our business."

"Of course it is," Evelyn said.

"Maybe they'd rather not have to listen to our advice about every little thing that comes down the pike," he told her.

"Advice is fine," Donna said. "Just as long as you're not insulted when we don't take it."

"They know my advice," Evelyn told her husband.

"What I want to know," Ed said, "is what's the news about that vacation? You two have any travel plans yet?"

"Harry hasn't said a word."

Ed took a swig of beer, leaving brown seasoning stuck to the wet bottle. "Just barge in. Lord hates a coward."

"Of course," Evelyn told him, "maybe they don't want our advice." She turned to us. "Our neighbor Judy Witt—her husband died last year from that collapsed lung—she just got back from the Poconos. She said she had a miserable time."

"What's that supposed to mean?" Donna picked the meat from her crab as if it were still alive. I took it and gave her a pile of claws.

"It means sometimes staying at home is a better vacation than going away," her mother said.

Ed wiped a streak of yellow fat on the newsprint. "It means steer clear of the Poconos. The place is a tourist trap."

"That reminds me," Evelyn said. "We were talking about going to see Fess Parker in *Oklahoma!* over at Painters Mill. Are you two interested?"

"Say yes," Ed told us. "I'd hate to see her have to go alone."

Donna wiped the seasoning from her hand so she could rub her eye. "Anybody else need a paper towel?"

"I take it that means no." Evelyn tossed a shell onto the pile. "If you have to go somewhere, think about the shore. Virginia Beach is nice. I like Atlantic City, too. We used to go there when we were little."

Ed weighed a crab in his hand. "I didn't know they had beaches back then."

"They were new that year."

"Matter of fact, I didn't know they had oceans. You must be younger than I thought."

She ignored him. "I'm ignoring you," she said.

"I'm not crazy about the beach, here in my old age," Ed said. "I get it from my old man. We'd go to the shore with a few other families, and we'd all be having a great time—swimming, lying in the sun, having a picnic, volleyball, you name it. My father would sit in a chair under an umbrella. Wouldn't swim. Wouldn't even wear a bathing suit. Said the sun made him itch. He sat out there in pants, a long-sleeved shirt, and a little cloth cap—I don't know why he needed it, 'cause it would've taken Napoleon's army to get him out of the shade. If he was really enjoying himself he might take off his shoes until his socks got hot."

Donna gingerly pulled out a firm wedge of snow-white meat.

"I don't think he can swim," Evelyn said.

"He claims that's not it," Ed added. "But nobody ever got the chance to find out. He's an ornery son of a bitch."

"Edward."

"Son of a gun." Ed winked at me and pulled a piece of shell from his teeth. "Ev and Dad never really hit it off. We'd be out on the porch, you know, going about our business at night, and my old man would sneak up and come bustin' out that door—"

"—Notice we were on *his* porch," Evelyn said. "I had to walk home."

"It was only two houses away." Ed turned back to me. "Anyway, they'd start arguing about one thing or another, and I'd go inside and read the paper."

"It's true," Evelyn said.

Ed scraped the gills away and dug out a fingerful of meat. "He and Mom fought like gangbusters. Mom's small, but she's a real wildcat. She loved to eat out, but Dad refused to go to restaurants. My brother and I took her once and our old man didn't talk to us for a week."

"Uncle Bill?" Donna asked.

"No, that was Connie. Before he left for California. Hell, I could tell stories about Connie."

"I'll bet you could," I said, anticipating one.

We were all silent except for the cracking and splintering of crab shells. For a moment I worried that Ed had taken it the wrong way; I enjoyed his stories. Then I saw he was just concentrating on eating.

"I'm glad my family wasn't like that," Evelyn said. "At least we all liked each other." She looked over at me. "In-law problems. You should be glad you don't have any."

Ed cracked a claw with his mallet. "It sounds worse than it was." He pulled apart the halves of the claw and studied them. "What it boils down to is this: your family is your family. You play what you're dealt."

No one else spoke. After a moment he went on.

"It's hard to be a good person," he said, "even harder to be a good parent. God knows it's hell being a good parent-in-law."

"Heck," Evelyn said automatically.

"I mean it," he said. "When you're a parent, you know everything about your kid. You can tell her to go to her room, or take out the trash, or turn off the radio. A parent-in-*law*, though—you've got to use tact."

Evelyn said, "We all know that's your short suit."

Ed was watching me, but I didn't know what he wanted me to say.

It was nearly dark when we topped the pyramid of crab shells. Donna pulled the knives and mallets out of the mess; I rolled the newspapers and shells into a ball and shoved it into one of the trashcans.

"It's the truth," Ed said when Donna and Evelyn went inside. He didn't look me in the eye. "It's hard to be an in-law. You do what you think is right, but . . . shit."

"What's the problem?" I pressed the lid onto the trashcan.

"I don't want you to think I'm butting in. I know it's none of our business, no matter what Evelyn says."

"But."

"I have a friend in the police department." He slipped a folded piece of paper into my hand. He waited, but I didn't want to look. I put it in my pocket.

"An old golfing buddy of mine," he said. "I haven't seen him in a while, but we go way back."

"You called him about this?"

He slapped his arm. The mosquitoes were starting to bite.

"No," he said. "I thought about it, and I knew that, if I was in your shoes, I wouldn't want you to do it, if you were me." He stopped, trying to see if he had said it right. "I don't live here, I don't know these people."

"You want me to call him?"

"He's a detective." Ed pressed the lid onto the other garbage can. "I haven't told Evelyn about this. Because I'm not sure what I'd do in your shoes. On one hand, what they're doing over there is wrong. It's illegal and all, but besides that. On the other hand, it's not like you're the sheriff or something, like it's your job to take care of this."

"It's not my job," I agreed.

"So what I guess I'm saying is, it's up to you."

He looked out across the yard. Lightning bugs glowed yellow in the dark.

"It's none of my business," he said. "I shouldn't have stuck my nose in."

We picked up the trashcans and carried them around front.

"Good thing they'll get picked up tomorrow," he said as we set them at the end of the sidewalk, near the mailbox. "These crabs'll stink in this heat."

Lying on the lawn. A beautiful woman. The yard has just been mowed—I smell fresh-cut grass. The woman wears a long-sleeved white shirt and jeans, but she has no face, no voice.

I want you, she is saying. *I want you right now.*

I move closer and she licks me on the nose. Her tongue enormous, rough as stubble.

Not out here, she says. *Not in public.*

She crawling. I crawl behind her, sniffing her legs, her rear. Lunging forward, I bring her to the ground.

Puts her finger to her lips, telling me to be quiet, crawls away. Stops at the door to Joe's house.

In there?

Nods.

Crawls in effortlessly, turns, takes off her shirt. No bra.

Bridging back on her shoulders, raises her hips, unsnaps her jeans and slides them off.

Motions for me to come in.

As soon as my head inside, doorway begins to shrink. Can't get shoulders through.

Come on, she says.

Lean forward, licking her thighs, her stomach, but she moves back. Twist my shoulders, jam one in.

Stuck.

Slowly, feet pushing against the ground outside, force my way into the doghouse.

Tells me to take off my clothes. Unbutton my shirt, feel cold and damp against my neck.

Belle nuzzling me. Joe behind her, sitting in an armchair, watching TV, holding a beer. Orioles playing Detroit.

What's the score?

He holds up one paw, telling me to wait.

Woman pulling my socks off with her teeth.

Hold it, I say. *I have to find out the score.*

Woman reaching for my pants. Belle picks up one of my socks and shakes it, ready to play.

Not now. Bad dog.

My pants off. Belle licking my calf, woman licking my neck. Woman climbs on top, long tongue scratching my face, leaving a trail of saliva.

Wait a minute.

Come on, woman says, kneeling above me.

Wait a minute, I say louder, trying to see over my shoulder. *What's the score?*

"Hey," Donna said. "Are you all right?"

"Umph." I could barely see her face in the darkness.

"You just said 'What's the score?' "

Fuzzy. "I must have been dreaming."

"So I guessed." She leaned down, nuzzling my neck. "Was I in it?"

Awake. "Sure," I told her. "Of course you were."

Chapter Sixteen

The Orioles ran onto the field. When the national anthem ended we settled into our seats on the third-base side, behind the dugout, loaded down with hot dogs and beer.

"A toast," Cindy said.

We raised our paper cups.

"To baseball," Press said.

Cindy groaned. "My husband, the romantic." She leaned across me to raise her cup to Donna's. "To a year of wedded bliss."

"Wedded bliss," we said. We touched cups; Donna made clinking noises.

"To the Baltimore Orioles," I said. "May we all live to see them win a World Series."

"And may you recover from your mental illness soon." Press was a Yankees fan.

"To puppies," Donna said. Joe and Belle had finally hit it off.

We touched cups and drank again.

"It seems like the wedding was yesterday," Donna said.

"It feels like a hundred years ago." I handed out packets of ketchup and mustard as the first Yankee came to bat. Dark clouds hung above us, but the weatherman hadn't predicted rain.

Cindy said, "Do the Orioles have anybody important? Should I know these people?"

"Not now," Press told her. "Buncha bums. Back in the old days, Babe Ruth."

"Baltimore to Boston to New York," I said, reciting by rote. "He won the World Series with them as a pitcher early in his career, then finished there in 1935. There's a great story about that." I stopped unwrapping my hot dog to tell it. "Ruth was awful at the end—he wasn't hitting, he couldn't field. But in one of his last pro games, against the Pirates, he hit three home runs. His last three. The third one went over the double-deck bleachers, out of the park. My father heard that game on the radio."

Cindy said to Donna, "Do you get the feeling we're supposed to talk recipes?"

The second Yankee batter hit a soft line drive into left field; he rounded first and stayed.

"If you think they're bad," Donna said, "you should've met George's father." Steve Barber got a new ball from the home-plate umpire.

"He played?" Press asked.

"Purely a stats man."

"And a foul-ball catcher." Donna squeezed my arm.

Barber got the third hitter to ground to Aparicio, who turned the double play to end the inning. I remembered another one of my father's stories.

"He knew a lot about players from listening to the games," I said. "It came in handy. People made bets against him all the time. They'd ask how many double plays were made by Tinkers and Evers and Chance, or to name the roster of the 1934 Cardinals, or what was Dizzy Dean's lifetime earned-run average. He knew.

"The biggest bet he ever won was at a bar in France when some American sailors said they had a man who could top him. There was an officer on their ship, they said, who knew more about baseball than anyone else alive."

Aparicio stepped up to start the inning for the Orioles.

"He took the bait, and the sailors made bets. The officer, an older man from Irwin, Tennessee, won the toss, so he went first. He named the top twenty home-run hitters of all time, in order."

Donna was impressed. "Could you do that?"

"I could guess at a few." Aparicio drew a walk on five pitches and trotted down to first.

"Steal coming," Press said. "But they'll get him."

"What did your father do?" Cindy asked.

"He repeated the list of home-run hitters. Then he gave their mothers' maiden names."

Press booed. Donna laughed and I slipped my arm around her.

"I don't get it," Cindy said. "He knew their mothers' names?"

"There he goes," Press said. "Dead meat."

Aparicio easily beat the throw to second.

"I think he meant that one as a lesson," I said, still thinking of my father. "He didn't want us to take that sort of thing too seriously."

Aparicio scored on a single, but the Yankees came back with two in the top of the third. Between innings, Donna asked Cindy, "Did you have to hire a sitter?"

"My parents. Mom loves to take care of them."

That was something I hadn't thought about: I had never had a baby-sitter. We had looked after each other.

"Do you leave them very often?"

"Not really—maybe once every other week. But it adds up. And to get a sitter you've got to call around, and they cancel on you at the last minute. We've got one real good girl in the neighborhood, but I'm glad Mom's there."

I told Donna, "We could hire one of your students."

"You don't know them like I know them." She asked Cindy, "Do they cry when you leave?"

"They go through stages."

Press kept his eyes on the field as he talked. "Sometimes Kimberly whines, but today I'm not sure they even saw us go—you'd be surprised how fast they get over that."

I thought of taking our son to his first ballgame, explaining it. Or our daughter—Pat loved baseball. But what about the years before they were old enough to care? And how many baseball games could we go to? Having a child wasn't necessarily going to bring Donna and me closer. It would sit between us.

After the Orioles batted in the fifth, I offered to make a run to the concession stand. The only vendor who visited our aisle seemed untrustworthy. "*Pea*-nuts!" he shouted. "Fresh roasted *pea*-nuts! I got peanuts that taste like chicken!"

"Anybody for ice cream?"

"You could twist my arm," Donna said.

"Sure," Cindy said. "It's hot out here."

I shuffled to the end of the row and headed down the concrete ramp. The inside of the stadium was dark and cool. Gusts of wind blew loose wrappers against people's feet. Souvenir sellers weighted down scorecards with jiggle-headed dolls, yearbooks with autographed baseballs on plastic stands.

It had never crossed my mind before. As I walked past gates leading up to the field, the voice of the public-address announcer hollow and distant, it struck me that it would be easy to disappear. I could be missing for the rest of the game, and Donna and Press and Cindy would have no way to find me. I could drive home, see Dusty, and be back before the crowd was out of the stadium.

There would have to be explanations and excuses, but that wasn't the point. It wasn't something I meant to do. It just crossed my mind.

I let it go one step further.

"Finally, you're here," Dusty would say. "I thought you'd never catch on."

Then I reeled it in.

I found the line for ice cream and stood straight, clearing my head. My first anniversary and I was thinking about another woman. There was no excuse. It was ridiculous.

Awful.

A phone call. I could walk to the farthest corner of the stadium, close the door on one of the booths near the stairs. No one would ever know. "God, it's you," Dusty would say. "We have to find a way to meet."

But I didn't really want to call Dusty—it was a silly idea, a perverse thought that forced its way in. Besides, I didn't know their number.

And what if someone was there? I imagined Grace pressing the receiver to her chest and calling upstairs, like a dormitory house mother, "Dusty! It's for you!" There would be a muffled answer, and a moment later she would come bounding down, answering the phone with the breathlessness of a teenager.

Dusty bounding down the stairs of the house next door. Stark naked. I pictured those callused feet I had seen in the driveway, those thin legs—

"No."

I said it aloud—the man in line ahead of me turned around. I smiled weakly and he looked away.

I watched the people near me, trying not to think. I imagined her face in the crowd.

Out on the field, the Orioles were at bat.

Concentrate on baseball.

If I didn't know that the game would end after nine innings, would I drive to their house? If I knocked on the door and she answered, would I go inside? And then what? Where would any of us stop, if we weren't afraid of who would find out what we had done?

A moment later I headed up the ramp with the ice cream. The dark clouds had drifted north, the threat of rain was gone. Press held his beer high in greeting. Donna smiled and waved. I walked up the concrete steps.

"You must have thought I was lost down there."

"I wasn't worried." She unwrapped the ice-cream cone and took a bite off the top, leaving a damp white border around her lips. The Orioles had runners on first and second, with one out. Boog Powell stepped up to the plate.

"Double-play time," Press said. "Ground ball to the right side."

Back with Donna, out in the sun, I felt optimistic. "You heard it here," I said. "Home run."

Donna smiled and squeezed my knee. "Too good to be true, but I appreciate the thought."

The third pitch landed deep in the right-field bleachers.

Chapter Seventeen

I stopped at the bottom of the basement stairs. Donna stood three steps above me.

"Close your eyes."

"Okay. Don't let me fall." She squinched hard.

I held my hand up in front of her face. "Here's the first surprise."

She opened her eyes. "Your ring!"

I finally remembered that I had taken it off while I was sawing. I had hung it on a nail, but it fell and rolled into a pile of dust near the furnace.

Donna kissed me. "I don't need anything else. Just keep it on."

"But there's more." She closed her eyes and I led her by the hand. I had sanded and stained and polished the bookcase, and before I went to get her I even dusted it.

"Open up."

"That's wonderful." She walked closer and looked it over.

Too fast. I recognized her tone of voice, the way she was looking at the bookcase. It was the tone and attitude I used as a kid when I opened a Christmas present I had found hidden in the attic the weekend after Thanksgiving.

"You weren't surprised."

"Sure I was." She rubbed her hands over the cabinet. "It's terrific."

"You don't like it."

She opened the doors at the bottom. "I knew you were good, but I didn't know you were *this* good." She closed the doors and opened them again.

"Tell me the truth—you weren't surprised."

Donna moved back to look from a distance. "Well, I knew you were making something—I'm not deaf. And we were just talking about bookshelves. This is wonderful, babe. Really."

That's one of the problems with Donna—when I ask her to tell the truth, she does.

She said, "It's for the dining room, right? The wood's a perfect match. It's lovely."

I pictured the oak in the dining room.

"That's just coincidence," I said. "I made it for here." The bookcase stood against the basement wall. It filled the space well.

"In the cellar?"

"Out of the way," I said. "So it doesn't . . . It would clutter the dining room. It's too tall. The room would feel cramped."

"It would be perfect. Let's try it."

Suddenly the bookcase was a monster. It was growing. I wanted to kill it.

"I still can't believe how good you are," she said. "I could never do anything like that. I'd probably saw off my fingers."

"The point isn't that I made it," I said, though that *was* the point, or at least part of it. "We needed a bookcase." I couldn't tell if she was getting the message. "It's something new for the house."

"Sweetheart, I know that. But why hide it down here? I want to show it off. When people come over, they can see what my talented husband made." She took my hand. "Let's just see how it looks."

"No," I said, moving past her. "Forget it. We'll use it for firewood." I started up the stairs.

"George?" Donna said. "Babe?"

"I'm going to cut the lawn."

I let the screen door slam behind me. It made a good solid slam—the spring was new. I stomped off toward the tool-shed, then stopped. I had just cut the lawn.

So instead I circled the house. By the time I reached the

backyard I knew I was being foolish, but after storming out of the house I wasn't sure how to get back in. I had never stormed out of a house before. I felt like a character on a television show.

Donna wasn't surprised, and she wouldn't leave the bookcase where it was. I should have known. I should have made something small.

As I reached the far side of the house I looked at the flowerbed by the patio. A thistle was growing in and around the bleeding heart. I hadn't been able to cut it without hurting the bush, so I had convinced myself the white flowers were pretty. Now I reached through the branches to the ground, felt for the base, and pulled it out by the roots.

The weed stuck to my hand. I pulled it away with the other hand and felt flesh tear.

The cut was half an inch long, with a tiny drop of blood growing on one end. I walked to the front steps and sat down.

I wiped the blood away. I was finished being mad, but it would be a mistake to go in too soon. I tried to decide how long I had to wait after storming out before I could go back in without looking foolish. Maybe I could walk to the store and get some milk. I would have, too, but I couldn't see me storming back into the house with it: "I'm sorry," I would say. "And to prove it, here's a gallon of two-percent low-fat."

So instead I just sat on the steps, stalling. The flagstones were warm. There was a nice breeze. I leaned back on my elbows and looked around.

Dusty was sitting on their front lawn, leaning against the side of their front steps, reading a book. She waved.

I started to call to her, then changed my mind—I didn't want Donna to hear me. That's why I decided to walk over. That and because I wanted to talk to someone.

"What's good enough to read on a day like today?" I had started to sweat from the heat.

"*The Hourglass Affair,*" Dusty said, reading from the cover.

I blocked the sun so she could see me.

"This guy leaves his wife and goes to South America or somewhere to manage a hotel. One day this chick checks in, alone, and says she's waiting for some guy from the States. It turns out they've been embezzling money from where they worked. Our guy finds out and runs off with the chick, but she doesn't have the bread with her—she has to pick it up in a foreign bank. Then her old man starts following them, and our guy—he already killed somebody, did I tell you that? That's how come he's down there—he sets traps to throw off the other guy. And some dying revolutionary is in town, hiding, so somebody wants to bomb the hotel."

"Sounds confusing."

"The worst part is, I've got to make up the ending. I'm missing the last ten pages." She closed the book. "I'll probably just kill the bunch of them."

"Where is everybody?"

"Grace and Eve went to Annapolis." She threw her hair over her shoulder. "Kristin's gone for a few days. Elvis is in the cellar."

Dusty was wearing her long-sleeved white shirt with the cuffs unbuttoned. She was sitting with her knees up, and I could see the inside of her thighs. I forced myself to look at a maple tree down the street.

"Where's Kristin off to?"

"She and Grace had a fight," Dusty said. "Grace told her to scram for a few days."

"What about Larry? I haven't seen him in weeks."

"He's around."

I realized I had been asking a lot of questions. She swatted something on her shoulder. I sneaked a look down, following her thighs up to the tail of her shirt, and still didn't see any sign of pants.

Dusty set her book on her lap. "You just come over to shoot the shit, or what?"

What could I say? I'm hiding from my wife?

" 'Cause if you've got a minute, you can try a mint julep. A friend of mine gave me the ultimate recipe."

It was like what happens when you're dating, or asking someone out on a date—a special tension in the air. Everything takes on a second meaning. It was something I had thought I would never be a part of again.

"They're my favorite," I told her. I had never had a mint julep.

We walked up the front steps, through the house to the kitchen, where Dusty took a glass pitcher out of the refrigerator.

"I haven't tried this yet, so it could be a total flop. It's only been in there a half-hour." She filled two tall glasses and added a long sprig of mint to each one. "So what's wrong?" We sat at the old yellow table. "You look like you just killed somebody."

I took a sip of the mint julep. It put Mrs. Webb's tea in the minor leagues.

She said, "You want to talk about it?"

I took another drink. "I've been living in that house twenty-four years, and every day I feel like it's getting smaller. Or bigger. Like I've grown up and it's turned into a doll house or something. But at the same time, it's more and more empty. Hollow." I finished my drink in one long swallow.

"Better slow down," Dusty said, filling my glass. "These things are potent." She added another piece of mint. "Maybe you need to clear your head. Pack up and get out for a while."

I sat back in my chair. Dusty crossed her legs and I saw her bare foot near my knee, under the table. It was cool inside, but the sun and the mint julep were coming on strong. I took another drink. "Donna doesn't want to go anywhere." A second lie.

"Not with your wife. On your own." Dusty turned her head just long enough for me to see the sun coming in through the window behind her. "What do you do to relax?"

I loosened the top button on my shirt. "I listen to music. I make things. I just finished making a bookcase. . . ." I dipped my finger into the mint julep, then licked it clean. "That's the latest. I made a bookcase. Big surprise. But when I showed it to her, she hated it." Three.

Dusty took a home-rolled cigarette out of a case on the table and lit it. "How come?"

"It just . . . looks homemade. My father made a lot of furniture, but when her parents need something they just buy it."

Dusty inhaled. She closed her eyes, concentrating, then opened them. "You still worry about what your parents think?"

I had seen her cigarette before—in a picture in the newspaper. "That's marijuana."

"Want to try it?"

"I don't smoke." I took another drink and put my hand next to hers. "You know who I'm named after?"

"Who?" Her fingers were long and thin, the nails blunt, bitten.

"Guess. A great American."

"Let's see." She put her elbow on the table and balanced her chin on her palm. "George Washington?"

"Wrong." I took the mint from my glass and chewed it.

"I give up. I can't think of any Georges."

"Babe Ruth."

She looked doubtful.

"Babe Ruth's real name was George Herman Ruth."

"What was your mother, some sort of trivia buff?"

"My father. He was a baseball fan. He named all of us after starters on the 1927 New York Yankees."

"Were they good?"

"Babe Ruth hit sixty home runs that year. The Yankees were in first place every day of the season. They won the World Series in four straight." I leaned forward. "And I know where your name is from. It's your hair."

"Wait a minute," Dusty said. "How many children were in your family?"

"Eight. We're missing third base—Joe Dugan."

"And you're all boys?"

"I have a sister. Our father used to say my mother fouled one off." I remembered the picture. "We played a game last summer. It was on the front page of the sports section of *The Evening Sun*." I tried to think about that, one of the last memories I had of my father, but I couldn't concentrate. "It was right before I got married. We all played our positions—Waite pitched, I played right field, the works."

"How did it go?"

"We lost, eleven to nine. I flied out three times."

Dusty laughed, but it wasn't funny. Our father had been disappointed.

"He's dead," I said. She didn't answer and I drank steadily, slowly, emptying my glass again. When I finished, she looked at me, and I looked at her. Neither of us spoke. Neither of us had to say a thing.

"I've been yabbering away," I said. "What about you?"

She sat back, arms lightly crossed. "What about me?"

I poured myself another drink. The pitcher was cool, slick with condensation. "Tell me something you don't usually tell people."

She reached out to push her glass toward the pitcher, leaving a trail of dampness on the table. "Some deep dark secret. A piece of me you can take away."

"Something you want to tell. Something about your past."

A half-smile crept out. "You can have it. Not that there was ever much there. I don't even remember my father."

"Mother?"

"You don't want to hear it."

"Sure I do."

She took a drag, holding it for a long moment before relaxing. "I have two sisters. One older, one younger. She raised us until I was nine, then left us with this woman she knew."

"Grace?"

"Another one." She stopped there.

"You never heard from her, never looked for her?"

"My baby sister tried once. I told her: It's a waste of time. As far as I'm concerned, the bitch is dead and gone."

I tried to imagine what it would have been like: what three girls had felt after being abandoned, why their mother had done it. I couldn't.

"I'm sorry."

"There we go—a little knee-jerk sympathy." She stood and filled my glass. "I don't need to hear it." She leaned back against the sink, shirttail halfway down her thighs. Thin, but no skeleton. Her neck was long and smooth, with a spoon-sized depression at the base of her throat. A place to rest your thumb. Your nose.

She said, "The first day we got here, when you came over, I said to myself, 'There's a guy in his twenties going on fourteen.' "

I wanted to look away but couldn't. I wondered if I should be mad.

"This whole place blows my mind," she said. "All this baking cakes and sitting in rocking chairs. I thought we were in a time warp. Like, you come over the first day, and I said, shit, this guy's putting a hit on me before we're out of the truck. Then you give me this line about helping out. Classic. Stone Age pickup lines."

"I was serious," I said. "I came over because you fell."

She exhaled smoothly. "I know it. That was the craziest part." She stroked her neck. "In a weird way, you're the wildest guy I've met in a long time. Your only problem is, this is the only place you know. You need perspective."

"I get letters from all over. Even Europe."

"You've got to see for yourself. These people will look different then. You'll look different. I didn't know who I was until I had been kicked halfway around the country."

Dusty went back to her chair. She put the end of her cigarette into a small metal clip.

"How many girlfriends did you have before you got married?"

"Three."

"Before your wife?"

"Two."

"You sleep with them?"

My face flushed. "What is this, confession?"

She let the tip of the cigarette drop into an ashtray. "Forget it." She stared at the thin column of smoke. "I'll tell you a story. This friend of mine and I went over to this other chick's pad to go out on a Saturday morning. This chick, the thing you have to know is, she was married. Not in a church or anything, but there was only one guy for her, right? She might as well have been. Married or dead. Anyway, according to her, we're the ones to feel sorry for. She's all the time giving us this crap about one guy, fidelity. That number.

"This Saturday morning I'm talking about, she was getting

ready, so we waited for her. Then we hear her old man's voice from upstairs—he yells down, 'Betsy, come up here.' She's embarrassed and all, so she says, 'I'll be up in a minute.' He yells down again, 'Betsy, come up here!' And she says, 'Just hold on a minute.' So then he yells down, 'Get your ass up here *now*, before I fuck the dog!' "

I tried to fake a laugh, and that's how it sounded: "Ha Ha."

"Strike one," Dusty said. "Threw you a curve." She squinted as she took another drag. "All I'm saying is, she said she was in heaven, but she was in prison. She just couldn't see it. Now, I don't know, but I bet there are some things you've been missing, and you seem to me like a curious kind of guy. If you know what I mean."

I took another sip from the mint julep. I didn't know what language we were speaking, but I wanted to stay in the conversation. "I guess I've always been curious."

"If you know what I mean."

I felt my face stretching into that idiot's grin. Dusty smiled back. I kept smiling—my face was splitting in half. Dusty took a long pull off her cigarette, then gave me an even bigger, friendlier smile, a smile that meant more than I could even think about. I wanted to die.

"Hey," Dusty said, "you have to run home now? Run home, home run. Babe Ruth." She put one hand behind her neck and rolled her head. "Sure you don't want to try this?"

"This is just fine," I said, tapping my glass. "Fabbo."

She laughed. "You get drunk fast."

I nodded.

"Lucky for us, I get stoned fast."

"Hey," I said. My brain was desperately trying to get a signal up to the front. A messenger crept forward through the smoke. I couldn't quite read the note, but I could tell it was important. "Look," I said.

Dusty stared back at me. "Hey. Look." She smiled as if we were sharing a secret.

I couldn't concentrate. The messenger disappeared in a cloud. "Marry me."

Dusty laughed until tears rolled from her eyes.

"Hey," she said.

"Look," I said. We both laughed.

"Look," she said. "You found your ring."

I held up my hand.

"So," she said.

"So."

"Does that mean you *found your ring*?"

"I don't know," I said. "I think it just means I found my ring." I took it off my finger and held it out.

She pulled back her hands. They were beautiful hands. "No rings for this chickee."

I put the ring back on my finger.

"Hey, look," she said, smiling again. "Seeing as how you're such a curious guy, you want to see the house? If you know what I mean."

"Hey," I said. "I'm curious."

We walked into the living room. The long curtains were barely open; the room was dark. The wooden floors were covered with a thick rug, but I lifted an edge by the wall. "My father put those boards there," I told her. I ran my fingers along the wood.

The long walls were deep blue, the end walls covered with mirrors. They had made the room an endless cave. The soft white sofa and two matching chairs were repeated as endless obstacles in a labyrinth, with a light hung over a low glass table to lead the way.

"Through that door in the corner," Dusty said, "is a room where we have a television and magazines and crap."

I put my hands on the back of the sofa, trying to steady them. "Like ours."

She just stood there, staring back at me. The longer the silence went on, the harder my heart beat.

"I had a dream about you," I said.

"I know," she said.

She walked past me, to the bottom of the stairs, and started up without turning. "My room is up here."

I watched her walk up, one bare foot followed by the other. I followed the lines of her legs up to her shirttail, and by the time she got to the top of the stairs I knew she wasn't wearing anything else. As she reached the landing, I felt I was watching a scene in slow motion, an accident about to happen. I followed her upstairs.

She was waiting for me. "The paintings are Eve's."

The stairway ended in front of the door to the bathroom. Two more doors were on either side of the stairwell. The downstairs layout was the same as ours, but this floor was different. The paintings on the walls were white canvases speckled with black paint.

"Guess what?" Dusty said.

"What."

"Guess what the paintings are of."

They looked like ink blots from a Rorschach test.

"Her mother and father?"

Dusty laughed hard, turning away from me, her knees bent. Her laugh wasn't hoarse like Grace's, and it wasn't a girl's giggle. It was a real laugh, but after a moment there was no sound.

"They're trees," Dusty said. "Eve says 'they capture the trees' personality.' "

She started to laugh again, then turned to me. "Hey," she said. She reached out. Her hand was small but firm, and warm. She held mine as if we had been friends forever. "Hey," she said again. "It's okay."

I faked a smile. "Look." It wasn't funny anymore.

"These are their rooms," she said, letting go of my hand to point to either side. She walked to the end of the hall, opened the door, and went inside. My feet weren't mine to command—they went after her on their own.

Her room was blue, not as dark as the room downstairs. There was nothing on the walls. A thick white bedspread flowed down to the rug. On each side of the bed was an old wooden end table, bare except for a candlestick. One held a short pink candle, the other was empty. On a desk on the far side of the room sat two leafy green plants and a record player.

"The music comes from in here."

Dusty answered from the other side of the bed. "Yeah. Records are in the closet." She turned to the window behind her. "I should get some air in."

As dark as they kept the house, the air was scented and cool. It smelled like flowers, but heavier.

Dusty struggled with the window.

"Do you need some help?" The words came naturally. George Willus, friendly neighbor.

"It still sticks in the frame," she said. "They were sloppy when they painted."

I walked up to help and she didn't move.

"One good push should do it," she said.

I stood behind her, reached around, and pulled at either side of the window. It wouldn't budge. I moved closer to get a better grip, and Dusty leaned back against me. She wasn't as stoned as I was drunk, and she didn't care about opening the window. I felt her back, small and hard against my chest, her hips against mine. Her hair traced a web against my cheek as I lowered my chin to her shoulder. She smelled like smoke.

I wanted to wrap my arms around her, but I yanked at the window. This time it flew open, surprisingly, like an eyelid of someone shocked from sleep. The summer breeze blew the curtain around us, flapping against our arms, our sides. Dusty turned to face me and I stepped back, toward the bed.

"There you go," I said. "Fresh air."

"Mr. Fixit."

She stood in front of me, only a step away. She bent down to pick a piece of lint out of the carpet. The tail of her white shirt rode up her legs, exposing a tan line. Her breasts, small and pale, hung free inside the shirt.

She straightened up, looking at me. She rolled the lint between her fingers. The breeze rustled the tail of her shirt against her thighs.

The message got through, a single word: Donna. Waiting for me. If she knew where I was, there might be nothing I could say. But if she didn't, it wasn't too late.

Dusty wasn't a beautiful woman, but at that moment, in her bedroom, two feet away from me, nearly naked, she was the most beautiful woman I had ever seen. And I stepped back.

"I was right about you," she said.

"So," I said, not even asking. "What's next?"

"And you were right about the name. Gold dust, for my

hair. My mother called me that." She turned and walked around the bed, into the hallway.

When we reached the backyard she showed me that she had taken nearly a half-foot of dirt out of the middle of what had been the old pond and pulled the vines off the steps. "I want to stock it with goldfish," she said. "Not those fat ones like you see in fountains in the city, but little ones, like you have as pets."

Standing outside, in full view of our kitchen window, I wondered where Donna was. Probably worrying, thinking I was still mad at her.

"Those aren't goldfish, are they? The big ones are carp." Dusty stopped when she saw I wasn't listening.

"We're going to have a baby," I said.

"Not me."

"Donna and I." I walked quickly toward the driveway.

"George."

I stopped and turned.

"That won't solve anything. That's not enough."

"I'm going to be a father," I said.

Dusty shut the gate behind me.

Chapter Eighteen

Donna hurried in from wherever she had been, stopping at the doorway between the kitchen and the dining room. I couldn't tell if she was angry or only anxious. A wave of shame washed over me.

"We have to talk," I said.

"I'm so sorry," she said, the words rushing out.

I was sober now. It hadn't been the mint juleps.

"*I'm* sorry," I said. For a moment I was actually going to tell her why. "I wanted to surprise you, and I didn't think. We should have talked about it first."

"No," Donna said. There was anxiety on her face, and guilt. "You spent all that time working and I was ungrateful." She came over and took my hand.

"You were not. You don't have anything to be sorry about."

We stood in the kitchen, awkwardly formal, both of us apologizing and neither ready to accept.

"I looked at the bookcase for a long time," Donna said. "If that's where you want it, that's where we'll keep it. But it is *lovely*."

"No, you were right. I didn't think it through."

"Oh, babe." She hugged me close. She had a darker scent than Dusty. "You made that beautiful piece of furniture and I didn't appreciate it. I'm the one who's selfish."

"You did appreciate it. You said so."

I held her tight, and understood there would be no resolution until I answered the question she wouldn't ask.

"I took a walk," I said.

"I looked. I thought you'd take Joe."

I didn't answer. I told myself it would be the last lie.

"Let's go bring it up."

"No," she said. "We don't have to."

"I want to."

"Are you sure?"

I told her I was, and I meant it; the whole argument was foolish, embarrassing. Whatever I had been trying to avoid by keeping the bookcase in the basement had been unavoidable from the day I bought the wood, or earlier—from the moment I had decided to build it.

"You get one last chance to change your mind," she said, leading me to the basement steps.

We went downstairs. Donna had unpacked our books and stacked them on the shelves.

"You're a sweetheart," I said. "You're too good for me."

"Opening boxes doesn't take any talent. This"—she rubbed the top shelf—"does."

We unshelved the books, packed them loosely in their boxes, and took them to the dining room. We cleared the space against the wall between the porch door and the dining-room window. It wasn't until we went back down that we found out the bookcase was too big to go up the stairs.

Later that afternoon, Joe and I were playing catch in the yard when the screen door on the porch groaned open.

"I just got a phone call from Virginia Mead," Donna said. "She's having an emergency meeting. Too important to discuss over the phone."

Virginia and her husband had originally come to the neighborhood in a cloud of controversy. They had only been moved in for a month when they called a meeting to organize the Community Association. Thanks to some flashy rhetoric and a roomful of apathy, Virginia had been elected president, her husband secretary. They campaigned for Kennedy among people who believed politics an impolite topic for public conversation, and when they proposed an open debate based on the candidates' literature, every mouth in the room was zipped and sealed. Not long after that, a rumor seeped out that Mr. Mead posed in the nude for classes at the Maryland Art Institute, and that just confirmed what everyone had suspected: these were wild, immoral people. But they both showed interest in the neighborhood, and they attempted to be friendly, and their Association had grown popular despite them. People enjoyed the excuse to get together. The Meads called meetings the first Tuesday of every month, but they didn't have much luck promoting rallies or petitions; instead we talked baseball and church suppers, and somebody always had raffle tickets to sell.

"About our neighbors?" I asked Donna.

"What else could it be?"

She waited for my reaction. She was barefoot, wearing shorts and a pale blue blouse. For a moment everything seemed just right: she was pretty and relaxed, the day was warm, the grass was cut. Even Joe seemed happy, jumping up and slobbering all over me. I had walked out of Dusty's bedroom just hours earlier, but I wasn't going to be part of any action to run them out of the neighborhood. Everything was fine the way it was.

"They won't need us," I told her. "I'd just as soon sit this one out."

Donna smiled and put her arms around my neck.

"It can't hurt to go," she said. "I'd like to hear what they have to say."

Bells vibrated softly to the rhythm of the idling motor. A man in a dark cap and a clean white shirt emerged from behind the truck.

"What'll it be tonight?" he asked pleasantly. He had a slight paunch and a well-worn smile.

"I need a minute to decide," Donna said.

"Take your time." The driver hitched at his pants. "I don't get stopped around here very often. Don't you folks eat ice cream?"

"Too many old people," I told him. "They're too slow to catch you."

Donna chose toasted almond and I asked for a red Popsicle. The driver opened a small door in the back of the truck. A wave of cool air rolled out as he stuck his head and one arm inside the freezer.

"You said it. Hit the nail right on the head." His voice was muffled, coming from deep inside. As he leaned farther in, fighting with something, his white shirt nearly disappeared inside the freezer, his legs became the stick for a giant truck ice-cream bar. The rustling stopped. "They move away."

He came out with frost in his hair. "Last Rocket I had." He put his cap back on and I handed him two quarters. "All the kids move away. It happens. Not in the city so much, but out here. Young families move, old folks stick together."

"That's what's happened, all right."

He gave me the change from a silver coin dispenser on his belt. "I shouldn't even bother coming through. Not worth it. Pretty neighborhood, though." He smiled and stepped up to the driver's seat. "You folks have a good night, now." He shifted into forward and the bells began again.

The Meads had pushed their furniture against the walls and into the dining room. The living room was filled. Virginia hunted for extra chairs while the others chatted, facing the fireplace.

"The Knights of Columbus are giving away a color TV," Mrs. Duncan told Donna. "Twenty-five cents a ticket, five for a dollar."

"Second prize is a smoked ham," Mr. Duncan said. "You can't hardly find a good smoked ham anymore."

I took two dollars out of my wallet and Mrs. Duncan burrowed into her pocketbook. She had the same general build as her husband—short, wide, rounded near all the edges—and she carried a pocketbook the size of a hatbox.

"You know, hon, I've sold two books of chances in the last ten minutes," she said, pulling out a fresh supply. "But these right here are the lucky ones."

We found two empty chairs and looked around. I wondered who had leaked the news to Virginia, and exactly how much she knew. For that matter, I wondered how much the rest of them knew—I hadn't been to Mrs. Webb's to catch up on gossip since the day Mrs. Wheatley had climbed all over Mr. Duncan's grammar.

Mr. Mead took his place behind a small table and put on his glasses, prepared to record the meeting in his mysterious shorthand. Virginia, even taller than usual in a dark red dress with vertical white stripes and high heels, her long black hair hanging severely down her back, strode directly in front of the fireplace, smiled, and then, as if suddenly remembering her task, tightened her lips.

"Thank you for coming tonight."

The conversation stopped. Mrs. Duncan stuffed a wad of bills into her pocketbook.

Virginia said, "We've asked you here because we feel a situation currently exists which we as a community must amend."

That's the way she talked. She tried to address the group with a combination of Philosophy Department jargon and her idea of how to talk to a five-year-old child. The first time I heard her I thought she was speaking for herself and her husband, but I came to understand that she spoke in the editorial "we." Everyone else probably thought she was schizophrenic.

"While this situation has only recently come to our attention," she continued, "it has existed now for over a month." She paused, letting the suspense build. I looked over at Mrs. Duncan. She was counting her chances without looking down, seeing who was left to put the squeeze on.

Virginia said, "The unfortunate truth is that certain new members of the community are engaging in licentious and probably criminal acts on an alarmingly regular basis."

A man in front raised his hand. "If it's licensed, what's wrong with it?"

It took her a moment, then Virginia shot him a look that she probably used in her classes. "Licen*tious*," she said. "Lacking moral discipline. Without sexual restraint."

Someone in front actually gasped. In our neighborhood,

sex was like diarrhea: everyone had had it, but no one wanted to talk about it.

Mrs. Bing spoke. "Why are we getting involved in somebody else's business?" People tended to pick up that editorial plural without thinking.

"As we said," Virginia repeated, "we suspect these acts to be criminal. Therefore, it is our responsibility to address them here."

Bill Steinkamp, the phone-company repairman, raised his hand. He liked to get to the bottom of things. "Just exactly what and who are we talking about?"

Virginia seemed pleased to make progress. "The parties involved are the three young women, the man, and the woman currently renting the house owned by Mr. L. V. Bellshaw. We believe, by the way, that these people bear no legal relation to one another."

Mrs. Lippert, a nurse at Sinai Hospital, raised her hand. "Do you mean to tell us that Bellshaw is supporting a home for fallen women?"

Virginia wasn't sure she had the euphemism right. She answered gently, "Do you mean a house of assignation?"

Mr. Mead looked up from his notes long enough to address his wife. "She means a whorehouse."

Mead lobbed the magic word into the room and the meeting exploded. Everyone spoke at once, some calling out to Virginia, others turning to people next to them, everyone registering shock and surprise. A few of the men grinned and, when their wives frowned, rubbed their necks, staring at the floor with unusual concentration.

"Order," Virginia said. "Order!"

"In our neighborhood!" someone shouted. "Women of lost virtue!"

"Lost nothing," someone answered. "They're selling it."

As the room began to settle, Virginia recognized Mrs. Coleman.

"What's the evidence?" Mrs. Coleman asked.

"That's right," a man called out from the back. "How much do they charge?"

A row of heads turned from the front, staring the speaker into silence. Virginia answered Mrs. Coleman.

"We've had reports of an unusual number of visitors to the house late at night, continuing until dawn. Nearly all of these visitors, as far as we can tell, are men between the ages of nineteen and sixty."

There was a pause just long enough that everyone heard Mr. Parsons comment under his breath, "Sixty? Congratulations."

"Call the police," said Mrs. Peach, sitting beside me. "Go to the phone right now and call the police." A number of voices rose up in agreement.

"It's not necessarily that simple." Virginia wasn't about to let anyone steal her show. "We could call the authorities and tell them our suspicions, and they would no doubt respond. However, that would have a number of adverse effects upon the community. Negative publicity for the neighborhood, for one. Also, we don't want to accuse anyone of criminal activity if, in fact, none has yet occurred."

I glanced at Donna, wondering what would have happened if she had seen me go over to Dusty's that afternoon. Would she be crying now? Would she have gone to her mother? Would she have thrown something at me? Sitting in the Meads' living room, she looked calm, detached. I felt distant too: unrelated, unwilling to agree with any of them.

"We might consider one of two courses of action," Virginia said. "We can either draft a petition, telling these residents that their current behavior is not in keeping with the standards established by the community, or we can draft a letter to Mr. Bellshaw, rendering him essentially the same information and requesting that he confront his tenants with our concerns."

I had to hand it to her; she could speak a mean sentence.

Mrs. Lippert slapped her knee. "We should call the police this minute. This is outrageous!"

"In addition," Virginia said, "we want to respect the privacy of the tenants."

"They don't want privacy," someone protested, "they want customers!"

"Again," Virginia said, restoring order, "they may not be

guilty. And if they are, perhaps we should allow them either to reform or to relocate quietly."

Her reluctance to prosecute was consistent with her liberal tendencies; what I didn't understand was why she had gone public with her information. It was possible she and her husband had called the meeting only because they knew eventual disclosure was inevitable and wanted to assert their authority. Whatever the reason, Virginia found herself being shouted down. The crowd took on the air of a lynch mob.

"They should be in jail," a woman cried.

"If in fact they are committing criminal acts—"

"Get them out of here," Mrs. Peach said. "Do whatever you have to, but get those harlots out of our neighborhood!" Most of the crowd shouted agreement, calling out suggestions and waving their arms, doing anything they could to try to be heard.

And then Grace walked in.

Everyone froze. Mrs. Peach stopped with her arm in the air. Mr. Mead, the only one who hadn't seen her, was scribbling furiously, trying to get everything down. When he glanced up, the pen died in his hand.

Grace took a cigarette out of her mouth. "Sorry I'm late."

She wore a light blue dress and a string of pearls. The dress was old, the pearls were bad imitations. She fit right in.

She looked over at Virginia. "Did I miss anything?"

It was the first time I had seen Virginia at a loss for words.

Mrs. Lippert spoke for her. Still angry, she said, "We've been told that your girls are ladies of the evening."

Grace had to chew off a smile. "Is that what you call them? Sort of dates you, don't it?"

Mrs. Lippert's jaw worked back and forth, a dummy without a ventriloquist.

Mrs. Peach spoke. "We want you out," she said. The artery in her neck bulged as she regained her courage. "We want you and your . . . your *people* to get out of our neighborhood. We don't need neighbors like you." I moved away from her.

"So that's what this is all about," Grace said. "And I didn't even get an official invite." She sized up the crowd the same way she had looked at Bellshaw's house the first day, and reached the same conclusion: she had her work cut out for her. "I guess you-all have a lot of nerve." She walked along the side of the room, squeezing between chairs. People pushed out of her way, partly to see what she was going to do, partly because they didn't want to run up against her one-on-one.

Grace reached a coffee table that had been shoved into the corner near the fireplace, across the room from Mr. Mead.

"You mind?"

Virginia half-shook her head, but she couldn't have known what Grace was going to do.

She picked up the phone and dialed the operator.

"Yeah, honey," Grace said casually. "Give me the police."

The living room was absolutely silent. A clock ticked in the hall.

"No, no emergency." There was a short pause before she said into the receiver, "Hold on a minute." She turned. "I gotta cop on the line. Which one of you wants to talk?"

I tried to press myself down into the floor, to disappear. When there was still no sound, I looked up.

A priest looking out over that crowd would have known he had delivered the sermon of a lifetime: every head was bowed, every eye was shut, every single person was praying fervently, *Dear God, take me now*. Even Virginia was studying the carpet. Mr. Mead was concentrating on his notes as if he had in front of him the sole remaining copy of the Gutenberg Bible.

When I dared to look at Grace, she had turned back to the phone.

"Sorry to bother you," she said. "I guess I've got the wrong number." The receiver dropped into its cradle heavily. A small breeze swept the room as the Community Association released its collective breath.

Grace spoke to the crowd. "Now we know what you-all are made of," she said. "Now we can get to the facts." She paused to puff on her cigarette. "I'm not going to lie to you," she said, looking at us through a cloud of smoke. "I spent half my life lying, and it never done me no good. Those girls and us, we're good people." A voice rose in protest, but Grace stared the speaker down. "And we have men over to the house. I'm not going to stand here and tell you they're boyfriends or cousins or anything else, because they're not. But our door isn't open to everything in pants. We don't go for your drug addicts or any other parts of your criminal element. I won't have it. We screen our guests. Most of them aren't much different from the people I see in this room.

"Here's what I want to know," she said, tapping her cigarette against an ashtray by the phone. "I thought we'd been decent neighbors. Then I turn around and see you aiming to stab us in the back. If we aren't bothering you, why do you want to bother us?"

Mrs. Middleman, sitting in front, spoke for the first time. "That should be obvious," she said. "You're breaking the law."

"Breaking the law," Grace repeated. Then: "There are a lot of laws in this country." She looked at Mrs. Middleman for a moment. "Don't you live in that big brown house down the street from us?"

Mrs. Middleman nodded hesitantly.

"Every morning I see you walk out to the bus, and I see you come back in the evening, and every day you walk right across the middle of Liberty Road. There's a law against that. It's called jaywalking." One or two people started to laugh nervously, then stopped themselves.

Mrs. Middleman was flustered. "You can't seriously be comparing what I do to what you do in that house."

"I bet we're not as different as you think. You married, honey?" A man in the back guffawed. "I'll say it again: if we don't bother you, what's the problem?" She turned to the rest of us. "Let me ask a question—do we give you any trouble?" She searched through the crowd. "George—you live right next door. Do we bother you and your wife?"

Everyone stared. I felt as if my face had burst into flame.

"Not at all. For that matter, you're probably the best tenants Bellshaw has had. And before we start pointing fingers, let's take a look at who called this meeting. That man over there, Mead—he stands in front of nineteen-year-old girls without any underwear!"

That's what I wanted to say.

Instead I cleared my throat. "Bother us? I guess not. I mean—"

"And there he is, a married man!" Grace poked at the air with her cigarette. "You just tell me. Right here, right now, I want anybody to speak up who thinks what we're doing interferes with the life you-all want to live."

No one answered.

"Another thing—when was the last time you saw that house looking so nice? When we got here it looked like hell—pardon my language. We've put flowers in, we keep the grass cut neat, it's all repainted. We're even getting Lenny Bellshaw to fix the sidewalk. Don't that tell you something?"

"I've noticed that," Mrs. Duncan said. "I meant to compliment you on your pansies."

"Thank you," Grace said.

No one else spoke.

Grace walked toward the door. "Any more questions? Complaints?"

Virginia scanned the crowd, waiting to see if everyone was finished. Even Mrs. Peach was quiet.

Virginia turned to Grace. "Well," she said, "we're sure everyone here would like to thank you for coming."

Chapter Nineteen

Warm and damp, a blanket of humidity lay heavily on the evening. Below thick clouds the sun balanced on the horizon. Our shadows stretched across the street as Donna and I walked home.

"I never would have believed it," I said.

She watched the sun.

"That Grace could turn the crowd like that. Just like Mark Antony."

Donna called good night to Mrs. Wheatley.

"Could you have done that? I couldn't have done that."

She didn't answer.

Our shadows floated over hedges and sidewalks, mailboxes, blending together and then separating. The tension might have been a person walking between us, or four people. The first few months we were married I would have pressed her, made her talk to me. Now I kept quiet, waiting.

We turned the corner and walked up Red Plum Lane.

"I wonder how she found out," Donna said, still looking at the sky.

"Virginia?"

"Grace."

But from her tone I could tell she already knew.

After Donna had told me about Virginia's phone call, I thought about what would happen. Once the truth was out—once everyone knew what went on at Bellshaw's house—there was only one decision they could reach. Dusty and Grace and the others would have to go. It reminded me too much of the conversations about Mr. Mead's poetry: people taking shots at someone who wasn't there to defend himself, people who didn't have any interest in hearing the other side of the story. I wanted to stand up for them, but I couldn't explain why. It had something to do with the easy way I could talk to Dusty and Grace, with the fact that Dusty and probably the other two as well hadn't had the benefit of the past I had had, and that from the start they treated that house as a place to be lived in, not just a temporary stop on some longer journey. There were the paint and the cut lawn and the oleander, those blossoms with the beautiful fragrance that no one thought would last a month. Planting it had seemed courageous, and it made me think Grace knew something the rest of us didn't.

I had written down the time and place of the meeting, then, thinking Grace wouldn't bother to go, added "IMPORTANT," and underlined it three times. Eve was in the backyard, working on the pond. I folded the note and asked her to deliver it.

As we reached the corner of Hobbs Quarry Road, Donna said, "Why are you doing this?"

"I thought it was the right thing." I watched my shoes stepping on their shadows. "I thought they deserved the chance to defend themselves."

"That's not what I'm talking about."

My feet barely seemed to lift from the ground before returning to meet their matches.

"I should have listened to my mother," Donna said. "The minute she found out, she told us to call the police. And until she said that, it seemed like the reasonable thing to do. But sometimes she makes me feel like I'm still living at home, like I'm sixteen again. My mother told me what to do, so I had to do the opposite."

We turned onto our sidewalk and stopped.

"That's not the reason," I said. It was more serious than that, I could tell.

"When I got out the binoculars, I was trying to teach myself a lesson. I said to myself, 'When you're pregnant, it's only going to be worse. You're going to look awful, and there's nothing you can do about it.' I said, 'There are always going to be other women around. Maybe not three of them next door, but there will always be someone to be jealous about.' I decided that it was my problem, that I had to learn to live with it. 'You've got a good husband,' I thought. 'There's no reason to be jealous.' "

She pulled her hair back and let it drop. I thought she was going to cry.

"So why," she said, nearly shouting, *"why do you keep talking to them?"*

I reached for her hand, but she backed away.

She said, "What are you trying to tell me?" Then she turned and hurried to the house.

I caught up to her in the kitchen. She stood with her arms crossed, her back to me.

"I was only trying to be friendly," I said softly.

"Who do you expect to believe that?"

I didn't answer. I believed it. At least, I had for a while.

"Why do you do it?" she asked again.

The question spread beyond me, enormous. Why had I followed Dusty upstairs? Why had I stopped? There were obvious reasons. Beyond them was something abstract, a contradiction between a dream I imagined with Dusty and a real life that seemed filled with painful endings. It was easier to daydream a life than to lead one, easier to replay the romance of beginnings than to continue past them.

"What's wrong," I said, fighting back to the details, "what's the problem with me giving Grace a note?"

Donna's anger turned to aggravation. "You don't understand why I would be upset about you spending time in a whorehouse?"

"I wasn't 'spending time in a whorehouse,' " I said, digging myself in deeper. "I was giving a neighbor a note."

"And the neighbor runs a whorehouse."

"You're starting to sound just like everyone else." I wanted to tell her that I had stepped back from Dusty. I had done the right thing.

Donna stared at the phone across the kitchen. I stood by the refrigerator and waited.

She said, "When I decided not to listen to my mother, just to wait and see what happened, I thought I was testing you. It was an awful thing to do, but that's what I thought I was doing. So maybe I deserve what I got."

"No," I said. "You deserve—"

"Don't you see? Your going over there is just like those letters you write. You're so desperate to get letters back—"

"—I am not desperate—"

"—and you have to talk to those people next door, but it isn't just to be friendly. You think you're missing out on something. Just tell me," she said, barely whispering. "What am I doing wrong?"

I wanted to put my arms around her, but I couldn't. There were too many lies between us.

"It's not you," I told her.

Neither of us spoke.

She brushed her fingers under her eyes. Her face was damp.

"I'm going to bed," she said.

It was a question. She wanted me to go upstairs with her. My answer would be a coded message, telling her everything was going to be all right.

I wasn't sure that was true.

"Well," I said. "I have to take care of some things."

The pins representing my brothers and sister, scattered, were still stuck into the maps in the basement. I sat on my old bed and looked at the six dots on the United States, two more on the ceiling, imagining lines that connected them. I considered calling them all, just to say hello and tell them I was about to talk to the others. We would be connected, then, in some momentary way.

But the phone call that told me our father had died was barely a memory compared to the speech he made after our mother's accident, all of us in one room. I thought of the long-distance call to Mark, the static between us. If there was anything to connect us, a web we all supported even as it supported us, it was spun from memories, the life we had spent together, and beyond that, our parents. Part of the loss we feel at anyone's death is the loss of the stories only that person could tell.

When I was young, looking at those maps, it seemed as if the whole world was waiting for us. Our father had been a traveler, his own father had never stopped. It was in our blood. On the other side was a contradictory urge, my mother's desires to know the world and to keep a home we wouldn't want to leave. I had dreamed of getting married and having a family and settling nearby, even as close as the house across the driveway. It hadn't sounded like much to ask for. I wondered if I had made the wrong wish.

Softly, a rumble. Again a moment later.

I turned off the light.

The wind had picked up, and I had to hold the porch door to keep it from slamming behind me. A bright line seared the night. I stepped to the railing and counted; the thunder came in three seconds, so loud that the porch seemed barely able to resist the force of it. Then, as if at the silent drop of a conductor's baton, the rain began.

My brothers and I didn't think twice about getting wet, and we weren't afraid of thunder and lightning. My mother would try to smile—thunderstorms terrified her—and Father would point out that if we stayed away from trees, there wasn't much danger. "You take more of a risk every time you get in a car," he would say back then, before my mother's accident.

That bad luck, the blind coincidence that put her in the path of a drunk driver, was the beginning of the unraveling, the first sign that the future I had planned would never exist. For a long time I punished myself by thinking about the accident, forcing myself to imagine the details: my mother's head hitting the windshield, her blood spilling onto her hands. Lying in bed, I jammed my fists against my forehead, hitting myself, trying to feel the force that had killed her. Those images became as vivid to me as if I had stood at that street corner and watched it happen—and still the pain grew dull. Three months after my mother died I finally slept nine hours straight without jumping awake, without the nightmares.

Then I found a new kind of pain: remembering good days. Times she had been happy, times she had made us happy.

Nights we spent talking about exotic places. Once while Pat and Father and I lived in the house alone, I was watching television and thought I heard my mother laugh. One night as I washed the dishes I heard her whisper, "Alaska."

And then one day I tried to hear her voice and couldn't.

Listening to rain tripping the leaves, pattering the bare dirt of the flowerbeds into mud, I tried to imagine the advice my mother would have given me. Whatever arguments she and our father had, they kept to themselves. They were quiet people, not the type to slam doors or walk away in the middle of conversations. When things weren't right, my father mowed the lawn or worked in his shop. The few times I knew my mother was angry—not momentarily upset, or unhappy, but truly angry—she emptied every cupboard and cabinet and drawer in the kitchen, cleaning with exasperating care, refusing help until she had restored order. In the eighteen years I knew her, she did it three times.

A sheet of light blinked twice, a false start. This was the first storm since the one that had driven Joe crazy, and he was quiet. He didn't mind water, but that night he had been caught outside, chained down, where he could see the lightning. Now he could hide. I imagined him curled in the house I had made him, his back to the door, safe and dry.

Lightning scared Donna too. She'd stare down at the floor, hoping to miss the bright light, the crack of the thunder. We laughed about it now, but there had been a time when, if we were together during a storm, I'd hold her in my arms and she'd burrow against my chest. She said she really did feel safer with me. I never told her that wrapping my arms around her made me feel strong. Now I imagined myself standing between my father's house and the storm, warding off danger, protecting her the way I believed he had protected us.

The next flash burst toward the north, and a siren wailed, calling for volunteers. A house had been hit, or a tree had fallen onto a car, or power lines were down. I looked out through beaded lines of water at the two large trees in our backyard, a thick elm and a towering tulip poplar. If either of them fell, the house could be chopped into splintered wood. There was nothing I could do.

The black sky rumbled. Donna wouldn't awaken if I disappeared into the rain, following my father, my grandfather. I held my hands out past the edge of the roof, letting the rain soak them. I stood there a long time.

Chapter Twenty

"George—have a seat. I can't find this note for . . ." Harry's voice trailed off as he raided the piles on his desk, juggling loose sheets and pads of paper in his search. "Got it." He picked up the receiver. "I'll be right with you.

"Hello, honey. Earl Rogers." Harry used a stage voice on the phone, projecting through all our offices. He was partly engaged in conversation, partly performing. He had thinning white hair, a bulbous nose, and slack cheeks. An old clown without his makeup. But when you knew him you lost the urge to laugh.

He covered the mouthpiece. "Old friend of mine. I'm embarrassed, I've known him so long." Then, booming back to the phone: "Earl? Harry. Harry Reynolds." He fumbled with his reading glasses and put them on. "Reynolds, for Chrissakes, over on Washington Avenue. What the hell's the matter—you senile?"

I had been working up my nerve for days.

"I thought maybe I'd write him a note," I told Press.

"Don't waste your time," he said. "The man doesn't read."

"What would you do?"

"Take that proverbial bull by the horns," he said. "Tell him what you want, and don't let him sidetrack you. If he doesn't want to listen, he'll make you forget why you're there."

"That's all? That's your advice?"

"There's no secret," he said. "But listen. The first year I was here, Harry had a guy working Virginia and West Virginia—Chester Ace. Whenever a customer had a problem, Harry would say, 'See Ace.' "

"I don't get it."

"His initial," Press said. "I think that's why he hired him. Anyway, Ace decided the company was cheating him on his expense account. He wanted the company to pick up his car insurance, maintenance, all that. He came in one day and told Harry he was robbing all of us, treating us like dirt. And so on.

"Harry wrote him a check for twenty dollars. He told him that should be enough to get his junk heap to an employment agency."

"Come off it."

"Truth," Press said. "Ask Janie. And the minute Ace closed the door, Harry called the bank and stopped payment on the check."

I squirmed in my chair as Harry's conversation wound to an end.

"Reynolds." He paused. "R-e-y-n-o-l-d-s. How the hell else do you spell it?"

He hung up and turned to me. "Senile son of a bitch wouldn't know his asshole from euthanasia. Probably never even *been* to Asia." He checked to make sure I got the joke. "If I ever get that old, somebody shoot me." He pushed the note to the side of the desk. "What can I do for you?"

The timing wasn't perfect, but I let it fly: "I want a vacation."

His eyebrows rose momentarily, then he went on as if he hadn't heard me. He took papers out of piles and pushed them into different piles. "I talked to the purchasing agent out at Tillerman's Sausages. He said he just gave you an order for four grand over the phone."

"That's right."

"I didn't sell it, and Press sure as hell didn't sell it. You'll be getting the commission."

I was happy and sad: the money was significant, but it probably represented Harry's only charitable act for the year.

"Thank you," I said.

"I had nothing to do with it. You'll be a salesman yet."

He was finished.

"I haven't had a vacation in two years, and—"

"There's still work to do down there," he said. "Sounds like you could get him to buy a few water heaters. He needs them."

"I know. But if I—"

"You don't get there soon, someone else is going to get in the door," he said. "The world don't stop and wait for you to make a sale."

It wasn't working. I called a temporary retreat.

Harry made a note to himself as he talked. "What do you mean, no vacation? A week at Christmas, all the holidays . . . this isn't the goddamn government, you know."

Suddenly I felt a crowd of people behind me. I heard Ed talking about his brother Connie, telling us to get away while we had the chance. I saw Dusty standing in her kitchen, telling me I had to make a move. I knew what my father had done, and when I stood on the porch in the rain I knew what my mother's advice would have been. In the end she had wanted me to go.

When I had finally gone upstairs, Donna was deep in sleep. I sat on the side of the bed, still dressed, and skimmed loose strands of hair away from her eyes and mouth. The worry and anger from earlier was gone; her face was peaceful, trusting. Looking at her, thinking of my parents in that same room, I realized our lives were caught up with the lives of others, living and dead, in a way that there was no running from.

"Hey," I said softly, shaking her shoulder.

She didn't move.

"Honey," I said, resting the back of my hand against her cheek. "Donna."

She blinked.

"Can you hear me?"

She opened her eyes, blinked again. "Uh-huh," she said sleepily.

"I have to go."

"What?"

"I have to take a trip."

She came awake. “You’re leaving? Now?”

“I want you to come with me.”

She reached for my hand as she closed her eyes.

“I know that,” I told Harry now. “I know this isn’t the government. But when I started, we agreed on vacation time after the first year, and I’ve never taken any. My wife and I need some time. I want a week.’”

Harry looked as if he’d just seen his ashtray jump up and do the fox-trot with his nail clippers.

“Sounds like somebody lit a match under your ass.” He looked straight at me; I locked eyes with him, refusing to be stared down.

Harry glanced out the window for a moment, then back at me.

“When?”

I plowed ahead, a kamikaze pilot going in for the final landing.

“Soon,” I said. “Maybe next week, or the week after.”

Hell, I could hear him say. *I’ll give you next week* and *the week after. I’ll give you a vacation for the rest of your life.*

Harry smiled as if he hadn’t heard right. “Where’s the fire?”

“I need time,” I said. “There are things I need to do. Family matters.”

He turned and checked his calendar, one a rep from Idaho had sent him. It came from a place called Fuzzy’s Cafe. The print above the dates said, “Try a Fuzzy Burger.”

Harry scratched his forehead, then set his glasses on the desk.

“Okay. Week after next.”

“Are you sure?”

“Goddammit, George—does the pope shit in the woods?” He wiped his glasses with a handkerchief. “That means Monday through Friday. The Friday before you leave is not Getting Ready for Vacation Day, and the Monday after you get back is not Coming Back from Vacation Day. You put in a full day before you leave—in fact, you’ll probably be in here late—and you be in here on time, ready to run when you get back. Is that clear?”

“Yes, sir.” I stood up. “Thank you.”

"You're welcome." He turned back to the note on his desk.

"I really mean it. I didn't expect—"

Harry cut me off with a look. "I can always change my mind," he said. "Business'll be for shit if it gets out I'm getting soft in my old age."

It was that easy.

The time passed quickly. Harry kept me busy, getting his money's worth for that paid week off, and at home Donna and I observed a truce, a peaceful period with an undercurrent of strain so slight no one else could have detected it. I spent the evenings recaulking the doors and windows, sealing the house tight. I didn't go over to Mrs. Webb's—I hadn't spoken with any of the back-porch crowd since the community meeting—and I didn't talk to any of them next door until the day before we left. I had avoided even looking at Bellshaw's house, stopping short of plugging my ears with wax.

Friday I got home late, and there was a strange car in the driveway. Donna was giving extra lessons to students who didn't think they could survive a week without her. Music drifted out the living-room window, stopped, repeated. As I got out of the car, Dusty came out of the house next door, on her way to the garage.

"Hey," she said.

I didn't answer. But we were leaving the next morning—what could happen? I walked over to the fence around their backyard.

"Where've you been?" She was in shorts and a man's blue button-down shirt not quite tucked in.

"Around."

She shook her car keys as if she were in a hurry, but she didn't move.

"So now you don't talk," she said.

In some conversations there are mutual silences, communication even more enjoyable than talking because of its shared subtlety. This was one of the others: an uncomfortable gap that threatened a break in negotiations.

Dusty said, "Goddamned men."

"That's not it," I said. "I've just been busy."

She stayed on her side of the fence, I stayed on mine.

I said, "I got a vacation. We're leaving tomorrow."

She shook her keys again.

"Mr. Family Man. I hear this all the time."

I couldn't tell how angry she was; I didn't know what to say. *Far from planning to come here, I meant to sail straight home; but I lost my bearings, as Zeus, I suppose, intended that I should.*

"I shouldn't have come. It wasn't your fault."

"Not my fault," she repeated to an invisible witness. "Incredible."

I remembered the way she had leaned back as I opened the window, the smoke and incense of her hair.

"Believe me, if I weren't married—"

"Just shut up," she said. But she still didn't move to leave.

"I wanted to let you know about the trip. We'll be gone all week."

"You want us to watch the house for you? Get the mail?"

I couldn't tell if she was serious. "Donna's parents are going to—"

But then she laughed, and she wasn't angry and she wasn't friendly.

"Mr. Curious," she said. "You want to see something?"

"What?"

"You have to come play in my yard."

I felt off-balance; I didn't know what she was talking about. But I knew what I should do.

"Right over here," she said. "Only take a minute."

I switched my briefcase to the other hand. Flute music was still drifting from our living room.

She opened the gate and I stepped through. I don't know what I expected—for her to hit me, or take off her clothes, or scream. She stepped to one side; I watched her. She held out her arm.

"What are you doing?" I said.

"Pointing," she said.

There were fish in the pond.

"We got them yesterday," she said. "One died already."

The pond was the size of an oval dining-room table, maybe

two feet deep at the center, clear and clean. Lily pads floated on the surface, dozens of tiny goldfish swimming beneath them.

"It's beautiful." Our reflections wavered on the water. There was a lily pad where my head should have been.

Dusty stood across the pond from me, giving the fish her full attention. A moment ago she had been tougher than I had ever seen her. Now she seemed young, absorbed in the simple movement under the water.

The fish swam above a yellow-and-orange design painted on the bottom, probably by Eve; it didn't look like anything. A smeared tick tack toe game. I couldn't remember the last time anyone had used the pond. I had known it was there, buried in the lawn, but I had never seen more than the concrete rim before the girls dug it out.

I said, "Do you remember I told you about Virginia Mead?"

"Should I?" Our reflections rippled as a fish tapped the surface from below.

"The president of the Community Association. They're the ones who had the meeting without calling Grace."

"What's new with them?"

I knelt down and picked a blade of grass, then dropped it into the pond. Two fish came up to the surface, looking for food. They pushed the grass in a small circle before heading back down.

"She wants something to do, a cause to fight for. I think she would be on your side, theoretically, but just about everybody else wants you out. I bet she'll help them do it, for the popularity."

"God damn." She made it two distinct words, thoughtful.

"I just don't see it," Dusty said a moment later. "It's none of their business." She dipped her hand into the water, then brought it out with her fingers pressed together, watching the drops escape and return to the pond. "What do you think?"

My reflection showed a stiff collar and a tie, a briefcase by my side. I wanted to tell her I thought of her as a friend, but I thought she might laugh. I wanted to say I would help them, but there was nothing I could do. The neighbors, the Meads, Donna's parents, Donna—together they were too strong. What

I really wanted, I think, was to keep anything from happening, to keep open the possibilities.

Then, kneeling in their yard in my suit, looking down at myself, I knew I had been ignoring the truth.

Only part of it was a daydream. They were in Bellshaw's house. I lived next door. Dusty was across the pond from me. Something was going to happen.

When I looked up, she was waiting.

I told her, "It doesn't matter what I think."

When Donna went up to get ready for bed I stayed in the living room, going over my checklist. I had told Mark we were coming, and called Pat in Virginia; she offered to put us up for a day or two. Joe was spending the week with Belle at Press and Cindy's. We had to pack the car in the morning. Other than that, everything was done.

I walked to the record player and flipped through my albums: Louis Armstrong, Count Basie, Wynonie Harris, Howlin' Wolf. I had gotten the first of them when I was in grade school. The cardboard was faded at the corners, rounded smooth. I pulled one out and let it play softly.

Finally, after fighting me all spring and summer, time was going to stop. There would be no job, no chores. No house. The last real trip I had taken ended with my father's phone call. Now there was no one to call me home. For the first time since he and our mother had moved in, the house would stand empty.

I thought about what my mother had hoped to do on the vacation she never took, but our wishful plans had concentrated on going and seeing; I didn't know what she had wanted to bring back with her. I thought about my father, wondering what he had hoped for that day he stood on his first ship, defiant youth, watching the land fade away like an obligation no one could make him meet. I closed my eyes and the music floated me back to an earlier time, a time when every day held its promise.

AUGUST

Why have you crossed the seas, if not to find out where your father's bones lie buried and how he met his end?

—Homer

He was a god.

—Joe Dugan, remembering
his teammate Babe Ruth

Chapter Twenty-one

We drove west toward Frederick, through Cooksville and Mt. Airy, then turned south toward Harpers Ferry and Charles Town. The traffic was light.

I had planned to drive fast, but it wasn't long before I realized that part of the pleasure of a trip comes from moving, the actual travel. Donna arranged the maps beside her, each one folded open in a firm rectangle, and on them she traced our crooked path through towns like Ridgeville and New Market, listing the names of the ones we'd miss this time out: Braddock Heights, Middletown, Myersville, and finally Hagerstown to the northwest, Gettysburg to the north, Fairfax and Warrenton to the south. Instead we had chosen to follow the Skyline Drive and the Blue Ridge Parkway, so we made our way through or near Clear Brook, Stephens City, Front Royal, Thornton Gap, Panorama Gap, Skyland, Hawksbill, and Big Meadows.

I wanted to stop everywhere: at the large towns because they seemed busy and self-absorbed, and at the smaller ones because they reminded me of home. Between towns were farms with roadside stands. Early on Route 26 we saw a thin black woman sitting in a kitchen chair just off the highway; beside her was a card table covered with green apples in orderly rows, and in the table's shade a cow, drowsing, flicked its tail. Before we had been on the road for long I found myself planning other trips.

"I know what you mean," Donna said. "But it wouldn't be right. I think what makes all the places we pass so attractive, what makes me want to pull up a chair and talk crops with some old man and his wife sitting on their porch, is that we're just passing through."

"You only want what you can't have?"

"Not exactly." Donna stared out at trees and farmland. "It's like the first time I heard the Shostakovich for piano and cello. I was in the dorm, in bed with the flu, watching the snow come down. Andrea, my roommate, had just brought some records from home, but I didn't feel like listening. She kept insisting, though, so just before she went to class I let her put the Shostakovich on the record player.

"I remember rolling over to try to shut it out, because I really wanted to sleep, and I didn't feel like getting up to turn it off. But then I started to listen, and I couldn't believe it. It sounds silly, but I felt as if Shostakovich was actually in the room—not the musicians, but him, standing by the doorway, like your mother would be when you were young, to make sure you were all right. It was as if he said: Here, listen to this, you'll feel better." Donna opened the vent on her side to get more of the breeze.

"I fell asleep when it was over. That night I had Andrea put it on again. I was wide-awake, so I tried to dissect it, tried to find out why I had liked it so much. I figured it out, I guess—but that's when I lost it." She paused, looking away.

"And that's what I mean about the driving. Sometimes I almost think it's better just to get a glimpse of things. If you want to play the Shostakovich, or if you want to compose like Shostakovich, then you need to go further. And if you do, you can enjoy the music as much, maybe even more, on a different level."

"Yes?" I asked.

"But it's a different kind of pleasure. It's not as emotional as that first time."

The countryside sped eastward, rushing behind us.

We stopped for gas in Berryville, Virginia. The town wasn't much more than two service stations and a diner. When I pulled into one of the stations a Mack truck roared past us, sending the dust up in clouds.

I opened the door and climbed out slowly, stretching my legs. We walked over to the Coke machine. A boy in overalls bounced a tire off a car on the rack and let it roll across the pavement.

"Won't take a patch," he said. "Fill 'er up?"

"Thanks."

The tire rolled toward the pumps, hesitated, then turned right. The boy ignored it. The tire built up speed going away from the station, hopped over a hose, bumped a telephone pole lying near the edge of the lot, and wobbled drunkenly; it drummed to the ground like a quarter on a table, settling in the sun.

I dropped the coins into the slot and opened the door for Donna. I got a root beer. Sam Cooke was singing "Cupid" on a radio in the garage.

I wiped my forehead with my sleeve and walked over to the boy.

"Sure is hot."

He nodded. "Ninety-five they said on the radio."

The ground and the pumps and the station, like the diner across the street and the pickup parked in front of it, were layered with dust. A black retriever panted in the short shadow of the truck.

"That's Amos," the boy said. "He's no dummy." After a moment he added, "Where you folks headed?"

He pulled the nozzle out of the tank and I handed him a five. "Nashville."

He whistled. "You've got a ways to go then. She's fine under the hood. You shouldn't have any trouble."

"Good," Donna said. "We don't want any trouble."

We headed south out of Berryville. Donna closed the first map and set it between us on the seat. A rectangle of missed opportunities. I looked down at it for a moment, then back at the road.

We listened to the radio for a while. We picked up one

station that played the Drifters and Otis Redding, but other than that we were stuck with country and western. I tried to find some baseball, but either they weren't playing in Bluefield or the local station didn't reach us. Donna turned to the weather—eighty-two in the mountains and clear—and then we heard the Coasters doing "Little Egypt." I sang along while Donna pretended to plug her ears.

Later we drove with the radio off, in awe of the mountains. It was clear on Skyline Drive and the Parkway; we'd heard some days the fog was so bad that people drove over the side.

We passed Rockfish Gap and Vesuvius, Bluff Mountain Tunnel and Peaks of Otter, and were approaching Troutville when I told Donna it felt like we were driving straight across the spine of the country.

"You mean like the Continental Divide?"

"Something like that. Like we're balancing on the top and eventually we have to slide off to one side." I remembered reading about Daniel Boone: in his old age, when he had moved to the wild frontier of Missouri, he was disgusted when a "damned Yankee" settled within a hundred miles of him. Looking out at the Shenandoah Valley, I tried to imagine what it must have felt like then, out in the middle of the country, but it was hard to see how he had felt caged in. I wondered what he was running from.

"Women," Donna said. "Explorers had a locker-room mentality."

"I don't want to hear this."

"If he were alive today, Daniel Boone would have a mobile home. You don't like North Carolina, you try Virginia. You get tired of Virginia, you move to Florida."

I said, "You ask me, it's a contradiction in terms. Homes don't move."

Donna's stomach growled and she looked at her watch. "Aren't you hungry yet?"

We stopped near Clayton Lake, not far from Dublin. We had left the scenic Parkway in Roanoke; it found Knoxville only after winding through the Great Smoky Mountains, and we were already running late.

The car kept the heat in, even with the windows down and the vents open, and we were damp and stiff. We were just to the west of the lake, on a hillside that sloped down to a river. The trees were tall and shady. It felt good to be outside. We unwrapped the sandwiches Donna had made and drank a thermos of iced tea and took a walk when we were finished.

It was quiet away from the road. We helped each other down the steep hill to the water and listened to the birds calling in the trees above us.

Donna found a flat stone. "Here it goes." She threw it and it sank.

"Bring your arm down. More of a sidearm."

"Don't I at least get to warm up?"

"Remember Chestertown?"

She picked up two more flat stones. "Remember sailing?"

After the wedding last summer we had gone to visit my aunt and uncle on Maryland's Eastern Shore. My uncle had a friend, a professor at the college there, who lent us a small sailboat. Neither of us had sailed before, but how hard could it be? We made great time heading downriver, enjoying the scenery, feeling like old hands. I had conquered the elements, Donna by my side.

Then the wind changed. First we stopped making forward progress, then we were spinning in circles. The sail swung hard, nearly knocking me overboard. I fought the boat, but soon we backed up past the pier where we had started, then went under the bridge into town, spinning backwards up the river. A motorboat pulled up and a friendly man with a sunburned face patiently explained something about forty-five-degree angles against the wind. We listened carefully, thanking him when he finished. I waited until he was out of sight, then dropped the sail and rowed to the pier.

We spent the rest of the day walking, skipping stones on the Chester River. When we were single, Donna would have politely ignored what had happened; we had been married for three days, so she rubbed it in.

She threw another stone. No luck.

"Here." I picked up a flat rock the size of a half-dollar and winged it. It skipped once, twice, three times before sinking.

"I thought Waite was the pitcher."

"Ruth used to pitch too. He was one of your all-around heroes." I reached down, found another stone, and gave it to her. "Keep your arm low. Try to throw it almost parallel to the surface."

Donna tossed the stone in her hand, trying to get the feel of it. She cradled it in the nook of her curled forefinger and cocked her head to the right. Leaning over and snapping her wrist, she let it go.

When I had picked up the stone it felt light, not quite right; maybe it was something about the weight, something about the tiny splashes it made as it skimmed through the shadows and out across the surface, that made it seem like something else, something that had the gift of motion for longer than a moment. It skipped once, twice, three times, and was about to touch the water for the fourth—when a long dark bird came streaming down from the trees and made a perfect catch, then took the stone to a spot out of sight on the opposite shore.

We continued on through Pulaski and Wytheville, Rural Retreat and Groseclose. The sun slid slowly lower as we passed Atkins and Chilhowie and Glade Spring, it hung in front of us as we counted the miles—longer now, as our backs stiffened and the silences stretched—from Bristol to Jonesboro, from Tusculum to Bulls Gap to Jefferson City, near the southern tip of Cherokee Lake. As we left Knoxville the glare off the hood made it hard to read signs; corners of bumpers and mirrors were blinding when they passed.

After sunset we stopped near Crossville. I called Mark to let him know we were still at least two hours away.

"We'll look for you around eleven, eleven-thirty," he said. I could hear his daughters in the background, laughing. "If you can't find us, give a call. It gets a little tricky once you get into town."

I hung up the phone and walked back to the car. Howard Johnson's orange-and-blue sign loomed over the parking lot.

We listened to the news and heard the scores for the day

and I turned off the radio. The silence was comfortable, the strain we had felt at home easing as we pressed forward, together. It was even more humid in Tennessee than it had been in Virginia or Maryland, but the night brought cool breezes. I felt a sense of accomplishment as the odometer methodically registered the miles to Pleasant Hill, toward Sparta and far-off Alexandria, pieces of Greece dropped into the middle of Tennessee.

We were between Smithville and Alexandria when I looked up to the left and saw a tiny dot of light brush across the sky.

"Look," I said. "A shooting star."

"What?" Donna was groggy, half-asleep.

I had never seen one before. I had been fooled—I had seen stars twinkle and airplane running lights move behind dark clouds—but I had never seen a real falling star, not that I could be sure of. I smiled. It was a good sign.

Then doubt set in. How could I be sure that's what it had been? I shook Donna's knee.

"That star," I said. "Do you think it really was one, falling?"

She didn't look up. I saw her reflection at a strange angle in the side window. "Fell a long time ago," she said. "Light speed. You know." She closed her eyes and tried to get comfortable, her head against the side of the car.

I wasn't sure that was right. I wasn't sure falling stars were really stars. I looked down at the soft green glow of the dashboard, thinking how strange they were. Pieces of living history—events themselves, or at least their images. Like newsreel footage that could only be shown once. I tried to imagine how it would be if lesser lights could travel so far, if someone standing on the moon tonight could watch George Washington waiting in Morristown while the British attacked to the north. The trick to seeing what you wanted would be to know how far to go: to Mars for the Restoration, to Saturn for the Trojan War.

I kept glancing up, over the reflected glare of headlights. After a minute I saw another one.

"Look!"

But Donna was asleep.

Two shooting stars! I wanted to pull over and tell somebody.

Instead I watched the sky. A few large stars flashed bright, threatening to go, but they were firmly in place. Or at least they were there whenever they had created the light that I was seeing. Since then, for all I knew, or even at the very moment I was watching, they were hurtling across the sky, out of energy, leaving their masks behind. One late night another traveler would look up and the masks would follow.

He and I would be bonded then. Unless two people are looking clearly at the same distant area at the same moment, there is no sharing it—one shouts "Look!" and the other turns, too late. Maybe somewhere someone else had seen it and had charted it neatly and could verify what seemed true but might easily not have been, but that wasn't the same as seeing it together, it wasn't the same as knowing.

When I was young I believed that everything I could think of had been done before: if I dropped a pen and it fell between my ankle and my shoe, standing straight up, I knew the same exact thing had happened to some kid in geometry class in China. If I lay on the grass and stared at a cloud, I imagined someone else—maybe across the street, maybe over in Montgomery County—was watching it at the same time. Now it struck me that it wasn't true: no one else had ever dropped a red Bic pen exactly like that, no one was looking at that cloud just then and thinking what I was thinking. In some significant way I was the only person in the world who had done those things. I was the only one to see those falling stars. And no matter how long, and how happily, we were married, Donna and I would always be different people, with two sets of experiences, like the picture in geometry class of two partially overlapping circles, the intersection of two sets. We were unequal sets with a few common members. For some reason I had thought we were supposed to understand each other perfectly, know each other completely, and act as one. I had thought we were failing.

It was late. I followed the signs and the bright lights to Nashville. Donna woke when we left the highway, and pulled from the bottom of the pile on the seat beside her a cruder map, one she had drawn from directions we had gotten over the phone. I turned on the dome light and she shielded her eyes; adjusting to the glare, she guided us in.

Mark walked out of the wedge of light shining from inside his house and opened Donna's door. Then he came around to my side and held out his hand.

Chapter Twenty-two

"Eggs and grits," Lisa said. "Your first Southern breakfast. How do you like your eggs?"

I stood in the doorway to the kitchen. There weren't any other plates on the table.

"Aren't you two going to eat?"

"It's ten-thirty." Donna reached over and squeezed my hand.

"No clocks, no alarms." Mark came in holding a cup of coffee. "You're lucky the girls didn't wake you."

I sat at the table and Lisa poured me some orange juice. "Scrambled sounds good, if it's no trouble."

Mark pulled out a chair and stretched out parallel to the table, legs crossed at the ankles, hands locked behind his head. Except for Earle, who had grown into a giant, he was the biggest one in our family—over six feet, with square shoulders and a Roman nose.

"You missed the twenty-five-cent tour."

"The house," Donna said, "is beautiful. Lisa's uncle did all the tile work in the master bedroom—it's gorgeous. And you should see the greenhouse."

"Greenhouse?"

"Lisa's," Mark said. "She grows ragweed and dandelions."

"Geraniums and orchids," Donna said, "and she's got a whole row of ribbons she's won."

"Don't be impressed." Lisa spoke over her shoulder as she

stirred the eggs with the end of a spatula. "There's no competition to talk of, not around here." She brought over a plate with scrambled eggs, toast, and a mound of something that looked like runny mashed potatoes mixed with birdshot.

"Is that new? The greenhouse?" I knew she had flowers, but from her letters it didn't sound like anything more than a window box or two.

"It's hardly big enough to turn around in." She held the frying pan in the sink; water hissed against the metal. "I'd like to get something bigger. It's real handy if you want to work with cuttings or keep things blooming in winter."

"We plant a lot."

"We *garden* a lot," Donna said.

I explained to Mark. "We keep the beds the way Mom had them. The house looks the same now as it did the day you left for college."

"Is it a house or a museum?"

Donna sighed. "You talk to him—you're his brother."

Mark held up one hand. "No domestic cases. Messy business." He stood and shook the coffeepot on the counter, then took off the top and looked inside. "I guess this means breakfast is over." He set his cup on the drainboard. "We thought you might like to do some sightseeing. But you were in the car all day yesterday, so you can veto."

"I don't mind," Donna said, putting her hand on my arm. "But I wasn't driving. It's up to you."

I swallowed a mouthful of grits. They tasted like runny mashed potatoes mixed with birdshot.

"That's why we're here. Let's see what this end of the world is like."

When I finished eating, Mark herded the girls into the back of the station wagon. He and I sat up front.

"We'll make the long drive first," he said. "The Hermitage—Andy Jackson's place."

He changed lanes, then looked over at me. "Lisa thought you should have a taste of what Southern artistocracy used to be. Those people were planning ahead for generations—their children, their grandchildren, their great-grandchildren."

"And he wants to see the furniture," Lisa said.

"One of my clients collects antiques."

Lisa leaned forward. "The problem is, if you just get one or two pieces, they don't match anything else. You have to redo the whole house."

"That's one problem." Mark looked at the rearview mirror to address Donna. "But the first one is that I'm not interested in collecting things. Not furniture, not old china, not antique toys—none of it. You go into some of the houses down here, it looks like nobody's thrown anything away for a hundred and fifty years."

"I'd like to collect some things," Lisa said. "Nice things. He would too, but he has to call his investments."

Mark told her, "As an investment, furniture is a bad idea. It appreciates slowly, it takes up space, and it can break. I don't want a house filled with thousand-dollar chairs no one can sit on."

Donna said, "A thousand dollars for a chair? I'd sit on the floor first."

Lisa nodded. "The prices can be ridiculous. But it's like buying artwork."

"It's *not* like artwork," Mark said. I had the impression they had covered this ground before. "Art is made to be viewed," he said. "You don't use it, you hang it on a wall. A hundred years ago a man built a chair so he could sit down and eat. Somebody traded him a chicken for it and used it for thirty years. Now someone else pays two hundred dollars and puts a red velvet rope around it."

He stopped to concentrate on traffic, and for a moment no one said anything.

"Some people buy old instruments," Donna said, "like Stradivarius violins, and don't play them, maybe they don't even know *how* to play them. And if you play one, of course, it can break. But you can have it rebuilt. It might not have the same historic value, but if you put it in a glass case you can only admire the wood, not the sound."

"What would you do?" I asked her.

"If I had a Stradivarius? Take violin lessons."

Lisa laughed. "I'd be too scared to pick it up."

"Seriously," I said.

Donna didn't hesitate. "If it could be rebuilt, I'd play it. You can't appreciate a good violin, or flute, or any other instrument, just by looking at it. The sound is everything."

"But here's the question," Mark said. "Would you buy a Stradivarius as an investment?"

"I guess it would be nice, if you love music," she said. "I don't know anything about the market. But if we had the money, sure."

Mark shook his head. "Go with stocks every time. Easier to liquidate, and they fit in a safe-deposit box."

Lisa told him, "What appeals to me about furniture is what Donna said about instruments. You can rescue it from somebody who's just going to keep it hidden away, and put it to use. That's what the man who made the chair would probably want."

Donna said, "If Stradivarius were alive today, he wouldn't sit in his shop and admire his old fiddles. He'd make improvements."

She didn't have to say anything else.

The trip took most of the day, and after a late dinner we played cards. Donna and Lisa went to bed at midnight, and I was tired, but Mark said he rarely slept more than four hours. We talked for a long time. After a while he suggested another ride, but I was in no hurry to get back in the car.

"Should we talk to Bobby? Have you heard from him?"

My eyes were bleary. The only light on in the house was the one over the card table. I felt like a suspect under interrogation.

"I got a letter a few weeks ago." I tried to remember exactly. It had been in June.

"Let's give him a try." Mark went into the kitchen and shuffled the contents of a drawer. "Every house has a junk drawer, right?"

I heard a soft cough from somewhere deep in the house.

"What I don't understand," he said, coming back with a scrap of paper and the telephone, "is why that's where you put everything you really need to find. All the garbage we never use is as neat as a pin." He read the number and dialed. "What do you do on a ranch in August?"

"Harvest?"

"Not a farm," he said. "You don't harvest horses."

He waited, but there was no answer. "What time is it in Kansas?"

"Are we in Eastern?"

"Central."

"Sometime around two."

He hung up, mildly annoyed. "Where could he be at two in the morning? He should be asleep."

I thought that was the end, but he wanted to try someone else. I suggested Pat.

"Aren't you going to see her? She'll be expecting it. Maybe Waite."

I wrote to Waite regularly, but I hadn't gotten an answer in months. Mark asked me if he was still in Spain and I said he was, as far as I knew.

"I've got that number somewhere." He went off toward the den without turning on a light.

A door squealed far away. I thought my ears were playing tricks on me: the sound seemed to come from the other side of the house, near the bedrooms. Soft footsteps tapped the hall floor.

Tracy appeared in the doorway.

"Where's Daddy?" She wore pink pajamas with a yellow elephant on the stomach.

"In the other room," I said. "He'll be back in a minute."

She walked over and climbed into a chair. Her nose was level with the edge of the table.

"Do you feel all right?"

She nodded. She looked wide-awake.

"That's good." I listened for Mark, hoping he'd get back soon.

Tracy wrapped her arms around her stomach. "Kathy's head fell off."

She didn't seem particularly concerned, and as far as I knew, there were no neighbor children sleeping over, so I let it pass.

"Her head got stuck in the oven."

So here it was—the niece test. I was supposed to make sense of this.

"Did your doll's head burn?"

"No," she said, giggling. She reached toward the table and picked up the deck of cards in her small hand.

"Was the oven on?"

"*Kathy's* oven." The subject held no further interest for her; she idly spread the cards on the table.

"Hey," I said. "Want to see a trick?"

She handed me the deck. So far, so good. I scooped up the loose cards and tried to think of something.

"Watch."

I stood two cards on the table, about three inches apart. Then I leaned the tops together, adjusting them until they balanced on their own, forming an inverted V.

I looked over at Tracy.

"That's not a trick," she said.

I sped up. Another inverted V went up beside the first one, a single card connected the two peaks, and a third inverted V balanced on that platform. It wasn't the Eiffel Tower, but at two in the morning the old hand-eye coordination was looking good.

Tracy sat up on her chair, mesmerized.

"Do more," she said.

I was adding two more cards to the bottom row when Mark came back with a blue piece of paper.

"What's this? Bozo's Circus?"

"Just entertaining the troops. Shake the table and I'll break your legs."

"Dad?"

"Yes, Tracy."

"Can I have some milk?"

Mark took a sip of his Scotch and went into the kitchen. I added a second pair of cards to the second level and put a card across the two peaks.

"Be careful," Tracy breathed.

Slowly now, balancing my elbows on the table, I set two cards on top, tipped them toward each other, and let go.

"More," Tracy said.

Mark came back with a yellow plastic cup with Mickey Mouse's head on top. A straw stuck out of Mickey's mouth.

"Did you come out because you heard the grown-ups talking?" Mark said. "Did you think you were being left out of something important?"

Tracy didn't answer. She held the cup in both hands while she drank.

"She's too cute for words," I said.

"I've built up a resistance to cute. They'll kill you with it." Mark turned to Tracy. "When you finish that, I want you to go to bed."

She stopped drinking immediately, and a line of milk found the bottom of her chin like a paint drip. Mark reached over and swept it up with his thumb as he dialed the operator. The call went through on the first try.

"Hello," he said. "Can you dig up Waite Willus?" Then, with the receiver away from his mouth, "This might take a minute. What time is it in Spain?"

I guessed. "Eight? Nine?"

Someone started talking on the other end, but it wasn't Waite—Mark listened to an explanation. I glanced over at Tracy. She had started to slump in her chair while we talked, but when I reached for two more cards to add to the bottom row, she perked up.

As I steadied them on the table, I wondered what Bob was doing away from his place in Kansas. He had a whole circle of friends I knew nothing about. As a kind of reassurance, I placed the rest of the family on a map in my mind: Earle in California, living with Uncle Dennis; Tony in Pennsylvania, living with Aunt Shirley and Uncle Buck; Pat in Norfolk, living with her boyfriend; and Lou and his wife in Alsace-Lorraine, in France.

"Portugal?" Mark said. He jotted something on the sheet of paper and hung up.

"Why don't we just write him a letter?" I added a third pair of cards to the second level. I could feel Tracy's eyes on my hands. "They can find him easier than we can. Probably faster."

"What are you talking about? I've got the number right—" The operator came on the line. After he placed the call I started again.

"What makes you think he'll even be there?"

Mark picked up his Scotch. "What's the matter—don't you want to talk to your own brother?"

I had to look through the top cards to see him. "Don't they do some kind of drills in the morning? Swab the deck?"

Mark shrugged and drank.

The air conditioning clicked on; the tower waved slightly in the breeze, but stood. I went to work on the third row.

The call went through and Mark asked for Waite.

"What's new on land, sailor?" Mark smiled as Waite realized who was calling. After a minute he nodded.

"Here," he said into the receiver, "I've got someone who wants to talk to you."

He handed me the phone. The static filled my ear, but behind it, like the voice of someone buried in a pile of laundry, I heard, "Lisa? Hello, Lisa?"

I couldn't think of anything to say. "Ahoy."

"Who is this?"

I pressed the receiver against my ear. "It's your pen pal from Baltimore."

"George! How the hell are you, slugger?" Waite was practically yelling.

I spoke up. "I'm good. You?"

"Great! What are you doing in Tennessee?"

I explained about the trip.

"Hey," he said, "what the hell is wrong with you two guys? I've got to be out of here in a minute. Why didn't you call at night?"

"You're supposed to be happy to hear from us." I had been hoping I wouldn't have to ask. "Do you get my letters?"

"You bet." He was enthusiastic. "They forward everything. Keep it up, buddy—I appreciate it."

We talked for another minute. He had just been transferred to Portugal and hadn't started into a regular schedule. He was in special training until the end of the year. He sounded anxious to go back out to sea.

I had written questions to Waite about what he was doing. Everything that came to mind now seemed too long and difficult to go into in a quick long-distance telephone call, to be yelled across the ocean.

"Are you happy in the Navy?"

"I just sent you guys caps."

"What?" The static was terrible.

"Blue baseball caps, with the name of the ship on it. I sent everybody one. You thinking of signing up?"

"What are you talking about?" I could hear my voice echoing in the house. "I'm a married man."

"Landlocked," he said. "This isn't a bachelor party."

"Do you have a girlfriend?"

"I've always got a girl."

"What's her name?"

"You gonna send her a birthday card? I've been working on M's lately. I went out with my first Maureen last week."

"You're dating a Marine?"

"Funny guy," he said.

He promised to write. Mark took the receiver for a moment before hanging up.

I said, "Didn't he sound great?"

"Bad connection." He crossed out Waite's old number.

"Sounds like he's still the ladies' man."

"Terminal teenager," Mark said. "He always wanted to be some kind of soldier, wearing that old Eisenhower jacket. And he never could keep a girl."

"You don't think he'll settle down, get married?"

"Sure he will. Three or four times."

"Nah," I said. "He'll grow out of it."

"He's twenty-eight," Mark said. "He's as grown as he's going to get."

He took our glasses to the kitchen, then came back for the phone. As he coiled the cord I picked up two more cards, reached up to the top of the tower, and leaned them against each other. They slipped and fell, but the rest stood. I took two new cards, set them carefully on the top platform, tipped the worn white edges together, and moved my hands away. This time they stayed. Smiling, I turned to Tracy.

She was asleep. Mickey's head rested against the yellow elephant, hers lay against the back of the chair.

I reached over and put my hand on her arm. "Hey," I whispered. She woke up instantly, without moving. "Look what Uncle George built for you." I stood, careful not to jar the table, and lifted Tracy into the air.

Chapter Twenty-three

The next morning, after another late breakfast, Lisa offered to take us to their country club for a swim. Donna and I put on our suits and reported back to the kitchen. The girls were still in their pajamas.

"It looks like I'll be another twenty-five minutes," Lisa said, bringing towels out of the laundry room. "Sorry. You can watch TV if you want, or just relax."

"Take your time," Donna said. "I thought we'd look at the flowers."

A brick path lined with large white stones wound through bright beds set off by the closely trimmed lawn. Lavender clematis covered a wooden fence around the perimeter, and in the corners were beautiful white ones with waterfalls of blossoms the size of quarters. One bed set yellow heliopsis against red day lilies, another was filled with phlox nearly three feet high: pink blossoms over a foot wide, others white with red eyes. In the back of another bed, purple liatris on four-foot spikes looked like mooring posts for three butterflies hovering at their tops.

"I don't know how she does it," Donna said. "She must spend all her time out here."

The yard looked like something out of a gardener's catalog. In addition to the shrubs and flowers and trees, there were two stone benches and a small fountain surrounded by daisies.

"Your mother would have loved this. She would have been in her glory."

I didn't see any simple pansies or African violets, and nothing was running wild. All the beds were geometrical, precise.

"It's great," I said, "really impressive . . . but maybe a little artificial."

"What are you talking about? They're flowers."

We walked through a break in an eight-foot hedge. The greenhouse stood in the back corner. Against the hedge were two beds of rosebushes, shades of pink and red.

"You have to see the orchids," Donna said.

The hot air in the greenhouse was both stale and fragrant. An open aisle led from the door to the far end, but the rest of the space was filled with flowers: geraniums on the left, orchids on the right. I expected standard geraniums, the ones my mother bought at the grocery store every spring. A nice, durable plant, but, as my father would say, nothing to write home about.

These were different. The flowers ranged from only an inch across to nearly six, and they were all colors—pink, crimson, purple.

"What do you think?" Donna said, looking to the right.

The whole thing—the greenhouse, the rose beds neatly mulched, the fountain and stone benches—it all looked like money. This wasn't a garden my mother could have grown. Mark and Lisa had a colored woman come in and clean once a week, and they probably had hired help for the flowers too.

Donna said, "She says she's got twelve species. I love the patterns—or the lack of pattern. Do you know what I mean?"

"Certainly," I said, glancing at the rows of orchids. "Very nice."

"We should try some. Near the porch, maybe?"

I wondered if my mother would have done all this if she had had the opportunity—fewer children, more time, money.

"I don't know if orchids will grow outdoors," I told her. "They might be too delicate."

"Then inside. In pots."

I could still picture my mother wearing an orchid Easter corsage.

Donna looked away. "I don't know why I waste my breath."

"Hold it." I put my hands on her shoulders. "I was thinking about something else, I'm sorry."

"Never mind." She was in her navy-blue one-piece with a yellow stripe. It looked good on her.

"Maybe we could try," I said. "I'll ask Lisa about them."

"Don't bother. I was getting carried away."

I turned her so she'd look at me. "If it's important to you, I'll ask her."

She put her hands on my chest—not hugging, not quite pushing me away.

"Some days," she said, "I think you're still living with your family, and I'm just in the way."

She could read my mind.

"It's not like that."

"Yes," she said. "Sometimes."

She traced a line from my chin to my Adam's apple.

"What would you do," she said, "if I asked you to turn over all the flowerbeds and plant grass?"

"Grass?"

"For me."

I hugged her close, but she pushed away.

"You wouldn't, would you. You couldn't."

"*All* the flowers?"

She sighed.

"Some of them," I said.

Not enough.

"A *lot* of them. If you were serious." I pushed the strap of her bathing suit off her shoulder.

"I'd believe it when I saw it," she said.

"I would do it." I pushed the other strap off her shoulder. "I *will* do it. Is that what you want?"

"Hey," she said.

"Hey what?" I tugged at the top of her suit.

"Hey." She put her hand to the neckline, holding it there. "We're going to the country club."

"Since when are you so excited about swimming?" I pulled the suit over her breasts, rolled it down to her hips.

"Lisa might come looking," she said, reaching for the top of my trunks. "She might find us."

I reached down to push her suit to the ground. "Then I guess we better hurry."

"This is perfect," Lisa said as I walked the girls back to their towels. They had matching plastic ducks around their waists. "Anytime y'all want to baby-sit, you just let me know."

"I don't know if I'd call it baby-sitting," I said. "It's more like practice."

Lisa had a towel sausaged over her eyes. She lifted it to check on on the girls—I had to help Jennifer out of her duck—then dropped it back into place. "Is this news? Are we knitting booties?"

Donna looked up and smiled but didn't give any signals.

"Just in case," I said. "We come down here, take the girls for a spin around the block, kick the tires."

"Let the buyer beware. You don't know the first thing about it until you start making payments. Kids are wonderful as long as you can dump them when you're tired of them."

"I used to baby-sit in high school," Donna said. "Even that got pretty wild some nights."

Lisa said, "Having kids is like moving to another country. You meet new people, you learn another language, it's all real exciting. Then you turn to go back to who you were and you find out they've stolen your passport."

Tracy and Jennifer were sticking eyes and noses into a plastic potato. I sat on the edge of Donna's towel, looking out over the pool. From a tall chair by the deep end, one of the lifeguards joked with a girl in a bikini.

"We're real lucky," she said. "They've been healthy. We know some couples who are always at the doctor, at the hospital. I don't know what I'd do with one of them in the hospital. The first time Tracy had a cold, when I heard that rattle in her chest? I was a wreck. It's one thing to live with two other people, it's something else when they're so small and helpless. They depend on you every minute." She brushed her arm where a fly had landed. "My momma used to tell me people who don't have children never grow up. And you know what I would say to that."

Donna laughed. "Don't you hate it when they're right?"

"The other big change is, you have less time for each other. Kids are always there. You want to go out, you've got to get somebody to take care of the kids. You want to make a nice dinner, you've still got to have food the kids'll eat. You want some quiet time together, you have to keep checking on them. And they have this instinct so that, as soon as you're really exhausted, trying to get a few hours in? They start bouncing off the walls. Even when I'm out shopping and they've got a sitter, there's always a part of you that's thinking about them."

"Stop!" Tracy said. "Stop it, Jennifer." Jennifer held the plastic potato firmly in one hand and pulled out the eyes with the other.

Lisa sat up and looked over at the girls, squinting.

"Jennifer is hurting Mr. Potato," Tracy said.

Lisa yawned and stretched. "Mr. Potato will be all right. You two play nice."

She looked out over the pool. The girl in the bikini dipped her toe in the water absently, one long leg bare to the world. Lisa said, "Just wait a few years, honey. See if you don't find something to cover up."

"I hear you," Donna said.

Lisa lay back down. "I'm no prude. Where I grew up, we went skinny-dipping all the time. But when they wear suits like that, somehow it looks like they're more than naked."

I thought of Dusty wearing her men's shirts and nothing else. Just as fast, I tried to get her out of my mind.

"Tell Lisa about our neighbors," Donna said.

I turned quickly. Donna was lying on her stomach, her eyes closed. I was starting to think there was a glass plate in the side of my head.

"There are new people in the house next to ours," I said.

"The one your father built?"

"Three girls and an older woman. They're . . . self-employed."

"God's truth? Right next door?"

"That's not what I meant," Donna said. "We looked out the

window one day and they were in the backyard sunbathing with no tops on."

"God, I hate that," Lisa said. "I don't deny anyone her youth, but do they have to flaunt it?"

Donna said, "There they were, half-naked in the backyard."

"Maybe I shouldn't say this with George around, but I still do a little of that myself. It feels real good, that sun all over you. Like warm butter."

Donna said, for my benefit, "In public?"

"Back between the greenhouse and the hedges. It's pretty well secluded back there."

"I noticed," I said.

"I used to do it with my girlfriends," Lisa said, "back when we all had stomachs like boards and no tush to worry about. I tell Mark, I'll keep it up until I start getting complaints. You know the dew is off the rose when they start asking you to keep your clothes on."

"Go ahead," I told Donna. "Get it over with."

She just smiled.

"What's going on?" Lisa lifted the towel from her eyes. "Did I miss something?"

Mark picked me up at the club, waiting while I changed in the bathhouse. As we drove into the city he pointed out local landmarks, and I slumped back in my seat, eyes even with the dash. It was nice not to have to drive for a while.

I said, "Are you happy down here?"

"You conducting a survey?"

"Details about your sex life are next."

We slowed at an intersection.

"Happy," he said. And then again, as if he were trying it out: "Happy. Do I go around with a smile on my face? Do I look out the window in the morning and say, 'It's good to be alive,' like something in a television commercial?"

"Really happy," I said. "Go back ten years and you would do it all again?"

"That's not a worthwhile question. If I had to do anything over, and I was the same person I was then, obviously I'd make the same choices—those are the choices I made. See that red-and-green building, brown roof?"

I followed his finger down the street to our left.

"Best Italian restaurant in Nashville. A dubious distinction. But since we got two of Guido's former employees to settle a grievance out of court, our wine's been free, and the service has improved remarkably." We turned right. "If you're asking me if I'm quitting my job, or divorcing Lisa, or putting the girls up for adoption, I'm not. If you're asking if I, as I am today, would still make the same decisions I made in the past, the question isn't worth discussion. I made sound decisions then. I make sound decisions now."

"Is that the short answer?"

"I'm on my lunch break." He looked over at me, then turned back to the road. "What's on your mind?"

"I've been thinking."

"It's never too late."

I wedged myself further down in the seat, the younger brother. "Sometimes I think of different lives I could have led. Things I could have done."

"Women you might have slept with."

I was going to deny it, but didn't bother.

"It's more than that," he said. "You wonder if you should have gone to school longer, or not as long. If you should have taken this job. If you should have gotten married when you did. If you should've gotten drunk a few more times when you were still young and carefree."

"Exactly." For the first time since we had pulled into the driveway Saturday night I felt close to him. We understood each other after all.

"You're asking if I wonder about that sort of thing?"

He looked down at me and I nodded.

"It's a waste of time."

I sat up, smiling, but he was serious.

"You must. Otherwise you wouldn't have known what I meant."

"Why should I wonder if Lynn Bauer would have gone to bed with me? Why lie awake and worry about whether I could've played Chopin if I had stuck with my piano lessons in fourth grade?"

He was watching the traffic, but I could tell he was still considering the question, elaborating on his argument.

"The past is like a steep hill dropping away behind you," he said. "You know it's there, but you have to keep pushing forward. Every time you turn around, you slide back a few steps."

"You have to look back sometimes. You're exaggerating." I aimed the air vent in the dash at my face.

"I could have married any one of a thousand women."

"Happily?"

"Let's say I could have been as content as I am now, and I think 'content' means for me what 'happy' means for you."

"That's ridiculous. Have you told Lisa?"

"Told her what?"

"This one-thousand-women theory."

"The important thing," he went on, "is to realize that, essentially, we stay the same. Whatever I do, I'm going to try to settle disputes using logic and persuasion. Whatever Bob does, he's going to spend half his time planning things out, then he's going to see his plans through. He's meticulous, and persistent."

"What about me?"

Mark pushed down his visor to block the sun. "You're getting the wrong idea."

"You know about yourself. You know about Bob. Tell me about me."

"You do it."

I looked out at the road. A boy in a convertible was singing with his radio.

"I'm reliable. Pretty reliable. I work hard. I'm sort of semi-intelligent. Smarter than a lot of other warm-blooded animals, but no genius. I mean well." A girl on a racing bike flashed by. "Sounds like a description of a dog."

"What's the problem?"

So as we drove through Nashville I told him the long version of the story. I told all about the girls and Grace and Larry, the strange crowd at their picnic, Elvis and her clothes.

I told him about Kristin and Eve sunbathing, and Dusty in the toolshed. I told him about going into their house, but I edited out the part about Dusty's room.

He put his right arm behind me, on the back of the seat. "That's no whorehouse. Those women aren't like that."

"That's what *these* women are like."

He slowed and waved for a pedestrian to cross the street.

"First of all," he said, "whores don't throw picnics for their customers, and they wouldn't have that kind of social circle. This Dusty wouldn't come on to you just for her own amusement. And the old woman wouldn't march in to your neighborhood meeting and admit what they're doing."

"You seem to be taking a personal interest in this case."

"I want you to get the facts straight."

"That's how it happened," I said. "Just like I told you."

"That's not how they operate."

There didn't seem to be any point in pressing it.

"So what's your advice?"

"See those red brick buildings?"

They were ahead of us—a college.

"Vanderbilt University."

"I'm looking for advice," I said.

He held up his hand like a traffic cop stopping cars. "I don't tell people what to do. I try to understand why they do it."

He turned off the main street. "Have you seen any travel ads lately?"

"Is that the end of the conversation?"

"Look at a travel brochure," he said, "any travel brochure—what do you see?"

I shrugged. "Hotels."

"Women. Women in bikinis, women in tennis skirts, women in evening gowns. Why do you think that is?"

"Women like to travel?"

"Men buy the tickets," he said. "A travel brochure says, 'Come to California'—or Hawaii, or Florida, or Paris—'and screw a beautiful woman.' "

"You're crazy."

"You're naive."

"What about women? They read those things too."

"Sure they do. And to them the brochures say, 'Come to so-and-so and *be* a beautiful woman.'"

"And make love with your husband."

He shook his head. "With a mysterious stranger. And the brochures work because life is not romantic. Life is hard work. Offer people romance, get them to believe in it, and you've got them sold."

"So what's the point?"

"Hawaii or a whorehouse," he said as we turned left into a large park filled with trees, "it's all the same. Don't get misled by the packaging."

"Hold it. You're telling me there's no such thing as romance? For anybody?"

"In movies," he said.

I looked out the window. Bicyclists made their way lazily along the shady road as couples strolled, talking. A circle of boys kicked a soccer ball. A woman pulled food out of a grocery bag, her dress the same yellow as the blanket she was kneeling on, making the whole thing look like an enormous bib. Everyone in the park looked sure of himself, as confident as Mark.

Ahead of us the trees thinned and finally opened to a large lawn. I saw the side of an enormous building sitting out in the middle, but a bus pulled up alongside us, blocking the view. When the bus passed I looked back.

"Welcome to the Athens of the South," Mark said.

The building was the Parthenon.

It was easily six stories high, and in the middle of the park it was as incongruous as a statue on a pitcher's mound. In my mind, in the picture based on my father's stories, the Parthenon sat in ruin on the Acropolis: one or two columns stood tall, the rest broken off near the ground, which was littered with chunks of dust-covered marble. There were no bushes or trees, not even grass. At the same time, I imagined the ocean not far away, just out of sight. Our father's ship waited for him. There was a smell of salt in the air.

But here it was, in the middle of a park in downtown Nashville, complete and gleaming white in the sun, like a skeleton in a well-lit biology classroom. We parked the car and got out.

Up close, without the trees and grass and soccer players, without Nashville, the Parthenon was wonderful. In an odd way, it was as familiar as my own house. I had sat beside it with my father.

Inside, on the long walls, were casts of the Elgin Marbles, fragments of the original sculptures. I tried to imagine the people who had walked through the Parthenon three thousand years earlier—I tried to picture Odysseus, the hero of our father's stories, striding in front of me, strong and authoritative. Instead I saw him jogging past picnics in a toga, trying to figure out how to cross the street.

We looked at a miniature of the East Pediment, a study for the full-size work outside. Helios was being pulled from the sea by four horses. But unlike the horses in the paintings at Haussner's, which looked like horses in paintings, these seemed real and important. They made me think of Donna's description of her audition for the Baltimore Symphony, music that made her whole body vibrate. One fluid line ran from the front-most tip of the horses, through their heads, through the arm of the sun god. I could feel them pulling him through the weight of the water.

I looked at the rest of the plaster casts and read the descriptions. Mark seemed almost anxious, as if he were afraid I wouldn't like it. I commented softly on everything, admiring, as if he had done the work himself.

Afterward we sat on a bench in the shade near the edge of a small pond. Three ducks waddled down the bank and dropped into the water. Mark leaned forward, elbows on his knees. I looked back at the building. It *was* beautiful, but at the same time, it looked all wrong.

Mark said, "He left some things."

"What?" I turned to him.

"He left things. A box."

"I thought you gave all that away—the clothes, that stuff?"

"This was a box of things he brought with him. Junk. Old books and papers. I haven't gone through them."

I didn't know what he wanted me to say. Mark and Lisa had been the ones feeding him at the end, driving him to the doctors and to the hospital, taking care of him. If Mark wanted the odds and ends our father left behind, he was entitled to them.

I said, "I wish I had been here. To help."

"There was nothing to do. We just tried to keep him comfortable, but it got to the point where he didn't even want to move."

"How did it affect the girls?" I thought of Tracy, two years old, learning to walk with a dying man in the house. Her grandfather. I wondered how Mark tried to explain it to them.

"That's not what concerns me." He reached down and pulled up a blade of grass. "A few weeks back, you called because it was the day Mom died. But she died six years ago. He died eleven *months* ago, and you never talk about it."

I looked out over the pond. The surface was dark, almost muddy. "So?"

"I think you're taking it hard."

"Weren't you just telling me not to wallow in the past?"

"This is different. You're ignoring it."

Father had worked as long as he could. Then he stayed home with Pat and me, either doing jobs around the house or reading or, on the worst days, lying in bed. It had been strange to have him stay at home, but it had been worse to see him in his old brown robe all day, to have to help him into the bathroom. When he was too weak to feed himself, the ambulance came to take him on the long ride to Nashville. His last real burst of energy, the last time I saw him the way I had known him, was when he came back for the weekend of our wedding. We all knew that he was losing the fight, that he was making one last effort. No one tried to stop him from bringing a photographer out to the softball game: we wanted to indulge him.

He died in front of the television late one afternoon. Mark phoned each of us, and that series of calls was Father's funeral. He had asked to be cremated without ceremony.

"Tell me how it happened."

Mark looked up. "You know."

"Let me hear it again."

He looked at me clinically, concerned.

"You were here," I said. "It's your story. Tell it."

He recited the facts without feeling. "Lisa and the girls were outside. I was working in the den. He used to like to sit back in our easy chair with the lights off and watch television. Ballgames, mainly, but eventually it didn't matter. That afternoon he was watching baseball. Somebody against the Yankees.

"Halfway through the game I checked to see if he wanted something to drink. I sat with him for a few innings. New York was losing, seven to three, and he bet me they would come back. I took him up on it, just to keep him interested."

"Seven to three," I said.

"What?"

"You remember the score."

"I watched until the top of the eighth, when the phone rang. When I got back the Yankees were rallying. You know how he watched baseball on television—never said a word. But when they got the tying run in, he didn't even look over."

Mark let the blade of grass fall from his hand. The ducks moved slowly across the water.

"Did he ever come here? To this building?"

Mark shifted on the bench. I knew what his clients must have felt: his attention focused on every word they said, his control.

"He didn't leave the house often, but he saw it." Mark wasn't enthusiastic.

"I would have liked to see his face the first time you brought him. I guess everything came full circle." I pictured the Parthenon in ruins, without a park and a pond and ducks, without families having picnics, our father sitting in the middle of whatever Lord Elgin had left behind. Then, years later, he was able to come here and go back in time, in a sense, to see what the Parthenon had been. It was a fitting ending to our father's journeys.

"I drove him here one Sunday," Mark said. "We took a

short walk, then sat in the shade. He was quiet, so I said something about bringing back memories."

A woman sat down on the edge of the pond, across from us. She began tearing slices of bread into pieces and throwing them to the ducks.

"George, I don't want you to get carried away over this. But he bought the *Odyssey* in San Francisco. He told me that. He carried it around until after he and Mom were married, when he took it out and started to read."

"He read it in Greece."

"Never."

"Sitting next to the Parthenon."

"He went to Greece, but he didn't get to go on shore."

I didn't believe it.

"He said it made him feel better, coming out here and making the story true. He even had his book in the car."

"But what about . . . what about the rest?" I thought of all the black pins and lines on the maps in my room. How much of it was wrong?

"It's not that important." I could tell Mark was wondering if he should have told me any of it. "He really did live on those ships, he traveled around the world. He just told a few stories." Mark said "stories," but he meant "lies."

The ducks made a tight circle around the crumbs. When the woman ran out of bread, they pecked at invisible objects just beneath the surface before spreading out across the pond again.

"Why do you think he did it?"

Mark leaned back. "It was entertaining. A little too neat, but a good kid's story. Remember those maps you used to have all over your room?"

"But if the rest of it was true, why bother to make that up? What did we care if he had seen the Parthenon?"

"That doesn't matter. What you need to understand is, true or false, he was obsessed with his youth. He never grew out of baseball. He named us after baseball players, he even died watching a game. He read one great book and reread it for the rest of his life, because the traveling he did when he was young was the most exciting thing that ever happened to him. Our father was a classic case of arrested development."

"He built those houses," I said. "He raised us."

"I see the same thing happening to you," Mark said.

"He was a good father."

Mark shrugged. "Being our father was the only role he left for himself. But it wasn't enough. He wanted to be a hero."

"That was romantic?"

"It's the wrong thing to want."

The woman across the pond glanced up at the sky, then called to the ducks. They ignored her, floating quietly.

Chapter Twenty-four

The moment we stopped waving I felt the dull anticipation I now knew came with a long drive.

"I'm spoiled," Donna said, settling into her seat. "Now I'm going to have to have a pool."

It wasn't just the pool at the country club. It was the two cars and the central air conditioning and all the rest of it.

She said, "Did you know they designed the house together? That would be fun."

"It isn't very big."

"Big enough. They could have another baby without being overcrowded—they've got that spare bedroom."

We moved onto the highway.

"I like older houses," I said. "Of course, it depends on the house."

"Of course."

"I wouldn't live in a shack just because it was old."

"Who would?"

I drummed my fingers on the steering wheel. "Imagine that you could live in any house you wanted. Except it has to be real—one you've lived in, or visited, or just seen."

"Could I redecorate?"

"Anything."

"I'd keep ours. Your father built it, he gave it to us as a wedding present. You don't give that up for central air conditioning."

That was the answer I wanted. But I had never thought of that house as ours.

We reached Norfolk late in the afternoon. Pat's boyfriend, Gary, met us at the door.

"Here's the man," he said. "The Sultan of Swat."

Gary was wearing dirty blue shorts and nothing else. He had thick dark hair and eyebrows, but hardly any hair on his chest. Pat had told me he was twenty-one; he looked about eighteen. He didn't offer to take either of the bags I was carrying.

I said, "This is my wife."

He nodded in her direction. "Howdy." He stood in the way as he held the door open, so we had to squeeze past him. Donna smiled nervously. I felt about fifty years old.

"Where's Pat? Is she here?"

"Still at work," Gary said, walking into the living room. "She'll be back soon."

I waited for him to tell me where to put our bags. He didn't react when I set them against the wall just inside the door.

"Come on in," he said, after the fact. "Have a seat." He hitched at his shorts and waved at the two empty chairs in the living room.

Except for a depression where he had been sitting, the plaid sofa against the far wall was covered with notebooks and papers. A basket of dirty laundry sat on what passed for a coffee table—a door lying across two heavy cardboard boxes stamped in blue ink, RED TABLE WINE. I had the feeling it was a joke. One wall was covered by shelves made of warped boards and cinder blocks. The television was on, and an open beer and a box of cookies sat on the table next to the laundry basket.

Gary pushed the newspapers on the floor into a pile and turned the sound down on the television. As we talked he kept glancing over at the set.

"Can I get you two a beer?" He looked at Donna for the first time. "I think we got a ginger ale if you want it."

"Beer's fine," Donna said.

The moment Gary stepped out of sight we exchanged a glance. Pat hadn't told me anything about the house except that it was small and the rent was too high. She had told me Gary was handsome and intelligent and funny, but that was how she described all her boyfriends.

Gary came back from the kitchen with two bottles of beer, unopened. "So how was the trip? Good?"

"So far," Donna said. She let the implication flop through the air, heavy as wet socks.

"Great." Gary sat on the floor, leaning back against the sofa. He was so casual that our sitting in the chairs seemed awkwardly formal, as if we were on thrones.

"I can't stand driving," he said. "I've never owned a car." He waited for us to act surprised. "Had a motorcycle for two years, but I sold it after I cracked up bad one night."

"How do you get to school?"

"We got a bike." He took a sip of his beer. "It's the only way to go."

Donna was sitting stiffly, not quite leaning against the back of her chair. "What about Pat?"

"It's not a long walk. Did you see that big toy store on the way in? The one with the giraffe in front? That's where she works. Hey, you two want a Mallomar?" He held the box of cookies out to us. "Yeah, she used to talk about getting a car, something used, but I told her: Man, cars are nothing but headaches. I know. My parents had a car."

I said, "Are you doing any work? Something part-time, after school?"

From the look on his face I might have asked him if he had ever been on safari.

He set his bottle on the floor against the sofa. "I'd like to," he said, "but the college keeps me pretty busy. I mean, I'm home during the day and all, but I have to think a lot."

Donna finally gave in and sat back. "What do you take in school?"

"International studies. You know, business, but foreign languages and things too. I want to go to New York and work for one of those big multilingual companies. A lot of them will send you overseas. You travel all over on their ticket."

The doorbell rang.

"Maybe she forgot her key," Gary said. He got up and walked around the corner to the door, out of sight. Donna looked over at me and wrinkled her nose as we listened.

"Hi, baby," Gary said. We heard a bag rustling, followed by a loud kiss. "Did you have a good day?"

"I'm dying," Pat said. "Get me a beer, will you?"

She came around the corner wearing her orange-and-yellow toy-store uniform. "George!" She hurried over and I stood up to catch her in my arms. She hugged me long and hard, then stepped back. "You look great, kiddo."

"You don't look too bad yourself." It was a lie. Her face was pale and thin, and she looked tired. I told myself it was because she was just home from work. No one in our family had ever looked so drawn.

"We didn't surprise you, did we?" Donna asked as she and Pat hugged briefly. "George told me he called."

"He did," Pat said, but she understood. "I'm sorry about the mess. Gary likes to spread out when he's home. Don't you?"

Gary had come back with a beer for Pat and another for himself. He pushed some papers to the side and sat on the sofa with his arm around her. He said, "Did you ask Debbie about bringing over the mattress?"

She ignored the question. "I picked up some chicken on the way home. You all can go to the kitchen if you want to start. I've got to get out of these clothes."

When she came back, Gary passed a roll of paper towels and we sat down to eat. The kitchen was small and dark. There was no window, only a fluorescent bulb across the ceiling.

"I just got a letter from Tony," Pat said. "He's playing drums with a group of guys up there—he said they just played at some high-school dance."

I had heard about the band, but not about the dance. I told her Mark and Lisa said hello.

"You'll have to tell me about them," Pat said. "And the

house. Is it nice? He calls, but I can't get a straight answer out of him. He said he'd send a picture, and six weeks later I got a postcard of the Taj Mahal."

Gary finished a piece of chicken and licked his fingers. "Isn't he the one that called in the middle of the night?"

"About a month ago," Pat told us. "Three in the morning. He never calls when I'm awake."

"He never calls us at all," I said.

"You're not missing much. Anyway, you're married." She said it as if I were dead.

Gary tore the skin off a breast. "He's the lawyer, right? Not for me, man. That's too much."

After we finished dinner, Gary left to go to a class. We helped Pat clean up, then went back to the living room. It was a small house.

Pat didn't sit down. "Let's not hang around here," she said. "You want to go for a ride?"

The sun cast shadows across small houses in need of paint and short fences crooked as bad teeth, dented trashcans without lids and a car rusted onto cinder blocks. Pat pointed us east.

"It's been so long since I've been in the back of a car," she said. "I feel like I'm back home. We were going to buy something used, but we decided to save our money."

"Is he saving too?"

"Well, not like that. But he's getting through school on grants. He's real smart. I know he doesn't look like he's doing much, but you'd be surprised—he'll just sit and drink beer for a few weeks, then all of a sudden he'll start working like nuts, days at a time."

"You're right," I said. "I'd be surprised."

"Hey, how about we just drive along the coast for a while?"

I said that would be fine.

"You don't mind using the gas?"

Pat was leaning forward from the back. I turned to look at her as we pulled up to an intersection. "Is money that tight?"

"You know how it is. Like Dad used to say, things can get pretty hard before they get any easier."

Something about that didn't sound right. First she had called me "kiddo," now our father was "Dad."

She turned to Donna. "It's hard paying for school these days. Mark offered to give me money to go to college, but what do I need college for? It's tough now, but after Gary gets his degree and we go overseas, this will all pay off."

"When are you going?"

"He'll be done in a year if he works hard. He's about a semester behind, which is why he's taking this summer course. Then we figure he'll get a job with one of the American companies that do a lot of international business. I'd like to go to Germany, but Gary says France. He wants to live on the Riviera."

"That sounds familiar," I said.

Pat didn't remember.

"Mom and I used to talk about sitting on a beach at St. Tropez."

"Gary really means it," Pat said.

Donna searched for the words for the next question. "Do you two plan to—"

"—get married?" Pat sat back for a moment, then came forward again.

"I don't want to start an argument or anything, but we sort of decided we'd just live together for now. We'll get hitched when he gets a job, so I can move with him. A lot of people think we already are."

"I guess they would," Donna said.

"Anyway, it won't be until he gets a job that we'll have some money, and that's when I want to have some children. I'd like to have one now, but we decided it would take too much time, and somebody's got to work. But it'll be a great way to raise kids, don't you think? Traveling around the world? Think about all the things they'll see."

She kept talking as we drove along the ocean. She told Donna how she and Gary had met at the beach. As I listened, I couldn't help thinking that she had left more than our house. Didn't she know what people must be saying? Didn't she know what our parents would have said?

* * *

That night they slept on a mattress on the living-room floor. We offered to go to a hotel, but I could tell it meant a lot to Pat for us to stay with them, as if having houseguests made them more officially a couple.

The bedroom smelled musty—a dark brown water mark stained the ceiling where it sagged in one corner—and it was cramped. One side of the bed was pushed against the wall, and on the other side was just enough room for the door to open. The dresser at the foot of the bed was crammed with hair sprays and deodorants, pennies and scraps of paper. We had to open our bags on the bed, then stack them in a corner. It took me a long time to fall asleep.

We woke up early, but Pat was already gone. Gary was sitting in the kitchen in a pair of jeans, reading the newspaper.

" 'Morning," he said. "Want some toast?"

He told us he was going to meet some friends at Old Dominion and spend the rest of the day at the university library. He invited us to follow him in the car to see the school, but we decided to go to the ocean.

"Sounds good," he said. "Maybe I could meet you out there." We discussed it halfheartedly until finally he decided he should try to work instead. He took a beer out of the refrigerator and set our dishes in the sink.

We drove to Virginia Beach. Lying on the sand, dozing in the sun while Donna rubbed suntan lotion on my shoulders, I thought of days we had spent at the ocean when we were dating. I remembered how proud I felt lying next to her.

"We don't have to leave tomorrow," I said. "We could just come down here and stay in a hotel. We wouldn't have to tell them."

"You would do that?" she said, lying back on her towel.

"Do you want to?"

"Let's make it a weekend at Ocean City. Thrasher's fries. Lemonade. We can even wait until after Labor Day, after the crowds die down."

Two girls near us turned on a radio. One was plain, the other was cute. The cute one rolled over, saw me watching, and smiled.

When she spoke again, Donna was serious. "You know, I think we did it."

"Did what?" But I could tell from the sound of her voice.

"It," she said.

"In the doghouse?"

"Are we talking about the same thing?"

"Greenhouse," I said. "I meant greenhouse."

"I don't think maternal instinct kicks in that fast. Before that." She put her arm across her forehead, shading her eyes.

Suddenly she seemed completely different. I wanted to put a tent over her. I wanted to pack her in a box of cotton.

I knew I was supposed to feel excited, and I did. But I wasn't happy-excited, the way I was when Bob and I went to our first Orioles game—this was happiness laced with fear. Having a baby was just asking for more pain. I felt as if I had reached the top of the first incline on a new roller coaster, and I wanted to see the engineering degrees of everybody involved in building it. I wanted to ask them: Do you know what you're doing? Are you sure this thing is safe?

I could feel my stomach tightening for a long free-fall.

I asked Donna, "Are you happy?"

"Uh-huh," she said. "You?"

I wriggled my feet into the sand and sat there staring out at the ocean.

She had a lot of work ahead of her. If she wasn't worried now, she would have plenty of opportunities soon. This was no time for me to let her down. Besides, all the moments of pure happiness I could remember were from my youth. Every important event since then had held the same vein of danger I could feel now. "Happy" was too simple.

I told Donna, "I'm excited."

She propped herself up on her elbows and looked out at the water. After a moment she turned and scooped sand onto my leg.

When my thigh was nearly covered she said, "I'm a little scared."

"Don't be. There's nothing to be scared about." But lies weren't right either.

"Not scared, really. Nervous."

"Nervous," I said. "That's okay. That's natural."

I watched as she covered up my other leg. The sand was warm and heavy, but it felt comfortable.

"Happy, too," she said. "Definitely."

"Good."

She stopped burying my legs. I wiggled my toes. The sand on the surface didn't move.

Donna jumped up, threw one last handful of sand on my chest, and ran down to the surf. She shouted at me to follow, then turned and dove into a wave. When her head broke the surface she was swimming away from shore.

The girls who had spread out next to us were on their stomachs, listening to "Runaround Sue." The plain one was snapping her fingers. The cute one caught my eye.

"Hi," she said.

I said hello.

"You from around here?" As she spoke she reached around and unsnapped the top half of her bikini.

"Nope," I said, lifting my legs from under the sand. "Just visiting." Before she could say any more, I headed for the ocean.

Pat met us at the door, still wearing her uniform. She looked like something left over from a party.

"Want a drink?" she said. "Anything? I was just watching TV." We followed her into the living room, stepping around the mattress.

"Gary must have forgotten to pick it up this morning," she said as I helped her lean it against the wall. I asked her when he would be back.

"Hard to tell. Some nights he's late at the library, other nights he goes out for a while. He'll call. Maybe he'll bring some people over." She seemed to brighten at the thought of company, then yawned. "I'm exhausted."

We found some cards and started to play gin, then Donna and I taught her how to play three-handed pinochle. It had been dark for a while when Pat grew noticeably more tired. Donna looked over at me and I stopped shuffling.

"Do you want to go to bed?" Donna asked. "You can take the one in the other room."

Pat sat up. "No, sorry." She laughed. "I didn't mean to doze off on you. Some hostess, huh?"

"Why don't you do that?" Donna said. "I thought maybe I would do some things in the kitchen. George and I didn't clean up too well after breakfast."

"Wait, no, don't do that. Gary will get it. I'll do it. No, stay here."

Donna had gotten up while Pat protested. "I'll only be a few minutes. You just relax. We've been acting as if you were on vacation too." She took two of Gary's empties into the kitchen with her.

Pat looked about to cry. She spoke softly, so Donna couldn't hear. "George, tell her to stop."

I put the deck of cards into the box. "She just wants to help."

Pat played with the bow on her uniform. She was past the crying now.

"What about you?"

"I want to help too."

She tugged at the ends of the bow as if to untie it, then reformed it slowly, firmly.

"I didn't know it looked so bad. God, that's pitiful, isn't it?"

"What are you really going to do?"

She pulled a pack of cigarettes out of the pocket of her uniform. She saw my eyebrows rise. "It's part of the new me," she said, striking a match. "Actually, I'm trying to quit."

She exhaled and leaned back. She looked more comfortable with the cigarette between her fingers.

"George, I've been knocking my head against the wall looking for work, and the best I've gotten is this cashier's job. I just can't make it. The money isn't bad—it would be plenty if it were just me—but I don't want to live like this. I just keep telling myself it's not for long."

"I don't want you to live like this either," I said. "And it could be for longer than you think. This whole plan with Gary getting some big job and going overseas—do you realize how it sounds?"

"He's not as bad as you think. He's smart, and he really cares about us."

"How can you tell?"

"I've been with a few other guys down here. I'm not keeping secrets. It's just that things changed so fast I figured you wouldn't even remember the names."

"I would too."

She put her feet up on the coffee table. "I bet you would. Good old George." She took a drag from the cigarette. "All I'm saying is, don't pity me. Gary may not be my dream man, but there's one thing I've figured out since I left home. As long as you keep dreaming, you wake up alone. Eventually you have to try to make one come true."

"But why this one?" I said. "This one doesn't look so good."

She smiled. "I don't know how to tell you. It looks good to me." She flicked her ash into an old jelly jar on the table. "We were all brought up to think that there was only one way to live, certain rules everybody had to play by. But there are a lot of ways."

"This is better?"

"Maybe," she said. "Maybe worse. Maybe just different. But I want to be the one that chooses."

We heard the water running in the kitchen as Donna worked on the breakfast dishes.

"We've all changed," I said.

She nodded slowly, chin tipped high, exhaling smoke.

"I guess we're still a family," I said, "but it's different now. We aren't the same people we were back then."

Slowly, drawing out the words for emphasis, Pat said, "You can say that again." Then, "Mark is into his lawyer thing twenty-four hours a day—he can't take time to write, he doesn't say anything on the phone. And now that he's making big bucks, that's all he can talk about. He calls and asks if I have enough for the rent, do I want a new car, do I want some money for this and the next thing . . . he means well, but spare me, you know? And Waite—what's he doing in the Navy? You can't think for yourself in the Navy. I thought that's what we were all fighting for."

"Fighting?"

"To get out of that house, to be ourselves."

I waited for the punch line, but she meant it.

"Not me," I said.

"Some of us," she said. "Most of us. That man was a tyrant. I felt like some kind of prisoner."

"What are you talking about?"

She sat back. "Maybe that's too strong. But he was such a cold fish. And there were those systems for everything—crews to clean the house, schedules for chores, a right and wrong way to do everything."

"Jobs had to be done."

"Even when he was sick," she said, "when you would have thought he'd talk to us—he'd just lie up there and read, or sleep, or watch baseball."

"He was dying."

"I just wanted him to be human." She flicked the ash from her cigarette. "Instead he was like a king or something. Like he had to die with honor. Like we weren't good enough for him."

"No. He was trying to do what he thought was right."

Silverware clattered in the kitchen.

She smiled. "Dad affected everybody differently. He was so strong, we couldn't help but have strong reactions."

"Still," I said. "There are things holding us together, things we have in common." I tried to express what I thought, what I hadn't been able to tell Mark. "Those years we were all together, whatever you think of them now, we share those. We're the only people who had that experience."

"Just being around Mom and Dad, those two particular people. Is that what you mean?"

"That's part of it." She understood, I was sure. We understood each other.

We sat at the table, thinking.

She said, "You know what he did to us? He made us all dreamers."

"That sounds like a bad song. Everybody dreams."

"Wait a minute, wait." She tapped the table, excited. "Listen. Tony wants to be a rock-and-roll hero. Earle wants to race cars."

"Since when?"

"Damn. I wasn't supposed to tell. Don't let him know, okay? He bought part of a stock car." She squeezed my hand, then let go. "Not part of it. Part interest, I guess."

"Bob wants his house in Kansas," I said, catching on.

"Mark got his Ivy League degree, he's a big-deal lawyer."

"Waite's sailing around the world—that's from Dad." I had never called our father that before.

"And Lou's a mystery man," Pat said. "There was always that side to Dad—it drove me nuts. Poor Lou."

"And you want to *marry* a mystery man. Some tall-dark-and-handsome guy who'll take you to France."

"Germany," she said. "I don't even know why." She laughed. "And you . . ."

"I'm left behind to hold down the fort."

"Is that how you feel? Left behind?"

"Sometimes." That was the way Mark had made me feel.

"Where do you want to go?"

I thought of the maps on the walls of my old bedroom, all the countries Bob and I had argued over, the places my mother and I had dreamed of visiting. I still wanted to travel—but call someplace else home?

Pat took my hand. "If you keep waiting for someone to tell you what's right and what's wrong, your whole life is going to skip by. If you want to stay in that big house and be a patriarch, just do it. You're a good guy, George. You're a family man."

"He would have liked that."

"You're a team player." Pat shook her head. "He had the whole thing, that whole myth built."

I considered telling her the truth about the Parthenon. But maybe she wouldn't care; maybe she already knew.

I said, "I'm the one who wanted to believe the story."

Donna and I were both awake when Gary came in. It was just before eleven. The light in the hall went out; I heard the sounds of a hushed argument. It went on for a long time, but I couldn't make out the words.

* * *

We took them out to a pancake house for breakfast. They thanked us, and I told Gary it was almost worth it just to see him fully dressed. He laughed and said it was a special occasion. I would have hit me.

When we got back to the house he helped us put the bags in our car; then I had a minute alone with Pat.

"See," she said. "He's not so bad."

I asked her about the argument in the night. She looked puzzled at first, then laughed.

"George, that wasn't an argument." She leaned close. "We were fooling around."

I couldn't look her in the eye.

She laughed again. "Sherlock strikes out."

Gary reached through the car window to shake hands before we left. "Good meeting you, Bambino. Now I'll know who she's talking about when she reads your letters to me."

We thanked them again and said good-bye. As we pulled away I glanced into the rearview mirror and saw them standing side by side, looking for all the world like a happy couple.

We pulled up to the first light.

"Navigator," I said, "prepare your maps."

Donna opened the glove compartment. "Maps prepared." She called out the first route number as we pulled away from the intersection.

Twenty-five

The yard looked like an open field.

We had been gone just less than a week, but there had been rain. When we walked to the door Friday night I felt the grass up around my ankles. Saturday morning I looked out the bedroom window and saw dandelions in clusters, yellow freckles scattered across the face of the lawn.

I waited until that evening to cut it, when the temperature dropped to the low eighties. As I watched the gold stream of gasoline pouring through the funnel, I thought of how many times I had done this, how many more times I'd do it in my life. I set down the can, went back inside the shed, and rolled out the riding lawn mower.

Ed and Evelyn had gone first class: the mower they bought had three speeds, crank start, a hitch for a fertilizer spreader, and a grass-collecting bag that rode along on wheels, like a motorcycle sidecar. The day after they gave it to us I made a test run so I could tell them it worked, but since then the lawn mower had been sitting in the toolshed, clean and white and expensive.

I pushed it out onto the driveway, leaned the seat back, and cranked the engine. I had been trying to follow my father's example too exactly. There had never been a rule about cutting the lawn with a push mower. If someone had given him a riding one, he probably would have used it. He wasn't the kind to let good tools go to waste.

I switched the starter; the engine sputtered and died. I was about to crank it again when I looked back near Joe's house and saw Elvis watching me.

Joe was still at Press and Cindy's. Elvis sniffed around the unoccupied doghouse, then turned back to me. She was wearing a reddish-orange jacket.

"How'd you get loose?"

She wagged her stump of a tail as I walked over, and she didn't seem to mind when I picked her up. She licked my arm.

"Good dog," I said. "You're a good dog."

I carried her across the driveway and set her down on the other side of the fence.

I cranked the lawn mower again and switched the starter; the engine sputtered, coughed, and died. I didn't feel like changing the oil, so I unscrewed the lid on the gas tank, hoping it was low. I looked down and saw Elvis staring up at me.

"Hey there, Houdini."

She wagged.

This time I just walked to the fence. She ran to catch up and took me straight to the hole.

I got some heavy wire out of the toolshed and closed off the space she had made between part of the fence and one of the posts. I was twisting the ends when their screen door opened.

Dusty stepped onto the porch looking like I had never seen her before. She stood tall on high heels and wore a pink-and-white-striped dress belted at the waist. She was wearing lipstick, and she had used blush on her cheeks. She looked angry.

"What are you doing?"

"There was a hole in your fence," I said. "Your dog got out."

"It's not my dog." She crossed her arms.

"I just closed it up." And when she didn't answer: "I can untie it if you want."

She sat on the top step and hugged her knees to her chest. I had seen her sit that way before, but now it looked awkward, dressed up the way she was. Elvis climbed the steps to sit beside her. Dusty pushed her down.

"I was letting her run away," she said.

"What did she do?"

"Somebody stole a hundred dollars out of my room."

I looked at Elvis. "She doesn't need clothes. What would she spend it on?"

Dusty didn't smile.

"Do you know who did it?" I rested my arms against the fence and leaned forward.

"Somebody who lives here. One of those bitches."

I wondered what this meant. I had always assumed they were friendly with each other.

"There isn't a person in the world I can trust," she said. "Not one. I figure, you have to tolerate people. You have to learn to live with them. And then they pull this shit."

"How do you know it was one of them?"

She wasn't listening. She looked down at the pond, thinking.

"This isn't working out," she said. "This whole deal is not working out."

Elvis climbed back up the stairs. Dusty didn't push her away.

"You look beautiful," I said.

She looked at me.

"Your dress. Everything. You look great."

She started to smile, looked away, and laughed.

"You crack me up." She imitated me. " 'You look beautiful.' " She laughed again.

I could feel my face flush. "I'm sorry I said it. I take it back."

" 'You look great,' " she mimicked.

"It's true." And it was, to an extent. She looked good in a dressed-up way. But it didn't look natural for her.

She put her hand on the back of Elvis's neck and rubbed her fur. "I got clowns all around me," she told the dog.

"Forget it," I said. "You look like a whore."

Dusty gripped Elvis tight. The dog squealed, but Dusty didn't let go.

"I'm sorry." I couldn't look at her. It was a cheap insult. "I'm sorry."

I walked away.

She said, "I *can* trust somebody."

I turned.

"I should have more faith in people."

"We're all different," I said, still trying to apologize. "There are no perfect friends."

"I need you," Dusty said. "To help me get rid of this dog." Elvis whimpered softly beside her.

"I thought you said it wasn't yours."

She ran her hand over the orange jacket, but when Elvis moved to jump down, Dusty grabbed her by the neck again.

"Are you going to help me?"

"How?"

She let go of Elvis's neck. "Open that hole in the fence."

I didn't care so much about what Kristin and Eve would think; I was worried about the dog.

"What are you going to do if she doesn't go? What if she hangs around?"

"I tried to get her to eat one of those leaves," Dusty said, pointing at the oleander. "It must've smelled weird. I could crush it up in her food or something."

I knelt on the gravel of the driveway and unwound the ends of the wire. Elvis watched from the other side, licking my fingers until Dusty told her to stop. When I was finished, I put the wire in my pocket.

Dusty walked over and nudged Elvis with her foot.

"Go," she said. "Scram."

Elvis sniffed the fence.

"She doesn't want to leave," I said.

Dusty pushed with her white high heel. "Take off."

Elvis hunched down and squirmed through the hole. She stood in the driveway and shook, then trotted over to Joe's house.

"Where's your dog?" Dusty said.

"With a friend."

Elvis sniffed around Joe's house, squatted, and marked a spot.

"She's leaving messages," I said. "He's going to go crazy when he gets back."

On the side of Joe's house I had built an overhang to protect his water and food bowls. Elvis snuffled the bowls; satisfied they were empty, she walked over to the tulip poplar, where Joe had left his scent, and sniffed all around the trunk.

"Hit her," Dusty said.

"What?"

"Hit her with a rock."

I looked at Dusty. She was watching Elvis.

"She'll leave on her own," I said. "Wait a minute."

Elvis sniffed some weeds, then lay down on the ground.

"She's not going," Dusty said. "Throw something."

"I can't do that."

Dusty reached over the fence and put a firm hand on my arm. "I would do it for you," she said, leaning closer. She was wearing perfume, something with too much alcohol. "You know what I would do for you."

The rock skipped a foot to Elvis's right. She glanced at the spot where it hit but didn't move.

"Try again."

The second one kicked dirt into Elvis's face. She stood up. She sneezed, then scratched behind her ear. She lay back down.

"I thought you were a hot baseball player. I thought you were Babe Ruth."

The third rock hit Elvis in the ribs. She yelped, spun in confusion, and ran through the hedges that separated our house from the Pattersons'.

"I owe you," Dusty said.

Late Monday afternoon Mr. Wheatley's bus came around the corner. He honked twice and stopped in front of the house.

I pulled my briefcase from the back seat, shut the door, and waved. I hadn't talked to any of our neighbors since we had gotten back, and I didn't want to talk to Mr. Wheatley, but he motioned for me to come over.

He was wearing a plaid short-sleeved shirt and old brown

pants stretched tight across the pockets, the cuffs high above white socks. His hand, resting on the gearshift, was thick and callused.

He asked me about our trip. I covered the highlights, but I could tell he was waiting to get to something else. Finally he said, "Has anybody told you the news?"

"What news?"

He looked at me secretively and said so softly that I could barely hear him over the bus's old, noisy engine, "About the letter committee."

I shook my head.

"Come on up."

I looked around, then stepped into the school bus, still wearing my suit, carrying my briefcase.

There were gum wrappers on the floor of the narrow aisle between the old green seats. I sat in the first row, across from Mr. Wheatley. A sign above the windshield said, NO STANDING OR RIDING BEYOND WHITE LINE WHILE BUS IS IN MOTION. Another said, KEEP HEAD AND ARMS INSIDE AT ALL TIMES.

"This is hot off the press," he said. "Emily talked to Ruth Middleman yesterday."

Mrs. Middleman lived down at the corner of Hobbs Quarry and Liberty, five houses past Bellshaw's.

Mr. Wheatley took off his Orioles cap and wiped his hand over his thin white hair. "Ruth told Emily she's been seeing cars down at the grocery-store parking lot late at night. Ruth hasn't been sleeping well lately—her back's still giving her trouble, and those pills she takes just make her dizzy. She says the cars start coming in around eleven o'clock. One at a time, off and on, all night. She says there's one or two people in each car, and they all walk this direction. Men, she says."

"We knew that. That all came out at the meeting." It was almost sad that it was so important to them.

"That's not the news," he said. "I guess Ruth told Dolly Bing, and Dolly told Elizabeth Lippert, and she told Virginia. So last night the five of them and Virginia's husband sat down and started to write a letter to L.V."

"Started to?"

"You know women. They were arguing about the dot over every i."

"What's the purpose of the letter?"

"To get those people out of there. They didn't give me the specifics. Get him to call the FBI. Get somebody to drop a bomb on the house and make the neighborhood safe for democracy."

I was surprised to hear him joke about it. "Why didn't you volunteer?"

"You and me and the six of them are the only ones who have heard about it." He nodded in the direction of Mrs. Webb's. "This hasn't even made it over to the back-porch crowd. I thought you and Donna should know, but I don't see any point in spreading it around."

He stopped and I looked up. There was something in his tone, and a look on his face, that I hadn't seen or heard before.

"Emily is all excited," he said. "You'd think Cooper had landed on the moon. You'd think the pope had come back to life."

"I guess it is a big deal," I said. "They're breaking the law. Grace all but admitted it."

"I know that." Mr. Wheatley slid the Orioles cap down onto his head, looking disappointed with me. "That's what Emily said."

He looked through the big windshield, then rested his arm against the steering wheel. The bus throbbed gently to the rhythm of the engine. "What upsets me," he said, "is what's happening to those girls. When I heard about it, all I could think about was our Linda."

I must have looked puzzled. Linda was married, training to be a nurse.

"About what could have happened if maybe she met the wrong people."

"I don't think you have to worry about that."

"Wait until you have a daughter. You'll realize you haven't yet worried a minute in your whole life."

He was right. I didn't know what I was talking about.

"Some people—and my wife is one of them—think that

there are good people in this world and there are bad people. You're brought up right or you're brought up wrong."

"Right," I said, willing enough to agree.

"The way I see it, just about anything can happen to anybody. Take yourself. You're raised well, finest parents you could hope for. But they both have to leave us while they're young, for reasons only He knows, and all eight of you are on your own. Anything could have happened. Who are we to say?"

I didn't have an answer.

"You figure you go off on your own, you could get into trouble. So you stayed home."

"Something like that," I said.

"But then what happens?"

I waited.

"Trouble comes to you. Moves in right next door."

I started to answer, but he cut me off.

"Now, I'm not saying anything," he said. "Don't take this wrong. I'm just saying, I know what it would have felt like if they had moved in next to *me* twenty years ago."

"Twenty?"

"Don't rub it in. One morning you'll start leaving your hair on the pillow too." He wiped his forehead. "Say, thirty years. Then it might have bothered me. Or back when I was your age."

I began to feel Mr. Wheatley was trying to tell me something he thought was important, something he wouldn't have said in front of his wife and the others on Mrs. Webb's back porch. I didn't know why he'd chosen me as his confidant.

"Bothered you how?"

"I think you know. Three young girls next door, waiting for business. Rita Hayworth they ain't, but there they are just the same. I was brought up good, and you were too, but if things were one inch different—if we were somebody else—"

"—somebody *else*," I said.

"Somebody without our character," Mr. Wheatley continued, "and our good fortune. That person could get himself into some trouble. Good upbringing and everything. Just an ordinary young man, has a few oats left to sow, sees a feed lot right across the driveway. Dangerous situation."

"Could be," I said.

"And who knows? Maybe *they* were brought up good. Maybe they were fine young girls. Wore white gloves to Mass, made A's in school."

I tried to picture Dusty in church. It strained the imagination.

"But their mother dies," he said. "An accident. Little girl on her own. Has some bad luck, runs into some bad influences." He looked over at Bellshaw's house. "A few bad breaks and that could be my daughter in there. A few bad breaks thirty-five years ago, that could be me pulling up in the parking lot at night."

"I'm not sure it's all that tragic." Or that romantic, I thought.

Mr. Wheatley looked at me as if he wasn't sure I was worth talking to.

I didn't know Linda Wheatley very well—she had been involved in things like theater in school, I had been playing baseball—so I thought about Pat, and how she left home when she finished high school. I thought about what had happened to her since then. I could imagine it.

He said, "That's what upsets me. I don't blame them. I blame whatever put them there. I don't know what to do about it, either."

"You said they're writing to Mr. Bellshaw."

"And what's he going to do?" He rubbed his fingers along the brim of his cap.

"Evict them. Get them out of the neighborhood."

"Something any one of those women could do if they had the nerve." Mr. Wheatley looked stern. "What gets me is, the way some of them talk, you'd think this was the Garden of Eden before apples."

"What do you mean?"

"Elizabeth Lippert," he said. "We used to call her Bumping Betty."

"And that meant . . ."

"Come on, George. You're a married man."

I still didn't get it.

"Used to be a song," he said. " 'The cats do the bumping all night long.' And Clarence Webb. I guess you don't remember him, but he got around in his time."

"After he married Mrs. Webb?"

"Nobody thought they'd stay together. They did it for Kyle, and then Clarence had his accident."

"And Mrs. Webb?"

"A good woman. But Dave Duncan—him and her were high-school sweethearts. There he is, over on her porch every day, making cow eyes like they were still sitting in class."

"And here I thought it was the apple pie."

"He'd eat mud pie if she fed it to him. Nearly fifty years now he's been hanging on her every word."

"Your wife," I said. "That's why she gets so angry with Mr. Duncan."

"Don't get the wrong idea. I'm not dusting off this prehistoric gossip just to stick up my nose. Like the Book says, Let whoever doesn't have any sins throw rocks. But when I see these people on their soapbox, I have to wonder what they would do if they could stand back and see themselves."

"So you don't think they should be writing to Mr. Bellshaw?"

"That's just it," he said. "I don't have a better idea. But having meetings and making speeches and getting six people to write a letter, that's just avoiding the issue. They can't see the woods for the trees."

We both listened to the engine.

I could remember sitting in Mr. Wheatley's bus nine years earlier, not in a suit but in a clean shirt and pants my mother had laid out for me, not with a briefcase between my feet but with a lunchbox and a bookbag. It hadn't been that long ago.

"I rode this bus to school," I said, looking down the aisle.

Mr. Wheatley nodded. "She's been rebuilt four times, each time a little worse than the one before. The day I retire I'm going to send her off a cliff."

"Must be hard work, driving this thing."

"Hell no," he said. "That's the beauty of it. I just sit here, look at what's going on, watch the kids grow up. Any moron could do it. Some days you look out and you see it's raining, snowing, you'd rather not drive, some mornings you want to stay in bed, but that's with any job. I walk out to the driveway and I'm at work. Nobody looks over my shoulder, nobody tells me how I'm doing. Every Christmas, parents give me enough fruitcakes to sink a ship.

"You know, they asked me to be a supervisor for the county, and I could have driven those big charter buses for the commercial lines. But they don't give you a raise because your job gets easier."

"I guess not."

"I have time to do just about everything I want to. Maybe I could have had big money in the bank, an expensive suit, and a foot-long cigar. But I'd rather be right here, talking to you." He glanced at his watch. "Except maybe I would have left five minutes ago. I'm late for dinner."

"I better go too." I moved to the bottom step. I owed him an apology, but there was no way to explain it.

"Didn't mean to talk your ear off," he said. "I just wanted to fill you in."

I stepped down, then he waved and shifted the bus into first gear.

Chapter Twenty-six

That night I finally sat on the floor of Pat's old bedroom upstairs and opened the box of our father's things that Mark had given me. Donna was practicing down in the living room; I recognized one of the Bach suites.

I had been torn about sifting through the last of my father's possessions. I wasn't sure what I would be looking for, and I was afraid to find clues that would contradict everything I had believed. I had started to think of the box as some sort of message, a final letter from my father; but he was no letter writer, and when I opened the flaps all I saw was what Mark had seen, if he even bothered to look: a box filled with old books and papers. I was almost relieved. It all looked meaningless, harmless.

Sitting on top was a weathered French-English dictionary. A yellowed paperback, the spine was gouged, and the covers came loose as I picked it up. I barely spread the pages as I looked through it, but crumbs of paper still broke off and dropped to the floor. I hoped to find notes, something in my father's handwriting; nothing was there.

Setting the dictionary on the floor, I brought out a thick pad of paper and fumbled with the edges before I realized that it was folded: a map. Opening it carefully, trying to keep the worn creases from ripping, I saw that it was a sea chart of some sort, showing shipping lanes and currents. There were no marks on it, no signs that my father had used it recently, or ever. It collapsed back into its folds softly, automatically. Why had he kept these things?

Then I found the one book I had expected. Wedged against the side of the box, standing on end, was his copy of the *Odyssey*. Any print that had been on the maroon cover had been worn off; it was dark and plain. Two of the signatures had come loose and been tucked back in place. I could picture my father holding this as he read to us, or propping it open as he sat in his armchair. Once it had been our father's book. Now it was an object, more real to me in memory.

Next were two more books, both bound in dark blue, yellowed and musty: *Advanced Carpentry* and *Wiring in the Home*. They were unremarkable, the sort of books he had kept in his workroom in the basement. Here, though, inside the covers, were figures written in his hand: page numbers. One led to a diagram of various types of molding, the other led to a long, eye-straining footnote about replacing fuse boxes. The title pages said that both books were published by the Coleman Press, in New Jersey, as part of a series called *For the Professional Builder*, first printed in 1936.

My father only rarely referred to books or manuals when he worked; his knowledge came from experience. He showed us how to mix cement and to sand off old paint, how to use a plane and a coping saw, always precise, never impatient with our ignorance. He did what he could to make us self-sufficient. He was proud that Waite had earned honors as an engineer in the Navy, and when he told strangers about Mark he referred to him not as a lawyer but as the son who had built his own house. If he had wanted to reward the one of us who had shown the most talent with tools, the best mind for design and construction, he would have given our family house to Bob. Instead, probably because he knew that Bob would, in fact, go to Kansas and build the ranch house he had always talked about, he offered it to Pat. She declined, saying that she didn't need it, knowing that he really wanted to give it to Donna and me as a wedding present.

When he died, he divided what was left among the others: his and our mother's combined savings, which weren't much; a variety of heirlooms and odd items that had accumulated personal value over the years; and the lot where Mark and Lisa had built their summer cabin, which our mother had inherited from an aunt. The land was left to Tony and Earle, but Mark paid them more than the market value and put the money into a trust fund for them. Lou had been left out—possibly because he had only come to my wedding because he happened to be in New York on business and, while he played in the softball game, he hadn't spoken to our father—but he claimed he didn't care.

I couldn't complain. I had the most valuable property our parents had owned. But in the will my father left Donna and me his deepest love and affection—no school ring, no locket of my mother's, nothing. I wanted to think that was why Mark had given me this box.

Beneath the books were wooden frames, glass-side-down, with pieces of shirt cardboard sandwiched between them. The first frame looked almost new, unlike anything else in the box: turning it over, I saw the photograph of all of us, smiling but embarrassed, posed on the field where we had played the softball game last summer, two days before our wedding, less than two months before Father died. I looked for Lou, expecting him to be sullen, but he had his arm around Waite's shoulders, grinning; he had been our best hitter. Waite was half-turned away from the camera, pretending to load up a spitball even though we were playing slow-pitch softball—the photographer from the newspaper didn't know any better. He had wanted Pat to put her hair in a ponytail and stick it through the back of the cap so that you couldn't tell she was a girl, but she wouldn't do it. He had me holding the bat like a lefty, trying to look like a slugger.

The caption said: "Members of the Willus family, of Hobbs Quarry Road in Snyder's Mill, are shown playing softball at a family reunion in Woodmoor on Friday. They might not look like world champions, but the roster is formidable: all eight children are named after starting players on the 1927 New York Yankees." After that came our names, our ages, and the names of the original players.

There had been others at the picnic: Donna and her bridesmaids, Ed and Evelyn, aunts and uncles and cousins, friends from school. Our father withdrew from crowds even when he was healthy, but that day he tapped reserves of energy we had thought long since depleted. Even so, he wasn't strong enough to bat, and he wouldn't umpire, so we made him lob out the first ball, and he was full-time first-base coach. He sat on a lawn chair a few feet from the hard rubber base and called encouragement to both sides, but we all knew which team was supposed to win. For the first inning we trotted out to our namesakes' positions, feeling self-conscious and even a little foolish, with Donna and Lisa rounding out our side. After giving up three runs, we let the photographer interrupt the game long enough to take the picture that got into the newspaper. Our father bristled at the "they might not look like world champions" line in the caption, and he was unhappy that they hadn't taken his suggestion and referred to the 1927 Yankees as the greatest baseball team of all time, but he was ecstatic. Later, even Tony and Earle, who hadn't wanted to play, said they were happy we had done it. Once.

I set the photograph next to the pile of books.

The next frame was older, and the photo, in sepia, was unfamiliar. A small woman with a thin smile and tight white hair sat in a rocking chair, her hands in her lap. You could tell from her eagerness that she was the one who had arranged for the picture to be taken. She looked prematurely old, as if she might have been ill for a long time in the past, but everything about her stood as evidence that she had done hard work. Her face had the leathery look of American Indians in history books, someone used to long days outdoors. Sitting on the porch steps, just below and beside her, a lean man who looked almost too young to be her husband wore a thin-brimmed hat with a dark band, a clean white shirt, dress pants, and suspenders. The picture was clearly posed—they were both looking at the camera, holding their breath—but the man hadn't been able or willing to draw up a smile. His chin was strong and angular, an anchor that pulled his lips tight as he stared at the camera. His left leg was drawn up behind the other, foot against the step, ready to push off if the photographer didn't hurry and get the job done.

Holding the frame firmly, I slid the photo, with white

edges that hadn't been exposed to light, onto my lap. On the back, in my father's handwriting, were the words "Mom and Dad at the farm. 1911."

My grandmother died when I was young. She came to see us once, before we moved, but I was less than a year old, and all I know is that the woman my mother had always considered unhappy and sharp-tongued had turned into kindness itself. She visited without her husband, my mother told me, and that seemed to make a difference; that and the fact that she was with her youngest of four sons and youngest of eleven grandchildren.

My grandfather was actually just older than his wife. He worked for the Baltimore and Ohio Railroad, and when he became a widower he headed west by train. Because of his work he had never been home for long stretches, and he had shown a penchant for drifting away, for days or weeks, so no one was surprised when he left for good. It had been as if he had reappeared from the dead when, on the morning of my seventh birthday, he came to visit.

I don't remember much about it except for what I guessed or was told, later, by my mother. Our grandfather hadn't known it was my birthday, of course. He didn't even know which grandson I was, when he came walking across the driveway. He stopped at the flagstone steps leading up to the front door, where I was banging at caps with a rock, said hello, shook my hand, and sat down. I didn't know Homer well enough then to know why (*The gods do disguise themselves as strangers from abroad, and wander round our towns in every kind of shape to see whether people are behaving themselves or getting out of hand*), but I was scared. He was tall and sinewy, and even in his seventies he looked like a man ready for a fight. Looks aside, he acted friendly. He asked me my name and how old I was, and when I said it was my birthday he said he wished he had brought a present. All he carried was a canvas bag. When he asked if my father was home I ran inside to find him, glad to get away.

Formal introductions were awkward, conducted in the front yard. When they were over our father invited the old man inside. We stayed out. At first none of us believed the man was really our grandfather; we thought he was a vagrant our father had taken pity on. Later, our mother told us he listened carefully to everything our father said, didn't talk about himself, and ate with his hands. But we could tell she thought more of him than we did, and that meant a lot. Unlike us, she had reason to dislike him. He hadn't come to the wedding. He could have—he was home—but he was unhappy with our father at the time. While Mom claimed she didn't hold a grudge against her father-in-law, our father was the only one disappointed when he left before dinner. The old man waved once as if to say: That's all I needed to know, sorry to bother you—then turned and walked southwest, across the driveway, toward Liberty Road.

I slid the photo back into the frame and reached into the box. Next was a baby picture. It seemed instantly familiar, but I couldn't tell which one of us it was. Nothing was written on the back. I imagined that I saw Lou's features, then Pat's. I looked again and saw myself.

Then there was one of my parents' wedding pictures, one I had seen before. They were standing outside the church, arm in arm. My father looked uncomfortable in a tuxedo. At the same time, the way he held my mother's arm said that if marrying her meant standing around in a tux all day, that was no trouble. Walk on a bed of nails? Bring them out. He looked consumed by happiness: happiness and pride. My mother was holding her bouquet a little too high, so it looked as if she were balancing her chin on it. Her mouth was spread in a wide smile, lips close together—she had always been self-conscious about her uneven front teeth. The two of them looked wide-eyed and young, nervous and unsure of themselves, nothing like I remembered them.

My left leg was asleep. I stretched it out and waited.

The box was half-empty. There were some faded newspaper clippings, none of which had any clear significance, and a postcard from Miami from Charlie, one of my father's brothers. After reading all of the articles, trying to puzzle out their importance, I put them on top of the stack of books. Then, reaching to the bottom, I brought out a small pile of thick paper folders.

The folders were off-white cardboard mats like the ones photographers use to display high-school graduation pictures. I opened the top one, and there, on the right-hand side, was a black-and-white autographed photo of Tony Lazzeri, the New York Yankees second baseman. On the left, under a piece of tissue paper, was a note on crisp white stationery, addressed to my father, which said, "Many thanks for your kind letter. I don't get as many requests for photographs these days, and am particularly glad to oblige yours. Hope your boy enjoys it. Sincerely, Tony Lazzeri." The picture was signed, "To Tony—Best Wishes for Success."

I read the note again, looking from it to the photograph and back. There was no date, but it had to be after Lazzeri had retired, and after my brother had been born. Why hadn't my father given it to Tony? Why hadn't he shown it to us?

My first thought was that it had been meant as a surprise. Maybe the time had never been right; he couldn't have forgotten it. I imagined our father about to pull his prize from hiding when, by sheer coincidence, Tony said he was sick of hearing about baseball.

Then I thought of something worse: maybe he had gotten it for himself.

The possibility tried to take hold, then fell back. Our father didn't have secrets like that. And he didn't have idols, not the 1927 New York Yankees or anyone else. Baseball didn't infatuate him the mindless way Hollywood stars fascinated teenage girls.

But I thought back to the game he had arranged for us to play, to the very idea of naming his children after men who played a game for a living. If that wasn't infatuation, what was? Why had our father's interest in baseball always seemed reasonable to me? Maybe all our parents and grandparents are mysterious to us, if only because their lives began, took shape, before we knew them.

The next folder was Lou's. There was no note, but the photograph, which showed Gehrig finishing a home-run swing, was signed, "To Lou." It was enough to be holding a photograph of Gehrig, but to think that he had been communicating directly to one of us, even if it was just long enough to add two words to a stack of autographed pictures . . . The next was Waite Hoyt, the stocky right-handed pitcher; the inscription read, "To my namesake—Best Wishes." In a note to my father dated September 15, 1940, Hoyt had written, "I hope he grows up strong. Tell him that a good pitcher has to throw fastballs, curves, and strikes, not in that order."

I flipped through the others quickly: Mark Koenig, Earle Combs, Bob Meusel, Pat Collins. After putting them aside, I opened the last folder carefully and, looking to the right, saw something odd.

Kneeling in the on-deck circle, two enormous bats on his left shoulder, staring straight ahead—sizing up the opposing pitcher, one imagined—the Babe was wearing a Boston Braves uniform. I had expected the pinstripes of the Yankees, but he was in Boston's red piping, the suit he had worn as a gate attraction before finally bowing out. In the picture he was enormous, out of shape but still ready to play. I had seen dozens, maybe even hundreds of photographs of him. Every one of them made him look bigger than life, awe-inspiring if not entirely heroic, but I always remembered something else: that awkward trot around the bases on those tiny ankles, that sad smile. He was the first great home-run hitter, the beginning of a new kind of athlete, but I could never see a picture of him without feeling that he represented the end of something.

The note, sent from Boston and dated July 1945, was typed: "Always enjoy hearing from the old fans; esp. enjoyed yr. kind letter. Photo enclosed." It was signed, simply, "Babe," but on the photograph he had scrawled in childish handwriting, "To another G.H.—George Herman Ruth."

The paper folder was heavy in my hands. There we were, the eight of us. When my father had called Tony and Earle to dinner, was he thinking of two other people? When he read to Bob and me at night, was he imagining talking to Meusel and Ruth? How did he link us in his mind, his heroes and his sons? I imagined for a moment that we had been cheated, that he hadn't really cared for us at all, but nothing could have been further from the truth. But why didn't he give us those photographs? Did he think we would make fun of him?

Even when he had been ill, it had seemed due to no

weakness of his own. It was a natural tragedy, like a hurricane or a flood. Yet he probably *had* worried about our reaction to those photographs, about whether he had been too self-indulgent with those names. He had probably lain awake wondering if he had acted the way a good father should. And yes, of course, there must have been nights when other possibilities threatened to seduce him—nights when he heard rain beating on the roof, knew that the rest of us were sleeping, and wondered if there wasn't still some way to escape, not the need to make the right choices for himself, which was inescapable, but the need to make the right choices for the rest of us. He had lain in bed staring at that same ceiling, imagining maps—imagining, even as he rejected the idea, his father's life, the possibility of walking away.

In the year since my father died I had only thought of how little I really knew about him, how much I wished I had asked him. We lived together for more than twenty years and we were nearly strangers. There was no explanation in that box of papers.

But as I sat on the floor of a room in a house he built, I realized what my father had seen the night our mother died, the night he finished his story with a line we didn't want to believe, an ending we hated, and him for telling it: he had seen his team. The look in his eyes had turned to sorrow, but for a moment we had found the unity he had tried to give us. He could only have proof, bittersweet, when his wife died.

Some of us had done what he expected and hoped, some of us surprised him. We were, finally, different, and there were too many of us to stay close. But the night my mother died we endured together the suffering that none of us could have survived alone. And five years later we took the field for that softball game, together in joy as well as sorrow.

Our father had to have known, better than any of us, better than my mother, that there are times when each of us feels we are alone, far from anything familiar and reassuring. No matter how closely related we are, no matter how much blood we share, we stand apart, pinpoints spread across a map too big to see. There isn't much we can do to bridge the distance in between: sign our name on a photograph for a proud father, or raise our children in a neighborhood that feels like home. Our father offered us those names.

His story about the Parthenon wasn't the harmless lie Mark made it out to be; it was a useful one. Babe Ruth left New York for Boston, where as an old man he hit three home runs in one game, including the longest home run ever hit in Forbes Field, one of the longest of all time. But there was another ending, one that gets left out of boys' books: five final games without a hit; a knee injury coming from age and poor health; obesity and alcoholism; the exhibition circuit, with opposing pitchers instructed to groove the ball for an old man losing his sight; rejection as a coach and manager; the slow, painful loss to cancer. I don't believe our father was trying to be our hero. I think he wanted us to be his heroes. But he must have known that heroes are romantic ideals, and that, no matter how much we try, we're all something less than we'd like to be.

I reached into the box to pull out the only thing left—a scrapbook filled with baseball clippings. There was a photograph of Lou Gehrig crying at Yankee Stadium, an obituary, and the whole issue of *Sporting News* dedicated to Ruth when he died in 1948. There were articles about the Orioles' first year. I tried to read the yellowed clippings, but tears crowded the corners of my eyes, and soon they began a slow march along my nose. They paused there before dropping down onto the scrapbook. I brushed them away when I heard a creak from the floorboard at the top of the stairs.

"Hey, babe—you okay?"

Donna was standing in the doorway, holding her flute. "It sounded pretty quiet up here."

I couldn't talk. Instead I fumbled for the team photograph from the newspaper and held it up, trying to smile. She came over and took it from me.

"Now, there was a great day," she said.

I turned away. Donna knelt on one knee and looked at the framed pictures and the books; then she opened the top folder and saw Babe Ruth.

"My god," she said. "This is for you."

I half-turned. "My father was always trying to tell us—" I couldn't finish. "I love baseball."

No. I was no longer a child; it was time to put childish thoughts away.

"You," I said. "I love *you*."

Donna reached for my hand. "I know you do."

A few minutes later she went back downstairs. That's when I called the police.

Chapter Twenty-seven

I didn't tell Donna I called. For one thing, I didn't want her to congratulate me, or thank me, or anything like that. For another, I didn't know what would happen. Ed's police-detective friend didn't sound particularly interested over the phone, and when he asked for my number and said he'd be in touch, I had the feeling he wasn't writing it down. Part of me was still hoping it would all just go away.

A few days later Donna greeted me at the door after work. Her cheeks were pink, and she seemed especially glad to see me, but she didn't say anything. I didn't know how she found out, but I wished she wasn't so happy about it.

"How was your day?" I said.

"Fine." She had a wonderful, beautiful smile. "Yours?"

"Same old stuff. Press and Cindy want to have us over for dinner."

She just stood there looking at me. Finally I kissed her and walked into the kitchen, taking off my tie.

"So," I said. "You got a phone call, and . . ."

"Nope." That smile was amazing. It made me want to laugh.

"Someone stopped by?"

"No."

What else would he have done?

"Did we get any mail?"

"Maybe male, maybe female."

I hugged her against the refrigerator.

"We have a bingo," she said.

"You didn't say anything. You didn't even tell me you had an appointment."

"I didn't. Mom called me to see if I wanted to go out this morning, so I tried his office and they had a cancellation." She leaned against my shoulder. "You don't know how hard it was to give lessons all afternoon."

"So your mother knows."

Donna held me tight. "No," she said. "You're the first."

"But how? What about her?"

"I told her it was just a checkup."

If she had told her mother first, I would have been angry. Since she hadn't, I said, "You could have told her the truth."

Donna leaned away, then kissed me again. "No," she said. "This is ours."

We stood between the refrigerator and the table, holding each other.

"Do you want to tell them?"

"There's no rush."

I pulled back to look at her. "You don't want to give them a call?"

"Well—"

I pulled out a chair and sat beside her while she talked to Ed and Evelyn.

If there had been any uncertainty left, it fell away. This was what I wanted. That didn't change the feeling that we were taking the first long plunge of a wild ride, but we couldn't keep our hands in the air; we had to take control. I wished there was some way I could tell my parents.

Donna held out the receiver.

"Hey there." Ed's voice was loud and happy. "Congratulations, son-in-law. I guess you had something to do with it. Just remember, if you start to get worried, feeling left out or confused or something, you know who to call."

"All right," I said. "Thanks."

"Evelyn. Once was enough for me." He laughed his showroom laugh. "That's a joke."

There was a pause, and when Ed spoke again he didn't

sound quite the same. "Seriously, George. If there's anything I can do—anything, I don't care how goddamned silly it might sound, or how long it might take—you let me know." He stopped again. "Shit."

The next few moments were awkward. After I hung up I asked Donna, "Was your mom happy?"

"She knows three good stores for maternity clothes. And she's been looking at cradles in the catalogs." She smiled, taking it all in. "She said she knew this morning, just from the look on my face."

That should have been me, I thought. I should have known. But maybe reading her mind wasn't the most important thing.

"Call Press," she said.

"I'll tell him later."

"No. Call him."

I tried to feel nonchalant while I dialed.

Press answered. "How's it going, Dad?"

I looked at Donna. I looked at the phone. I felt like a psychic, or no, the opposite of a psychic—everybody could read my mind.

I said, "How'd you do that?"

"Cindy went to the vet today. We've got six coming."

"You mean Belle?"

"No, Cindy's having puppies. Joe's in big trouble."

"How about that."

"The vet ran his hand under her belly and said he could feel them in there, just waiting to pop out. Cindy's all excited. She's trying to explain it to the girls. This makes the four of us parents, or grandparents. We're going to have to get some champagne."

He finally slowed down, but the moment was gone. There seemed to be too much of a chance for some kind of confusion.

"That's great," I said, "because that's exactly what I was calling about." Donna was giving me a funny look from across the kitchen table. "I meant to ask you at work," I told Press, "but I forgot all about it." Donna mouthed the words, *Tell him.*

"Six puppies," I said, trying to find a way out of this

conversation, "and Joe and Belle, that's eight—we've almost got enough for a team."

"A team of what?" Press said.

"An all-dog baseball team. We could tour the country. I could stand at home and throw the tennis ball for, you know, the hits, and they'd be at their positions, all around the field—Donna and Cindy could sew them little uniforms, with pinstripes, and we— "

"You just keep thinking," Press said.

Donna had her hands over her ears.

"Look," I said, "can I call you back later? I just remembered something I have to do."

"Sure." He sounded puzzled. "I'll be here all night."

I hung up.

"Joe and I should go for a walk," I told Donna. "We're going to be fathers."

We went out to dinner to celebrate. Maybe it was the wine, or maybe I was getting old and soft, but whatever it was, I gave in to wallpaper. "Just the baby's room," I told her. "We'll see how it looks." Donna said she already had it picked out. She wanted to paint our bedroom pale blue, and she had a new color scheme for the bathroom planned, but there was something else I wanted to do first. When we got back to the house I took her to my old bedroom in the basement. Together we took down the maps.

Chapter Twenty-eight

"Mr. Willus?"

An official-looking man in a dark business suit stood outside the kitchen door.

I nodded, guilty.

The man leaned closer, peering in, and drew a billfold from his pocket as he spoke. I half-expected him to pull out one of Terry Gleason's old dirty pictures.

"I'm Detective Ramsgate, from the Baltimore County Police Department? We talked on the phone."

Clipped to the billfold was a badge. I had never seen a real policeman's badge; it looked like the ones hall safeties had worn in elementary school, only smaller.

"I'd like to speak with you and your wife."

Now that he was at the door, I wanted to send him away. I still hadn't told Donna, and this wasn't how I wanted her to find out. But I stepped back and let him in.

Donna was drying her hands on her apron. When she saw the detective she caught her breath.

He stood just inside the kitchen, as if he wanted to be sure he could make an escape. He was an older man with sagging cheeks, crow's-feet at his eyes. He almost looked worried. He wasn't the sort of policeman you picture when you imagine brave men keeping the streets safe at night.

"I'm sorry to interrupt your dinner, Mr. Willus, Mrs. Willus, but I'm here to ask your permission to use your house as an observation point. We're going to be watching the building across the driveway for a few days. You are not obligated to allow us to use your house, but we would certainly appreciate your cooperation." He spoke quickly, distractedly, as if he had memorized the words and was afraid he might forget something.

Donna concentrated on the detective for a quiet moment. "Walter?"

The detective glanced at his polished black shoes, then nervously smoothed back his hair. "Hi, Donna."

"I guess you've never met George." She turned to me. "This is Walter Ramsgate."

"We met at the door," I said.

He reached over to shake my hand, then remembered to put his billfold away. His hand was firm but clammy, as if he had been sitting next to an air conditioner.

Donna said, "Walter's an old friend of Dad's. They used to play golf together all the time. He used to come into our living room and toss me up in the air—remember?"

Detective Ramsgate looked over at me, trying to decide whether to allow himself a grin.

"Sure I do," he told her. "You were a cute little girl."

We all stood in the middle of the kitchen, staring at each other.

"Well," Donna said, "what a coincidence this is. After all these years."

Ramsgate looked at me. I stared back.

"Coincidence," I said.

"Certainly is," he said slowly. "It's a small world."

"Would you like anything?" Donna asked him. "Iced tea?"

He waved his hand. "Thanks, but no. I really shouldn't stay. My partner is waiting in the parking lot down the street."

"So," she said, turning to lower the heat on one of the burners. "You're here to watch our neighbors?"

Ramsgate checked with me, then answered. "We've been put on the alert by an observant citizen," he told her. "We're here to follow up on a tip. Started work yesterday, as a matter of fact."

Donna crossed over to the counter for a bowl of string beans. "It was Virginia Mead, wasn't it."

Ramsgate said, "I'm not at liberty—"

"Mrs. Middleman?"

He fingered a button on his suit coat. "Don't be alarmed. If there comes a time when you could be in personal danger, we will certainly give you complete protection."

I tried to picture him defending us from Grace.

"Will you be the only one here?" Donna dropped three handfuls of beans into a pot of boiling water.

"One other fellow," Ramsgate said. "My partner, Sam Raleigh."

"How long will it take?" I asked him.

"Two or three nights. Four at the most. From about nine until three—that's the inconvenient part."

"You and your partner are going to stay in our house until three in the morning?"

"Don't feel forced," he said, confused. "You're under no obligation."

We were all quiet.

"That's okay," I said. "It will be fine."

Ramsgate took a form out of his inside coat pocket and unfolded it. "If you'd just sign this—it says you allow us on the premises, you retain all of your rights, that sort of thing."

I signed.

"If you folks have any questions, just give me a call. Otherwise, we'll be here tomorrow night." He handed me a business card with his name and rank and phone number and a tiny policeman's badge up in the corner. "Donna, it's good seeing you again. George, good to meet you." He backed toward the stairs, keeping an eye on me all the way. "You all have a good dinner, you hear?"

When he left, I locked the door. I took the three steps up to the kitchen slowly, staring down at the toes of my shoes. When I had both feet on the yellow-and-green linoleum I looked up. Donna was watching.

"You?"

I nodded.

She hugged me.

"I love you," she said.

I didn't regret calling Ramsgate; not exactly. As long as those girls were next door, as long as Dusty was in that house, there was too much of a chance that I would keep doing things I didn't mean to do. I had held another woman in my arms. I had thrown rocks at a dog. Calling Ed's friend was a sign of defeat, but I didn't want to know what would happen the next time Dusty asked me to do her a favor.

"Don't love me for this," I told Donna. I hugged her in return and sat at the table. She watched me for a moment, concerned, then served dinner.

"You did the right thing," she said as she took off her apron and sat across from me.

I held up a forkful of ham-and-noodle casserole, watching the steam rise and join the column of steam above the string beans.

The neighbors wanted to fight away crime, and Mr. Wheatley worried about what was happening to those girls and the men involved with them. Ed worried about his daughter. But I couldn't help but wonder if all of us—Ed and Evelyn, the neighborhood, Donna and I—hadn't taken the whole thing too seriously. If Dusty and the others seemed more exotic and attractive in my mind's eye than they really were, they weren't nearly as evil as other people saw them.

Now there wouldn't be any scandal, and the neighborhood would be saved. Community Association meetings would return to ordinances about leaf burning and repainting the fire hydrants. Ramsgate and his partner would come and take the girls away. Sometimes it seems a shame, but life is rarely as dramatic as we think we'd like it to be.

"I'm glad," I told Donna. "I'm glad you think it was the right thing to do."

She picked up her fork, dipped it into her string beans, and raised them to her mouth. She pursed her lips and blew softly, breaking a soft dash in the cloud of steam.

Lying in bed that night, I thought about our trip, and what it had felt like coming back to the same streets, the same driveway, the house where I had always lived. I knew the sound of a car pulling onto the gravel, I knew where a corner of flagstone was missing from the second step by the front door, I knew the not-quite-straight crack in the plaster that ran from the stairwell in the living room to a point above the left side of the fireplace. By closing my eyes I could see the messages my brothers and Pat and I had scratched into the red brick of the chimney outside, and the deep valleys we had cut into the red wood pillar and the dark brown beam in the basement. Walking from the bedroom to the bathroom, I knew where to step on the old hardwood floors to make the least noise.

Before Donna and I left for our trip I had imagined what it might have been like coming home from that other vacation, the one that was cut short. My mother and father would have come outside, smiling. My brothers would have been working and playing and arguing. I would have gone down to my room in the basement and carefully charted a line representing the places I had been.

But that was all past, and it wasn't what I wanted now.

Chapter Twenty-nine

Eve sat on the front steps next door, her black hair pulled back in a long braid. She was concentrating on a sketchpad, occasionally looking up to check her subject.

I crossed the driveway one last time.

"Is Dusty here?"

Eve kept sketching.

"George—how's life treating you?" Grace's raspy voice came from behind the screen door. Smoking a cigarette, she propped the door open with one foot.

"Is Dusty here?"

"Should be back in a few minutes. She went out to pick up a few things."

I wanted to say something, but Grace wasn't who I had come to see. She looked across the street, then around the yard, then flicked the butt of her cigarette onto the grass before going inside.

I knew that if I left I wouldn't come back. I waited, following Eve's line of vision. In front of her were the lawn, a maple tree, the sidewalk, and the road. I looked down at her pad and saw crooked lines and shaded areas.

"What are you drawing?" It looked like a storm cloud over a yard sale.

"What it's like to be sitting here, drawing."

I looked at the pad again. "Which part is you?"

"Not a portrait," she said. "It's a visual representation of what it's like for me to sit here and draw."

"Ah."

"Don't act interested."

A pickup came around the corner, but it wasn't theirs. I tried again.

"How long have you known Grace?"

"Since the beginning of time." Eve erased a part of a line, then lightly brushed the paper clean with the back of her hand. "She's one of those people you remember as soon as you meet her."

"I know what you mean."

"That's not what I meant. She doesn't remind you of someone else. You don't have to have known her before, you just have to be prepared for her."

I looked back at Eve's drawing. Sideways, it looked like a St. Bernard in a plaid sport coat.

"Like somebody you see somewhere," she said, "and they do something for you, or say something—you don't have to know anything else, right? With some people, you find out everything that fast. Like Dusty."

"Dusty?" Eve was a talking tornado; I couldn't tell where she would touch down next.

"You know her before you ever meet her."

"She makes herself a part of you," I said.

"No. That would be unselfish." She stopped drawing. "Here's Cinderella."

Dusty turned the corner in the pickup. Eve stood and brushed off her shorts.

"See you later," I said.

She walked up the steps and into the house without answering.

I met Dusty at the garage. She scrambled down from the driver's seat holding a grocery bag. "You two have a nice chat?"

She was in worn jeans, her shirtsleeves rolled up past her elbows, like a ranch woman in a cigarette ad. Every time I saw her I was surprised: her face was a little thinner, her complexion was a shade lighter, she was bonier than I remembered.

Something radiated from her that made her seem to see more, to know more than she did.

"I guess we talked," I said. "I'm not sure. I don't think we see eye to eye."

"That's a good sign."

The garage was hot and dark, with a faint smell of gasoline in the air.

"So," I said. "Have you seen Elvis lately?"

Dusty raised her eyebrows. "Do you have news? Or did you come to collect?"

I stepped back. Kneeling by the pond, I had failed her. I had lied to myself, too. It did matter what I thought. And now there was a way I could make it up.

"I came to do you a favor."

"They haven't bought another dog," she said. "Don't tell me—you're going to save me from all this."

"I think you should take a vacation. Go to the ocean."

"Is that where you want to go?" She smiled, and for a moment I could imagine being on the beach with her.

"For a few days, at least."

She shifted the grocery bag and wiped sweat from her eyes. Her shirt clung to her chest.

"Don't ever gamble," she said. "You don't have the face for it."

"What about Larry?"

"What about him?"

"Is he ever around?"

"Downtown." She reached back and lifted her hair off her neck. "He doesn't get too close. He was pissed when we had to use his car."

I could feel the sweat prickling my nose.

"So you're one of them now," she said.

I looked at an oval oil stain, a black eye on the floor of the garage.

"One thing I've learned about the past," she said. "When you remember, you always try to change things. Make it better or worse."

I looked up.

"Don't do that," she said. "You were the one most worried

about this whole thing. More than anybody. It's been something to see."

"I've got to go."

"What's the rest?" she said. "What do you want from me?"

She came closer, moving the grocery bag to her hip, and I thought of what was missing.

"Tell Grace."

"Tell her . . ."

"That anything could happen, any day now."

"It's every fish for herself," she said. "None of them never done anything for me."

The other times I talked to her, she didn't have that hardness in her voice; or maybe she did and I hadn't noticed.

"You owe me," I said.

"She can't just take off. And if I tell her what's up, she won't leave anybody behind."

"I don't care what you have to say."

She leaned back against the truck. "Why not just get this beach thing out of your system? You need to get out of here, take some chances on your own."

"You don't understand," I told her. "Going away doesn't tell you anything. It's the coming back."

I left her alone in the garage, leaning against the pickup.

Donna's parents wanted to be there for the stakeout. Ed said he just wanted to see Walter Ramsgate, his old golfing buddy, and Evelyn said it really wasn't important, but they pulled into the driveway at seven, before we had even finished dinner. When we were through, ten minutes passed, then fifteen. Finally Ed said, "Time's wasting. Cut the cards, Grandma," and we put up the table.

"I wonder if they'll arrest them tonight," Evelyn said.

Ed opened the bidding with one spade. "You've been watching too much television. In real life this stuff is boring as all get-out."

I bid two clubs.

"They've got to arrest them sometime," Evelyn said. "Two hearts."

The knock came a little after nine. We all stood up.

"I'll get it," I said.

The detectives were at the door on the side opposite Bellshaw's house. Standing on the porch in dark suits, carrying thin briefcases, they looked about as inconspicuous as buffalo.

Ramsgate introduced his partner, Detective Raleigh, who looked young enough to be his son, thin and quiet and suspicious of everyone. Raleigh seemed impatient while Ed and Ramsgate talked golf.

"You ever figure out that slice?" Ed asked.

"The left hand," Ramsgate said. "I was leaving it open."

"What did I tell you?" Ed sat back. "I was playing last weekend and this fella I'm partners with tells me, 'You know your problem? You're standing too close to the ball—after you hit it.' It's hell when your partner starts talking like that."

"We should get together sometime," Ramsgate told him. "Maybe one weekend?"

"We've got a match Saturday, but maybe Sunday . . . you still over at BCC?"

Raleigh cut in. "I'll get started."

Ed stopped him and said, "You and I ever play golf?"

Raleigh looked him over, then shook his head. "No sir."

Donna led the detectives upstairs, her parents right behind them. I brought up the rear. In the hallway Donna stopped and said, "You'll want to use the window in here." She pushed open the door to the bathroom. "You can see the road." Ramsgate stuck his head inside, looked around, then turned off the light.

"And the side?"

Donna led the way to our bedroom. Raleigh crossed the room and pushed back the curtains. After looking down at the driveway and the porch next door, he dropped them back into place.

"Good," he said. "Very good."

Ramsgate didn't seem to know whether he was supposed to act the part of a detective or a friend of the family. "Thank you, Donna, George. We won't bother you a bit."

He was standing in the middle of our bedroom. Ed and

Evelyn had squeezed in beside him. Donna stood in the doorway. Suddenly the house seemed small.

"Well," Ramsgate said, "I'll go to the . . . facilities." He edged by us and headed down the hallway.

Raleigh didn't look up. He pushed the window open higher, parted the curtains, took out a notebook, and knelt down next to the laundry basket.

Evelyn's curiosity got the better of her. "Is there something we can do to help?"

Raleigh's gaze never left the driveway.

"Act natural," he said.

When we got back downstairs Evelyn turned off all the lights except for one next to the card table.

"Mom?" Donna asked when she finished. "You mind filling us in?"

"So we can see," she said. "If we hear somebody outside, I'll turn off this light and we can see who's out there."

"What about seeing who's in *here*?" Ed said. "I can't tell the ace of clubs from the ashtray."

Evelyn pulled the lamp closer. "Let's try it. If nothing happens, we'll put the lights back on."

Nothing happened, but the lights stayed off. It felt as if we were playing poker in an Edward G. Robinson movie—all we needed was cigar smoke clouded over our heads.

We usually talked while we played, but after a while, because of the anticipation and the darkness, we grew quiet. The room was silent except for shuffling, followed by the soft snap of single cards placed on the table. After two hands like that, Ed broke the spell.

"I knew I had seen that kid," he said. "Raleigh. He used to play baseball with Doc Moody's son."

"That was years ago," Evelyn said. "You wouldn't know him from Harry Truman."

"He was that kid—you remember—he was the one who couldn't hit." He turned to me. "This friend of ours, Doc Moody, his son was a big baseball player in high school."

"Leo," Donna said. "Leo Moody."

"Played for Bill Hurley," her father said. "Friend of mine

from Woodlawn. Doc and I used to go out to watch the games, and there was this one kid who had a thing for getting hit by the ball that you wouldn't believe—one game he got hit in the head three times. I never saw anything like it. He used to put his toes over the edge of the batter's box and crouch down with his head over the plate, awkward as hell. People would pass out watching him."

"This was Raleigh?"

"Guys on his own team would yell, 'Use your head!' and they meant it. I'd be surprised if the boy isn't brain-damaged."

"Edward."

"I'm serious—the kid was beaned twenty, thirty times just that one summer."

"Are you sure it's him?" Donna asked.

"I'll bet you a hundred bucks. You can probably still see the seams on his skull."

Just then we heard footsteps crunch gravel; Evelyn dropped her cards and smothered the light.

"Battle stations," Ed said, not leaving his chair.

Evelyn shushed him and made her way to the window at the bottom of the stairs.

"What the heck." Ed stood up to join her and caught his toe on the table leg. "God *damn*," he said, and Evelyn shot him a look we could see in the dark.

The footsteps grew closer. Straining to listen, I heard the squeal of the gate next door. The footsteps disappeared as the night visitor crossed the grass, but we heard him take the wooden steps up to their porch, and then three quick knocks.

Donna's parents' heads were silhouetted against the screen.

"A code," Evelyn whispered.

"What code?" Ed said. "He wants them to open the door."

A moment later the screen door creaked open and snapped shut.

We waited.

There was nothing else to hear.

Ed stood and called upstairs, "You get him?"

A muffled sound came from overhead. Heavy footsteps crossed the floor directly above us. Raleigh spoke from out of sight, at the top of the staircase. "We would appreciate it if you could speak at a conversational volume," he said. "We are attempting to be discreet." And then: "We saw a male Caucasian, probably in his late twenties or early thirties, enter the house currently under surveillance." His heavy black shoes crossed over our heads as he walked back to the bedroom.

"What did I tell you?" Ed said, groping his way to the card table. "The kid's brain-damaged. He thinks *they're* trying to be discreet? We're the ones playing bridge with the goddamned lights out. Jesus H. Christ in a coal mine."

"Watch your language," Evelyn said.

"I would if I could see it."

Evelyn switched on the lamp. After the next deal, Donna won a hearts bid; I excused myself.

Upstairs, I knocked softly on the bathroom door, then reached in and turned on the light.

Ramsgate spun around on the toilet seat. He had a pair of binoculars he'd let drop to his neck so he could shield his eyes.

"We have to keep them off," he said. "They might get suspicious."

I thought it might be more suspicious if Grace noticed there was an extra car in our driveway and only one dim light on in the whole house, but I didn't say anything. I switched off the bathroom light and Ramsgate picked up his notepad. I asked him how he could see what he was doing.

He held up his pen. "It's got a little bulb on the end. See?" He pushed a switch and a small tunnel of light cut through the darkness before catching one of the buttons on my shirt. He turned it off and put the pen in his pocket. A car passed outside; he parted the curtains and raised the binoculars to his eyes. A breeze came through the window.

"Excuse me," I said.

"Yes?"

"If it's all right, I'd like to use the toilet."

He repeated it softly, as if it were a clue that had been eluding him. "The toilet," he said. "Of course." After a moment he let the binoculars drop to his neck and made a note on his pad. I reached for the light switch.

"No," he said, standing. "Keep a lookout while you're in here. If you see anything, I'll be right in the hall."

My stay in the bathroom was uneventful. Inside, I could dimly make out Ramsgate's jacket draped over the shower rod. Outside, the street and sidewalks were bright, gleaming with reflected moonlight. I watched, not sure what I was looking for: nervous teenagers? Unfaithful husbands? Men so ugly or mean-spirited that there wasn't a woman in the world they could charm?

No one was out there. I buckled my belt in the dark, then opened the door.

"You see anybody?" he asked.

"Mr. Bubbles," I said. "On the edge of the tub. And he's got that silly grin on his face."

"Who?" Ramsgate said. Then: "Oh. A joke."

"I hate to say it," Evelyn said, enjoying every syllable, "but I told you so." We picked up our cards. "It was only a matter of time. You should have never had anything to do with them, from the very start."

"We haven't had anything 'to do' with them," Donna said.

"You've lived next door, haven't you?"

"That's right," Ed said, fanning his cards. "This line about staking out their place is probably a load of crap—they think you're in cahoots."

Things calmed down for a while. Donna and I concentrated on the game, playing aggressively, and won the next rubber. Evelyn wasn't herself: she didn't answer Ed's bids, and once she even played out of turn.

Ed cut the deck. "What's wrong with you, partner? You playing a different game?"

"I can't understand why it's so quiet," she said. "You said there are three girls, and we've only seen one person go in. Is it usually this quiet?"

Maybe we had been playing too long. I couldn't stop myself. "Wednesdays are their busy nights," I told her. "Double coupons."

Ed cracked a wide smile. "Fridays are two for one."

Donna was getting tired too. "That's the problem," she told her mother. "Tonight must be ladies' night."

Evelyn glared at all of us. "I don't know how you can think this is funny."

"You want to see somebody over there?" Ed said. "I'll go if you don't start trumping George's diamonds."

It wasn't long before Evelyn got what she wanted. We took a break, and Donna went upstairs while I refilled drinks. A car pulled into the driveway.

I watched from beside the sink. An old Plymouth rattled to a halt by the garage and two men got out. They talked softly, joking as they walked to the gate. Their words were carried away by the breeze. They stopped for a moment, finishing their conversation, then took the steps up to the porch door.

"They were old men," Evelyn was telling Ed as I came back to the living room. "They were your age."

"Must be a senior citizens' cathouse," he said. "Maybe it's a public service."

Donna sat quietly, arranged her cards, then put them down. She said, "When you went upstairs, did he ask you to 'keep a lookout'? With the lights off?"

I nodded.

"When that car pulled up, I thought he was going to jump in there with me. I think I ruined his night."

Ed shook his head. "They're both foul balls. I always said Walter had a screw loose."

"You never said anything of the kind," Evelyn told him. "I wonder if they're going to raid it now."

"Not until we finish this rubber. Get your ducks in line."

She tried to concentrate, but Donna and I won anyway. It was our lucky night. We played until after eleven, and by then we were all yawning. After tallying the final points, Ed sat back, stretched, and beat a short drumroll on his stomach. "Ready to call it a night?"

"I guess so," Evelyn said, reluctant. "I wish we knew what they were going to do."

She lingered in the kitchen. Ed and I walked out to the car.

"Well, son-in-law," he said. "If I can do anything else for you—"

"You've done plenty," I said.

He rubbed at a spot of dirt on the windshield. "More help like mine you need like a hole in the head."

"It all worked out."

"It was none of my business."

"Yes," I said. "Of course it was."

"I had no right—"

"Every right in the world."

We stood there for another minute, quiet.

Ed took out his keys. "You can thank me for one thing, I guess. When was the last time you had an armed guard while you were on the pot?"

After they left, Donna and I stood on the sidewalk and looked at our upstairs windows.

She said, "Are they really going to stay until three?"

The moonlight reflected off Ramsgate's binoculars in the bathroom. I waved. "Do you think they copied down Ed's license-plate number?"

"Listen to me," she said. "Where are we going to sleep?"

I shrugged. "In our bedroom."

"Not with that police detective I'm not. I don't feel safe with him in there."

We took our time putting the glasses in the sink and taking down the card table, hoping they would get the message. Finally we went upstairs.

"Hi," I said from the door to our room.

"Can I help you?" Raleigh never glanced away from the window.

Donna stood behind me, offering silent support. "Look here," I said. He didn't, and I lost my momentum. "How much longer do you think you'll need to watch?"

"Two, three hours. Hard to tell, really."

"Oh." I paused. I felt a finger in my ribs. "We'd like to go to bed now."

"Tell us if we disturb you."

"Well," I said, "you see, this—"

"We sleep in here," Donna told him. "This is our bedroom."

Raleigh dropped his pen. "Make yourself at home." He giggled.

I had had enough. "Why don't you pack up and move out. You can watch from the kitchen."

Raleigh stood, admonished. "Certainly. Of course." He picked up his binoculars and briefcase. As he passed us I looked for tiny indentations in his skull.

We took turns with Ramsgate in the bathroom, brushing our teeth in the dark and giving him time in between so he could be sure he wasn't missing anything.

We slipped into bed silently.

"Shoot," Donna said.

"What."

"I should have told them where the iced tea is." She started to get out of bed.

"They're detectives," I said. "If they want something to drink, they can find it."

A moment later we heard a tentative knock at our bedroom door.

Raleigh asked, "Hello?"

I spoke up. "Yes?"

"I left my pen."

I got up and walked to the window. The pen was on the sill. I opened the door two inches.

"It's not just a normal pen," he said. "It's got this little light bulb on the end, so when you have to write in the dark— "

"I've seen it," I said.

I closed the door and got into bed. Donna rolled into my arms.

"Listen," I told her.

"What."

"There's no sound."

We held each other for a moment, straining to hear. Joe barked twice, then stopped. There was no music from the house next door.

"Good night," she said.

I hugged her. "Good night."

Detective Raleigh called in from the hallway, "Good night."

Chapter Thirty

Three nights were all they needed. Friday evening, Ramsgate called.

"We won't be coming by." He said it as if he and Raleigh were turning down a dinner invitation. "If you're interested, you might look out the window around ten." He thanked us officially for cooperating with the police department and hung up.

"That's all?" Donna sounded disappointed. "Do you want to call my mom and dad?"

They had asked us to let them know, and it might have been just as well to treat the whole thing as a night's entertainment. But I didn't want anyone else around.

There was nothing for us to do, but we couldn't do anything else. After dinner we took our time with the dishes. The rest of the night seemed to be open, empty: a lull before an event neither of us would celebrate. We stood in the kitchen, aimless.

"Well," Donna said, straightening a dish towel that was already straight. "Backgammon?"

"Sure. Music?"

"Your choice." We went to the living room. She set up the board in the middle of the sofa while I flipped through our albums, looking for one in particular, one I wasn't going to recognize. After a minute's search I found the title on the spine and slipped it from the shelf. The cover didn't look like much. Black with white letters, a childish drawing of a man and woman dancing. I set the tone arm down lightly.

We rolled for first move; Donna's six over my four. Without looking up, she said, "Since when are you listening to Shostakovich?"

"I thought I should hear it. This is the music that raised the dead."

"Cured the flu," she said. "Beethoven raises the dead."

We played, listening to the sonata for cello and piano. It wasn't bad. Shostakovich wasn't in a league with Ray Charles, but who is?

Between turns we both watched the clock on the mantel.

Donna moved a blot. She asked me what I had done with the picture from the softball game. "I wanted to put it up," she said. "Our copy is in the scrapbook."

I had considered hanging all of those pictures: the baseball players framed beside their letters, my parents' wedding photograph, the yellowed shot of my father's parents, the mystery baby. But it was enough to be living in my family's house; I didn't want them staring at me from the walls.

Still, the picture from that softball game might be the right one to keep in mind. It was something my father and brothers and Pat and I had shared, but it meant a lot to Donna and me too. It was our beginning.

As the game picked up, we concentrated on our rolls. I had better board position, but my dice were all low numbers. Donna edged me out with double fours.

"Great game," she said.

"Dumb luck. Again?"

As we set up, I heard something familiar—something on the record.

"Hey," I said.

Donna looked up.

"That sounds like Gershwin. *Rhapsody in Blue*."

She listened. "A little."

I got up and moved the tone arm to where the piano came in.

"Okay." She nodded. "I hear it now."

"That explains everything," I said. "This is Gershwin."

"I don't *like* Gershwin."

"But you like this, right? And he stole it from Gershwin."

"I'm starting to like it less," she said, "and let's not jump to conclusions."

"Wait a minute, hold it. You're telling me, after all this time, you don't like this now because you know it's from Gershwin?"

"I was just kid—"

"What if Chopin got his melodies from Count Basie? What if I told you Brahms stole from Blind Lemon Jefferson?"

"Enough," she said. "I enjoy Shostakovich, I'm not fond of Gershwin. But if you appreciate this sonata because you think it sounds like some overrated jazz mishmash, that's fine."

"You just can't admit it. The guy's a thief."

"Play."

I won the first roll and got off to a good start. I liked backgammon because it was simple, and I could win. Donna preferred cards. Her backgammon strategy was to make the game interesting. If she had a big lead and got the chance to move her last man past me, she'd open one up instead. She liked to see what would happen.

While she was making the game interesting, I was thinking of mistakes I had made.

In some important way I had betrayed her. I didn't sleep with Dusty, and I didn't walk away that night I stood on the porch in the rain, but not because doing those things was wrong. I hadn't acted out of courage; I had been afraid of what would happen.

I wanted to explain that to her, but at the same time I realized that telling her wasn't enough. I wanted to be like Donna's father, who did what he thought was right even when he knew we might not want his help. I wanted to be determined, like Ed's brother Connie, who took a picture of his wrecked car as proof of his story, left the past at the bottom of a hill, and climbed back up to the road to California. When I thought about my father and the mysteries of his travels, his building the houses, his giving us those names, I was willing to accept that the most important things we do may be the ones no one else will ever fully understand.

Donna covered a yawn. "Go. It's your turn."

I rolled. Shostakovich finished and the record player switched off.

"I'm glad we didn't call them after all," she said, glancing up at the clock. "The show's getting off to a late start."

Summer was almost over. Soon the pennant races would draw to a close, and October would bring the World Series. My mother's chrysanthemums, the last of the late bloomers, would brighten the front of the house. I would run the gas out of the lawn mower and drain the oil. The leaves would turn from green to red and yellow and brown and fall, and we would spend weekend afternoons in light jackets, raking them into piles.

The baby was due in early April—just in time for opening day. Actually, I was still hoping for a girl. Raising a son seemed harder, complicated by reflections I'd see every day: me in him; my father in me. He and I would play catch for a few years, as my father had with Mark and Waite before leaving them to teach the rest of us. He'd play pickup games with his friends, maybe even letter in high school. Then he would quit. I could hear Brian Lindbaum's father predicting the future from the front seat with all the confidence of a boxing announcer at a rigged fight: "You're not going to care *one bit* about baseball," he told us. "All you'll be thinking about is girls." True enough—but what then?

I wondered if, when our son was my age, or in my situation—married, about to have a child—he would think about him and me, part of an endless succession of fathers playing catch with sons, and if he would realize that we threw the ball to each other in part because there were so many things we couldn't do so easily, things we couldn't be sure would be caught with the reassuring snap of horsehide on leather.

Maybe we would be different. There were things I *could* tell him, or try to—stories he should hear. There would be room for misunderstanding and disagreement, but I could attempt to tell them the way I thought they should be told. Then they would be his to believe or disbelieve, remember or ignore.

Anything could happen. I thought for a moment longer, then groaned.

"What's wrong?" Donna asked.

"What if he's a musician? What if he wants to play the flute?"

"What if she's a carpenter?"

"Boys run in the family."

"I'll tell you what," she said. "If it's a boy, and if he does, I promise to teach him 'Take Me Out to the Ballgame.' "

"It's not the same." I rolled the dice. "What if he—or she—doesn't like baseball *or* music? What if it's an insurance salesman?"

"We'll love it as if it were our own." She walked to the record player and hunted for an album.

"Let's have some real music."

"You had your turn." She put a record on the turntable and set it spinning.

A string bass beat out a fast dance rhythm as a booming voice sang:

Got a cold-blooded woman lays steel on the railroad tracks
Got a cold-blooded woman lays steel on the railroad tracks
She got a hug like a bear, she almost breaks my back.

"Since when have you been a Big Joe Turner fan?"

"Ssh," she said. "Listen."

I said ooo-ouch stop, baby you hurtin' me
I said ooo-ouch stop, baby you hurtin' me
But it feels so good from my head down to my knees.

"Now, there's great poetry."

"You missed it," she said. "He lifted that phrase from Wagner."

"What?"

"The Ring cycle. His estate could sue."

"I'm not listening to this."

"Astonishing similarity." But she couldn't keep a straight face.

"If that's true," I told her, "I'm sure it's an improvement."

That's when they came. Three police cars pulled up in front of Bellshaw's house and two more turned onto the driveway, one of them blocking the back gate. They didn't use their sirens, but the revolving red lights moved in slow circles, illuminating the night.

Donna and I sat at the bottom of the stairs and peered out the window. The lights fell on the front porch, where I had helped them carry in their furniture; on the house itself, which was my father's, then Bellshaw's and, for a while, theirs; on the rear upstairs window—Dusty's; and on the backyard, where she and I had stood across the pond from each other. The beam swept the driveway and crossed our faces. Donna squeezed my hand.

The red lights continued to circle silently, casting a vulgar glow over their house, ours, the neighborhood. Finally, after twenty minutes of the scraping static of police radios and single policemen going in and out of the front door, unhurried, something happened. There was a small commotion, and then two policemen came out with a big man in a straw hat between them. The man kept his eyes to the ground, but as he got into the back of a patrol car he ducked, remembering the hat. Just beyond the police cars, standing in the shadows, a crowd had begun to gather: teenagers who had been loitering in the parking lot of our grocery store down the street, other people I couldn't quite make out. It seemed rude for strangers to be watching.

Next out of the house came another man, smaller, who looked scared, worried someone would recognize him. He tried to hide between the policemen. Innocent, his face was trying to say. Guilty of a lesser crime. After a short pause, two of the policemen went back in. One brought out Kristin, unnecessarily handcuffed. Behind her came Eve. Walking them to the cars, the policemen looked like clumsy groomsmen escorting bridesmaids up the aisle. A third policeman stopped in the doorway to the house, and for a moment I thought

Dusty had let me down; but then he turned and shrugged, empty-handed. Grace was gone.

The patrol cars with the girls pulled away from the curb. One of the remaining policemen turned and, giving in to an urge to act the part of a television cop, cupped his hands and told the crowd, "You can all go home now. The show's over."

Donna smiled and rested her arm on my knee. "Great."

The crowd lingered, but when they realized that there was nothing more to see, they stepped back into the darkness, then disappeared. It was midnight and the house was empty.

The next day the neighborhood buzzed with the news. The first call came from Mrs. Duncan.

"You know, hon," she said, "I had a lucky feeling. I knew I should've stayed up late." Before she hung up she told us that a couple from Old Court had won the color TV.

Mrs. Webb was next.

"I worry about those oleanders," she said. "If that woman doesn't come back soon, you might want to water them for her."

The phone rang constantly. Donna answered questions while Mr. Wheatley and I sat out on the front steps drinking beer and watching movers empty the house. Larry must have sent them, but I didn't see him, and I didn't ask.

"Just between you and me," Mr. Wheatley said, "I'd have given a week's pay to have been a bug on their wall."

I said I knew what he meant.

"Not that I approve," he said. "And it's not as if I ever took part in that sort of thing, even when I was young. But it's hard not to wonder."

"It's impossible," I said.

We sipped our beers and wondered. After a few minutes, it seemed healthier to change the topic.

"You do much gardening?"

"Me?" he said, looking around for someone else. "George, I couldn't grow mold on month-old bread."

"We were thinking about putting in some bulbs on either side of the walk," I told him. "Tulips, daffodils."

"Isn't it a little late?"

"Fall bulbs. For next spring."

"That would look right pretty." He took a drink. "Daffodils. They're the kind with the green parts"—he made the shape with his hands—"and then the flower up on top?"

There are at least two kinds of appreciation: the fresh excitement of the new, and the subtler pleasures of the familiar. If it applied to music, and to small towns on narrow highways, maybe it held true for neighbors. I asked Mr. Wheatley what his schedule looked like for Sunday.

"Church in the morning," he said. "Then I set and read the paper. It's a full day's work."

"Donna and I thought you and Mrs. Wheatley might like to come over for dinner."

Mr. Wheatley looked over as if he had just gotten me into focus. "You're sure you want to do that?"

I glanced across the driveway. The movers had the sofa balanced on the back of the truck.

"To tell you the truth," he said, "I guess I wondered if you weren't ducking your head."

"What do you mean?"

"You haven't been so much in the thick of things lately. Maybe those stories I told soured you on us. Maybe you're tired of talking to all us old farts."

"I've just been busy," I told him. "Taking care of some things. Since when are you an old fart?"

"Right answer. I'll have to ask Emily about Sunday, but I'm sure she'd be delighted." He stood and stretched, then set his bottle on the steps. "I better be getting home. What do I owe you for the beer?"

"I'll put it on your tab."

For a few days I watched the mail, only half-expecting a postcard from Ocean City: a shot of waves rolling up to the boardwalk, where pretty girls in swimsuits would be showing off their tans. But we had said our good-byes.

The last we heard of any of them came a week later. During a heavy rain, late in the night, Mrs. Webb heard a strange noise, something bumping against her door. Bravely she looked out. Nothing was there. Then she looked down and saw

Elvis, still wearing a ragged band of cotton. With a new name—Duchess—Kristin's poodle grew old and fat, content to spend humid summer afternoons half-listening to the slow conversations of the back-porch crowd, half-dozing between the oleanders. Naked.

New people came to Bellshaw's house: a middle-aged couple with three children. Two boys and a girl. The children were well-behaved and their father didn't drink. He drove a dump truck for a local company. The family seemed like a good addition to the neighborhood until, with Bellshaw's permission, they pulled out the old fence, covered the backyard with stone, and paved it. The father parked his truck where the pond had been. We tried to tell ourselves that the parking lot was a sign of permanence, of commitment, but the trucking business must have gone bad soon afterward; in June, almost exactly a year after the girls had pulled up in their dirty green pickup, the house next door stood empty again. Dandelions came up around the edges of the cracked asphalt. Bellshaw drove by on Saturdays to make sure no windows were broken, waved his cigar at us, and left.

Donna and I were as happy as two people living in a world full of endings could be. In the spring I had told Harry I needed a raise to support my family, and when he stalled, I moved on. It had been a year for that. One quiet night as I stood by our bedroom window, rocking the baby softly against my chest, I could have sworn I heard the beginning of a melody. I looked out, listened a moment longer, then let the curtain fall back into place.